PRAISE FOR

Rites of Spring (Break)

"Terrific...wound tightly around an expert conspiracy plot and a bumpy, convincing love story...Though *Rites* is not an overtly political novel, it would be insensitive to ignore the parallels between Amy's travails and the quagmire in Iraq: This is a story about how to deal with perpetual war carried out unpredictably and unconventionally—how to survive, while keeping your sense of humor, when you've been targeted by an invisible enemy whose demands your pride will not permit you to meet. It's very funny, also: After Amy almost drowns as a result of someone tampering with her life jacket, her head is 'whirring' so hard that you could 'pour some rum in [her] skull' and make daiquiris."
—*New York Observer*

"As tension escalates, Peterfreund adds an appealing romance subplot.... The novel moves fast, packs some laughs and does its job as a light diversion."—*Publishers Weekly*

"Once again, Peterfreund mixes mystery, romance, and typical college high jinks.... It's an ideal summer read—whether island bound or not."—*Booklist*

"*Rites of Spring (Break)* is an entertaining quick trip into college life at an elite university. Classes, final papers, applications for grad school, secret societies—all this and the personal and secret society life of the main character are portrayed in clever, witty terms...the best of the series that includes *Secret Society Girl* and *Under the Rose*.... Amy is quirky and endearing.... The story has good pacing, consistent characters, and enough action to make things exciting."—*Romance Reviews Today*

PRAISE FOR

Under the Rose

"Deep within the Rose & Grave secret society at Eli University, the secrets even members aren't privy to make Peterfreund's second novel impossible to put down.... Peterfreund offers an intimate view of the modus operandi of a college society.... Readers will be absorbed by the juicy romance plots."—*Publishers Weekly*

"Diana Peterfreund has performed a minor miracle; she has created a sequel that works. The entire cast is back from *Secret Society Girl*, and boy, are they hiding some secrets.... Ms. Peterfreund has also managed to weave a very credible, complicated mystery into the plot, with more twists and turns than you would believe. *Under the Rose* is definitely worthy reading for this summer."—*Romance Reviews Today*

"Cross Dink Stover with Nancy Drew and Bridget Jones and you get Amy Haskel, the sarcastic senior at transparently disguised 'Eli University' who briskly narrates this winning mystery."—*Yale Alumni Magazine*

"Peterfreund pairs romance and suspense in a picaresque university setting with a few surprises thrown in for good measure. Readers who picked up the series debut will be excited to continue the adventures of Amy and her cohorts. The author doesn't spend too much time rehashing the first book, but new readers will get swept up in the sexy story in no time."—*Booklist*

"*Under the Rose* is every bit as involving and hard-to-put-down as its predecessor—perhaps even more so.... If college life is a kegger, Peterfreund's series is a cocktail in a sugar-rimmed martini glass, sophisticated and easily gulped but delivering a satisfying kick."—*Winston-Salem Journal*

PRAISE FOR

Secret Society Girl

"The action is undeniably juicy—from steamy make-out sessions with campus hotties to cloak-and-dagger initiations."—*The Washington Post*

"[A] tell-all book about secret societies at Ivy League schools... Think *The Da Vinci Code* meets *Bridget Jones*."
—*Toledo Blade*

"*Secret Society Girl* succeeds.... Ms. Peterfreund's descriptions of the ambitious Amy Haskel's collegial life are both vivid and amusing."—*New York Observer*

"Cheerful, sensible, with just enough insider's scoop to appeal to the conspiracy theorist in everyone... Readers will cheer on the not-so-underdog as she faces male alumni and finds that membership does indeed have privileges."
—*Tampa Tribune*

"Thanks to a quirky, likable protagonist you'll be rooting for long after you've turned the last page and a provocative blurring of fact and fiction, *Secret Society Girl* provides the perfect excuse to set aside your required reading this summer and bask in a few hours of collegiate nostalgia."
—Bookreporter.com

"Fun to read—full of quirky characters and situations."
—*Booklist*

"A frothy summer read for anyone interested in the collegiate antics of the secret rulers of the world."
—Bloomberg News

"The plot is a winner."—*Kirkus Reviews*

Tap & Gown

AN IVY LEAGUE NOVEL

Diana Peterfreund

DELTA TRADE PAPERBACKS

A Delta Trade Paperback Original

Published in the United States by Delta, an imprint of The Random House Publishing Group, a division of Random House, Inc., New York.

DELTA is a registered trademark of Random House, Inc., and the colophon is a trademark of Random House, Inc.

Library of Congress Cataloging-in-Publication Data
Peterfreund, Diana.
Tap & gown : an ivy league novel / Diana Peterfreund.
p. cm.
ISBN: 978-0-385-34194-3
eBook ISBN: 978-0-553-33859-8
1. Women college students—Fiction. 2. Greek letter societies—Fiction. 3. College stories. 4. Chick lit. I. Title.
PS3616.E835 T37 2009
813'.6—dc22 2009004145

Printed in the United States of America

www.bantamdell.com

BVG 9 8 7 6 5 4 3 2 1

Book design: Carol Malcolm Russo

For Kerri

I hereby confess:
Everyone wants to be
one of us.

You've heard the legends, I'm sure. You arrived on this campus in a state of awe, of wonderment. Maybe you're the latest in a long line of students bearing your family name to matriculate to our fine university. Maybe you're a celebrity, or foreign royalty, or a sports star, or a genius at the near-lost art of lute playing. Maybe you're a Westinghouse scholar, a national debate champion, or the valedictorian of an elite, East Coast boarding school where your name was on the register from the moment you were born. Or maybe you're none of the above. Perhaps you're just handy with the SATs, rocked grades nine through twelve, and charmed the heck out of the middle-aged lawyer who interviewed you one evening in his satellite office on behalf of his alma mater. Whatever way it happened, you ended up at Eli.

And from the moment you stepped on campus, you heard about us.

For all that we were secret, we remained one of the constants of your college career. You could hardly get to your freshman dorm without passing our tomb. And you wondered, even if you wouldn't admit it to your roommates or your singing group friends or your lab partner, what it would be like to be one of us. What did we do in there, sequestered, sacrosanct, silent (except for the occasional scream)?

You hoped someday you'd find out.

The season is upon us once more. We, the members of Rose & Grave D177, are graduating and are thusly charged with the tapping of new souls to fill our robes, to take up the torch of our traditions, to stand beside us as members of this illustrious, rarefied order. It is a lofty duty, and one that no man (or woman) should undertake lightly. We are the standard bearers of a new world order. We are the key to the life you've only imagined.

You will be judged. Will you be found worthy?

I hereby confess:
I like being his.

1.
Pledges

I've decided that life is a bit like a standardized test. Not putting down an answer because you fear it could be wrong *will* lower your overall score. Now, as many of my friends (and a few of my enemies) will tell you, I have a tendency to overanalyze. I'm aware of this characteristic within myself, and I do my level best to overcome it. As a result, I have occasionally been known to make snap decisions that, in retrospect, were probably mistakes.

Then I remember what those nice folks at the Princeton Review told me, back when I was a green seventeen-year-old terrified I'd never get into college: Narrow down your options and make an educated guess.

But be careful. You never know where that decision is going to take you.

Almost a year ago, I accepted the tap from Rose & Grave, Eli University's most powerful, exclusive, and notorious secret society. I knew my life would change. What I didn't realize was how. I figured my induction into their order would net me some contacts in my preferred field, add extra oomph to my resume, and provide an insurance plan for the future that loomed just beyond my next set of final exams.

What I didn't expect was that it would open my eyes to a whole world of my own potential. I no longer even wanted the job I'd once hoped Rose & Grave would help me get. I also didn't count on a host of new friends, some of whom I'd never dreamed of associating with before—a few of whom I'd actively disliked. I certainly never knew how much danger one little club membership could result in, though I'd spent the last year being threatened, thwarted, chased, conspired against, and even once—bizarrely— kidnapped.

But most of all, I didn't realize that the following March, I'd be sitting on a couch that looked like it had been fished out of the trash, staring at a guy I'd never even have looked twice at, and wondering if I dared answer the following:

Amy Haskel, are you in love?
A) Yes
B) No
C) Insufficient Data to Answer This Question

Oh, hell, it's C, which is why there was no way I was going to let our Spring Break fling end. He couldn't do the secret hooking-up thing anymore? Fine. We'd try something new.

"I'm really sick of secrets," I said, and kissed him.

Brilliant as Jamie Orcutt is, it took him several seconds to parse the meaning of my statement. When he did, the kiss turned from hesitant to heated in no time at all.

Somehow we shifted from a relatively decent and G-rated side-to-side to something that rated the sort of parental supervision we had zero interest in at the moment.

And, say what you will about how the couch looked, it certainly felt comfortable once I was sandwiched deeply between the cushions and Jamie. I clung to his shoulders as if I were drowning and he knotted his fists into my shirt, sliding the material away from my skin as his mouth moved south over my throat.

"Ja..." I said on a sigh, and then, as his tongue flicked over my collarbone, "Puh..."

He lifted his head. "You are never going to get it straight, are you?"

"Unlikely." I slid my hands down his back, to where his sweatshirt ended and his skin was bare. "It's tough enough to even think of you as Jamie and not as—" *Poe.* I stopped myself in time to avoid the fine that punished us for using our society code names beyond the confines of the tomb.

"This is troublesome," he said. "But then again, that's *your* society name." He tapped my nose.

Bugaboo. Yes, and he'd probably had a hand in choosing it, too, now that I thought about it. Malcolm wouldn't have been so snarky on his own. "You want to know what's even more troublesome?" I scooted up. "Our real names rhyme."

He chuckled. "Yeah, they do. I never thought of that."

"People are going to laugh whenever they say things like, 'We should invite Amy and Jamie to the party next weekend' or 'Let's go on a double date with Amy and Jamie.' "

He frowned. "I'm now required to go on double dates with your friends? Maybe this isn't such a good idea."

Especially since the majority of said friends had no particular love for him. "I'm just saying, 'Amy and Jamie' sounds a bit pathetic."

But he was smiling. "I was just thinking how nice it sounds."

I blushed, and just as quickly, the concerns started crowding into my head. What kind of person gets into a relationship less than two months before graduating from college? Was I mad? Jamie was in law school, here, at Eli, for the next two years. I had no idea where I'd be. When I left town at the end of May, there was no way our relationship would be ready for the long-distance thing (if it even lasted until then), and I had no intentions of sticking around New Haven for a boyfriend I'd just started dating. This was silly. I was setting myself up for an even worse heartbreak come commencement.

"I should go," I said.

"What?" He shook his head in disbelief. "I don't think so. You can't just show up on my doorstep, drop this bombshell on me, then disappear."

"I have work to do . . ." I began vaguely.

"You just got off a twenty-hour car trip." He caught my hands in his. "You have relaxing to do." His thumbs slid over the scabs on my wrists and we both winced. He looked down. "I'm glad I wasn't there that night," he said softly. "I don't think I would have trusted myself."

"You? Mr. In-Control Poe?" Crap.

He wagged his finger at me. "See? You can't keep it straight. And yeah. I might have killed that kid."

"You wouldn't have been alone." Half my club had wanted to kill Darren Gehry for drugging me and dragging me off in a twisted, dangerous version of what the teenager had convinced himself was a society prank. I was the only person who understood that we might have been to blame for giving him that impression.*

My hands escaped Jamie's and twisted around each other in my lap. He noticed, in the way he has of noticing everything.

"Stay here for a while," he said. "I'll cook something

*And some of my friends were still muttering the word "Stockholm" in my vicinity.

for you and we can talk. You can ask me all those personal questions you've been so relentlessly curious about, and I can..." He trailed off.

He could what? Give me a foot massage? Seduce me? Lecture me about the importance of tofu in cuisine? He knew everything about me already. He had exhaustively researched my past when they'd tapped me into Rose & Grave. Scary thought. I'd never before dated a guy who could name all my elementary school teachers, who knew every one of my worst fears and how best to exploit them.

It's kind of like dating your stalker.

"We're a little past first-date conversation where I'm concerned," I said. Of course, back when he'd done all that research, he'd felt nothing for me but contempt. In Jamie's opinion, I hadn't been good enough for Rose & Grave. He'd changed his mind now, though. Right?

He cupped my face in his hands and kissed me, and all my fears dissolved. "We're a little past first dates, too."

———

After dinner, Jamie walked me back to the gates of Prescott College. I swiped my proximity card at the sensor and pulled open the door. "Well," I said.

He rested his hand on the bars. "Well." A flash of memory: Jamie gripping these same bars last semester as we shouted at each other. I wouldn't let him in, and I'd left that evening with George. George, with whom I'd been sleeping in a no-strings-attached affair that now seemed beyond alien. *Who was that girl, Amy?*

"Come up for a minute," I went on. "You've never seen my suite."

Here's something new: When Jamie looks at me now, his eyes, those cold gray eyes of his, almost smile. I didn't know eyes could do that.

We wandered through the courtyard, which remained mostly devoid of students. Spring Break had come to a shuddering stop as folks drifted back to campus. Some of the windows overlooking the courtyard were illuminated, but the suite I shared with Lydia remained dark.

Jamie caught my hand as I crested the steps to my entryway and tugged me back into his arms.

I laughed inside the kiss. "If this is supposed to demonstrate our new ability to kiss in public, you picked a pretty pathetic venue. No one's here."

"Baby steps," he said, as I unlocked the door to the entryway. As I wrestled with the doorknob to our suite, he nibbled along the neckline of my shirt. I flicked on the lights to the common room, but Jamie showed no interest in our décor; he just pulled me onto his lap on the couch and started kissing me for real.

A moment later, someone cleared a throat.

I looked up to see Lydia and Josh standing in the doorway to her bedroom. The former looked amused, the latter, gobsmacked.

"You're home!" Lydia said, then looked at Jamie. "And you have a guest."

I slid off Jamie's lap and we stood, knees knocking against the coffee table. "Just got home," I said. "I didn't realize you were here."

"Clearly," my best friend replied, not even trying to hide her glee. She shoved her hand at Jamie. "I'm Lydia, Amy's roommate."

"I've heard about you," he said. "Jamie Orcutt."

"Nice to meet you."

He then turned to Josh. "Jamie," he said, and stuck out his hand.

Josh shook himself free from shock. "Um, Josh," he said, a moment too late, and with a complete lack of believability.

Lydia rolled her eyes at the boys. "Give it a rest, you two. I know where Amy spent her Spring Break. Where else could she have met him?"

Jamie looked at me, eyebrows raised in disapproval. But Lydia wasn't about to let an opportunity like this pass her up. "So, what college are you in, Jamie?"

"I'm at Eli Law, actually," he said.

"Oh." Lydia frowned. "I thought you were a . . . senior." Meaningfully.

And now Jamie did smile. "I was a . . . *senior*. I graduated." He looked at me. "Your definition of 'secret' differs from most people's."

I shrugged. "Some things are impossible to hide."

"Apparently!" Josh blurted.

Everyone stared at him.

"I guess you want to catch up with your friends," Jamie said at last. "I have some reading to do anyway."

I thought of him walking all the way back to his apartment, alone, in the dark. But what could I do? There was no way I was about to invite him to spend the night. He gave me a quick kiss. "I'll call you."

As soon as the door closed, Lydia let out a strangled squeal. "Oh my God, Amy!" She grabbed my hands and led me over to the couch. "That was a boyfriend 'I'll call you.' You have a *boyfriend*. I leave you alone for two weeks and you have a boyfriend. And he's cute! And he's tall! And he's at Eli Law, which means he's brilliant, too! Tell me all about it."

"Lydia," Josh said. "Leave her alone. She's had a traumatic week. She's not—"

"Thinking clearly?" I finished for him. "Is that your theory?"

Lydia waved her hand at him dismissively. "Shoo. We're having mushy-wushy girl talk now."

But Josh was not the type who could be shooed. "Who else knows?"

I lifted my chin. "Whoever wants to." George, to start with, and probably anyone else who'd ridden back to Eli with me in the van. "It's no secret." Did Josh expect me to make a formal announcement?

"I want to hear everything!" Lydia pressed. "Did all this happen before or after...you know."

Before or after I was kidnapped, she meant. I wondered what else in my life was going to fall under that particular "before or after." I didn't want it to be like that.

"We've known each other for a while," I said. "And our feelings just...blossomed."

"Like fungus off rotted meat?" Josh snarked.

Lydia whirled on him. "Would you get out of here? You're ruining her story."

"It's okay, Lyds," I said. Josh's reaction was the one I expected. "We can talk about it later. Tell me all about Spain."

"Spain was great," Lydia said. "But I need to hear about your adventures."

"Specifically, the one where you were almost killed," Josh added.

Ugh. Maybe I should have gone with Jamie.

———

At the first society meeting post–Spring Break, the knights who hadn't been with us on the island tiptoed around me like I was one of the more precious of Rose & Grave's relics. I suspected that there had been some sort of "don't grill Amy as to the details of her ordeal" e-mail sent around prior to the meeting. Probably by Josh, for whom it was all well and good, since he'd gotten the scoop from me

already. For all I knew, he'd since drafted an "official version" for the next club newsletter. *Spring Break with D177—
sabotage, kidnapping, and the near-drowning of one of our own!
Turn to page 3 for pictures!*

Of course, it didn't help that tonight I played "Uncle
Tony"—society code for the evening's master of ceremonies. I sat on an elevated dais in the Inner Temple, displayed before my fellow knights, feeling the bumps and
edges of the carved wooden back of the Persephone throne
through both the wool of my robe and the knit V-neck I
wore underneath. After so many months, I could practically read the images through my skin: The series of ridges
beneath my right shoulder blade were the grove of trees
from which Persephone was snatched by Hades. The sharp
point digging into my spine was the root of the pomegranate tree. And the round bump rubbing up against my tattoo
was the humped back of the mourning crone Ceres became
until her daughter emerged—oh so temporarily—in the
spring.

Poor Persephone. She gives in to temptation for one
moment, indulges in one tiny bit of comfort and luxury,
and gets trapped in the underworld forever.

I scratched the scabs on my wrists.

"Bugaboo," Soze said, in a tone that indicated it wasn't
the first time he'd called my name. I snapped to attention.

Right. Dragon's Head. While the majority of us had
been off campus for Spring Break, rival society Dragon's
Head had, in the latest volley of a long-standing war, broken into our tomb again and, what's more, finally figured
out how to infiltrate our most precious sanctuary. They'd
come into this very room, the Inner Temple, and...left
a note.

Let me repeat: Left. A. Note. Last time we broke

into their tomb, we'd hidden one of their most prized possessions—and that was only because we couldn't figure out how to outright steal it.

Why they hadn't stolen anything while they were inside ours was the big mystery. They'd been trying to breach this space for decades—and when they finally do, they had nothing better than mail delivery planned? The room had been thoroughly searched, both by the few Diggers who'd stayed on campus for the break and then again when the rest of us came home, and we could neither find anything missing nor anything (like a microphone or a camera) left behind.

But no one really believed that Dragon's Head went to the trouble of getting in here just to drop off their calling card—least of all me, the target of their ire for most of the semester.

"Are you feeling okay?" Thorndike asked me. She and Angel exchanged glances. "Maybe tonight wasn't the best time for you to be Uncle Tony...."

"I'm fine." I turned to Soze. "You were saying?"

"I wanted to know your thoughts on my proposal. You were the one who bore the brunt of Dragon's Head attacks last month."

And he apparently thought my condition too fragile to put up with anything else.

Soze's theory, from what I understood, was that the letter they'd left—"It's not over, Dragon's Head"—was not, in fact, a belated Valentine's Day card, but rather, a notification of cease-fire until each society had completed the tap and initiation process this spring. Apparently, this was standard society M.O., like armies not attacking on holidays.

Though from what I knew of history, armies had great

success attacking on holidays, when people were the least prepared. Just ask George Washington. Or Anwar Sadat.

"I think it's risky," I said at last. "I don't trust Dragon's Head at all."

"But historically—"

"Historically," said Thorndike, "society pranks were just that. Pranks. But that's not what we've been dealing with lately, is it?" She glanced at me.

I bit back a sigh, tempted to stand and scream, *My name is Amy Haskel and I'm a kidnap victim. Can we all just get over that now?*

"I'm not discounting any of that," Soze said. "However, the fact remains that we don't have time right now to concentrate on a feud, and neither do they. The tap period is upon us."

"So we can either take their word at face value," said Angel, "or spend time and resources we can't spare distracting us from tap."

"Which may," said Big Demon, "be their idea all along, seeing as how we usually compete for the same juniors."

I couldn't argue with that. And I was sure, were Poe here, he'd probably be saying the same thing. "So we leave this mess for next year's club to clean up?"

"The feud has been going on for generations," said Puck. "We're not going to end it before graduation."

Everyone could agree on that, and when no one came up with any more objections, Soze spoke again.

"I'd like to get this settled, and move on to new business. I've got not one, but two theses to finish this month. So, how about we call it a day and talk about tap?"

Bond raised his hand. "I motion that, barring any new evidence, we table the feud with Dragon's Head and assume they are doing likewise."

The motion was seconded and passed with astounding alacrity. Soze wasn't the only one with a thesis coming due. Visibly relieved, our secretary began handing out little booklets, bound in heavy, faded card stock, curled with age and as soft as felt beneath my fingers. The pages were thin, yellowed typing paper, the text uneven and clearly hand-typed (complete with corrections). The title page read "TAP PROCEDURES" over a red, hand-stamped symbol of Rose & Grave. How many decades of clubs had been using these same books, these same procedures? I wondered if Josh had spent any time going through each one, crossing off the word "men" in favor of more gender neutral terms.*

"The time line is as follows," Soze said. "We choose a preliminary tap list, which may, in fact, be larger than our actual tap list, and then, over a period of three weeks, we winnow this group down with the help of meals, parties, and formal interviews. During these activities, the potential taps should remain not only unaware of the society's identity, but also of the true nature of the events."

"Please," scoffed Juno, who, over Spring Break, had cut her curly hair into a fetchingly short, ready-for-prime-time coif. "I know I wasn't on campus for this last year, but are any of you saying you honestly had no idea why some random senior had suddenly befriended you and popped up everywhere you went?"

"You're right," said Graverobber. "I knew exactly what was going on."

"I knew it was a society courting me," Angel said. "But I also knew the Diggers didn't tap women, so I had no idea what to think."

---

*Upon closer examination...no, he did not. Then again, two theses.

"I thought you just came to the parties as a selling point for us," Graverobber said to her with a leer. She ignored him.

"To tell the truth," said Puck, "I found the whole following-around thing a little off-putting. Dude really cramped my style." Lil' Demon, sitting closest, jabbed him. "What?" he complained. "It's true."

Soze cleared his throat. "At the conclusion of all this merrymaking, we pick our tap list, and a few alternates, in case a tap, for some reason, chooses to reject us when we show up at their door."

"How often does that happen?" asked Lucky.

"In the past? Almost never," said Angel. "The way my father tells it, usually the knights are able to weed that element out before Tap Night. It's rare for Rose & Grave to get an answer on Tap Night that isn't 'Accept.' "

I wondered how the society managed that while simultaneously keeping their identity and purpose a secret and would have interrupted again to ask, but Soze was getting a distinctly impatient look on his face. If his theses were in that much trouble, maybe he shouldn't have spent the last two weeks gallivanting around Spain with my roommate.

"But with the kind of year we've had," he went on, "I can't make any guarantees. I think we should have at least two alternates."

"Who chooses the alternates?" asked Juno.

Soze took a deep breath. "That's Rule Number One. We *all* choose *all* the taps. Every decision made from here on out must be a unanimous choice. Who we tap, why we tap them, and most of all, how we go about it."

Robed heads nodded all around the Inner Temple. Of course. The whole point of this society was to create a sense of unity and camaraderie among its members. Why wouldn't we all have to agree on this, our most important task? But how could fourteen such different individuals ever agree on not one, but fifteen people to tap?

"So in the interest of ease and consistency, I move that we follow the pattern set by last year's club, which builds upon the traditions of the order. The tap list should be composed of persons who most match the demographics of each of the current knights."

"Including gender?" Thorndike asked.

"Yes."

"I oppose."

Soze rubbed his temples.

"Uncle Tony recognizes the opposition of the Knight Thorndike," I said.

She stood. "Such a motion would forever lock the male-to-female ratio of the society into uneven terms."

"So what else is new?" asked Kismet. "We've already locked it into uneven terms on the basis of race and sexuality, if we're honestly required to 'tap our own demographic.' It's a completely stupid system."

"The alternative," argued Juno, "is to see people of your own mind-set become unrepresented in this group."

"So now you're in favor of affirmative action?" asked Lucky.

"I'm in favor of protecting what's mine," Juno replied.

"I think it all works out," said Angel. "Can anyone here argue that we haven't tapped the right people for this club?"

Everyone got very quiet, and I studied the gavel in my hand. If they were going to name names, it would almost certainly be mine. I was never supposed to be a member of Rose & Grave. I hadn't attended their parties and events. Instead, I was a last-minute substitute when my big sib, Malcolm, got into a fight with the girl he was supposed to tap.

"It's easy for you to make that point, Angel," said Thorndike. "Rich, white, East Coast legacies are in no danger of losing slots in this society. You've already got one of each gender in this club." She pointed at Puck. "Do you want this club to be permanently two-fifths women?"

"What would be fair to you, Thorndike?" Soze asked. "Seven of fifteen?"

"How about eight?" asked Lil' Demon. "That would match more with the actual demographics of Eli."

"I think the number of women we have is just fine now," said Graverobber.

"No," said Thorndike with a sneer. "*You* think we've got too many."

"That too."

"My problem isn't with the numbers," said Bond. "It's with the restrictions. I can easily make an argument that the proper replacements for ourselves are not necessarily of the same gender, just as they were not last year. Every woman in this room was tapped by a man who thought that, in all other respects but gender, she would carry on his legacy within the Order." He shrugged. "Why don't we do it like that? Tap according to merit, and worry about the gender and other demographic breakdowns as a secondary concern?"

Cue another half hour of rigorous debate. This did not bode well. If we couldn't even agree on how we were going to pick the taps, how in the world would we ever agree on whom we'd pick? I recalled Poe's description of last year's deliberations. He claimed to have argued against the inclusion of women until his voice gave out. Was this how it worked? The person with the energy to debate the longest was the one who won? The knight willing to browbeat the others into little puddles of mental and physical exhaustion got his or her "unanimous" vote by default?

From the raspy sound of Soze's voice, he'd reached the end of his rope already. "Can't we just trust that D176 knew what they were doing when they designed it the way they did?" He looked at me with a plea in his eyes. What? I was supposed to jump to the defense that D176 were some kind of masterminds, just because I was dating one of them? My personal mastermind thought the plan his brothers had devised was a terrible one, and had made that perfectly clear to me on the steps out front last spring.

Although that wasn't all I'd heard about last spring. Their so-called secret deliberations hadn't been entirely secret, either. Malcolm had told me, at least, how they went about choosing who would be assigned a female tap.

"They didn't design anything," I said. "They drew straws to see who would be the ones to tap women."

"So you think we should draw straws?"

"I think if the argument is that we should do it like D176, then we should base that argument on the way they actually did it. They didn't assign gender tapping responsibilities to certain knights, which is what we'd be doing if we said all the women had to tap women. They did it randomly."

"I could roll with that," Thorndike said. "Fifteen of each, and we all have a 50/50 chance. With the understanding, as I said before, that transgendered people are to be considered according to their self-defined gender identity—"

"Tell me again," Lucky said, "which of us you think is going to be looking to tap someone transgendered?"

"You have a problem with that?" Thorndike snapped.

And on it went for another half an hour.

"My problem," Soze said wearily, "is that I don't think they had fifteen of each. I think they picked the ratio of six to nine and drew straws that way."

"*Gosh,*" said Puck. "If *only* someone in here had the phone number of a patriarch, so we could call and verify. *Who* might have that on her person?" He looked at me. I shrugged and pulled out my cell phone. *Let's just finish this and go home.*

"So what?" Thorndike says. "Poe's word is now our law? Haven't we spent this entire year doing basically the opposite of whatever that dick says?" She glanced at me. "No offense."

Whatever. A few months ago, I would have been glad to hear someone else say it. And even if I was offended that she was impugning my boyfriend, I had to admit that Thorndike had a point. I hardly ever agreed with Poe's take on society traditions, and he outright hated ours.

Funny how I'd forgotten all of that down there in the Florida heat. Was it saltwater poisoning that had so addled my brain? Back at school, in this tomb, I was constantly reminded why it was that I had always butted heads with my now-boyfriend.

Whether or not he could help us in our present predicament wasn't the point. I didn't want to turn to Poe at the first sign of trouble or discord. We could do this ourselves. We didn't need the help of patriarchs. For once, I wanted to prove that we, the knights of D177, could handle something on our own.

Especially since it was the last chance we'd have to do so.

I put my cell phone away and sighed.

Forty-five minutes later, Puck was either nodding off to sleep or pretending to, Angel had lapsed into silence, and both Lil' Demon and Graverobber had long since given up any pretense of paying attention. Big Demon appeared to be counting the stars painted on our ceiling. I was pretty sure Lucky was surreptitiously checking her e-mail on her iPhone. (Either that or she was texting Tristram Shandy, who also had his head lowered and his robe-draped hands hidden underneath the table.) Kismet, Frodo, and Bond looked wearily on as Juno, Thorndike, and Soze battled it out. I leaned my left elbow on the carved armrest of the throne, rested my chin in my hand, and watched.

And watched.

And watched.

I couldn't even think of anything more to say at this point. I wasn't entirely sure what the scope of the argument was anymore. I'd had it in my mind fifteen minutes ago . . . but now all I could think about was my five-page-a-day diet to get my thesis done on time. I guess tonight's schedule was shot. My right hand dangled the gavel over the side of the armrest, the nape of my neck grew irritated from the rasp of the robe against my skin, and my left foot began to go to sleep.

CRACK!

Everyone looked up. I scrambled off the throne to retrieve the gavel from the floor. "Sorry," I said, tripping over my robes as I climbed back up the dais. "You were saying, Thorndike?"

"No," said Angel. "I think *you* were saying, as Uncle Tony, that we need to *get the hell on with this.*"

"I agree," said Lucky. "Maybe dropping that gavel was an act of God."

"Persephone," said Juno.

"Whatever. It means the time for discussion is over. I second the Knight Bugaboo's motion that this debate be brought to a close."

"Um, all in favor?" I said, leaping at the opportunity.

Unsurprisingly, the motion passed.

"So what are we left with?" Lil' Demon asked. "I can't even follow anymore."

"Fifteen of each marble, and we pick at random," Soze grumbled. "This is going to be a disaster."

"It's only fair," Thorndike said smugly.

"Fine!" Soze crossed the room and from a cabinet withdrew a vase and a leather bag filled with marbles. "For the purpose of this operation, black marbles will be for men, red marbles for women—no discussion, okay?"

Thirteen heads nodded. Soze counted them out, poured them into the vase, and shook it around. "Everyone pick, but keep your hand closed. We'll reveal them at the same time."

He walked around the table, and each knight picked a marble. He approached me, and I stuck my hand into the vase, rooted around a bit, then closed my fingers around one and pulled it out. The glass sphere felt cool and solid inside my fist. Soze picked last, then held the vase out to me again. "As the evening's Uncle Tony, please pick a second marble for our missing fifteenth member."

"Our what?"

Soze cleared his throat and mumbled, "Howard."

I did, with my left hand.

I spoke. "Knights of Persephone, rise." Around the table, everyone stood and held out their fists. "At the count of three: one, two, three."

Everyone opened his or her hand. My right palm held a red marble, my left held black. I glanced around the room, making a quick calculation.

Nine black. Six red.

Exactly what we already had.

I hereby confess:
I don't always get what I want.
In fact, I don't always
know what that is.

2.

Concessions

"I can't believe it," Josh said, punctuating his sentence with a well-aimed kick at the edge of the walk. "All those hours, wasted."

"Were I a religious man," George said, strolling along the deserted sidewalk two steps behind us, hands resting easily in his jacket pockets, "I'd say this was the universe's way of telling you people to chill out."

Josh stopped dead and whirled around. "Well, maybe if you picked up some of the slack around here, we could. You've never taken society matters seriously enough."

"Yeah," George replied. "Wonder why that is?"

Not entirely true. George knew when to take it seriously, and when it was just a bunch of stuffy traditions that ought to be ignored.

I stepped between the two of them. "All right, guys. It's late, we're all tired, we're all a little in shock over the outcome. Let's just table any more discussion until tomorrow, okay?"

Josh turned and stormed off down the sidewalk toward

Prescott College. George shrugged and fell into step with me. "I do think there's something to this 'universe' theory of mine," he said.

I murmured in assent. Maybe there was. How else to explain the results? Hours of debate, and we ended up with exactly the same ratio as our class.

"Or maybe it was just the universe's way of telling us that D176 had it right?" George continued.

I didn't have the wherewithal to respond to that one, either. Upon seeing the marbled results, I'd immediately called the meeting to a close, and the other knights were smart enough to agree it was a good move. No one had the energy to react in any way that was either useful or wise. Demetria, in particular, looked ready to implode. We'd deal with it tomorrow.

I looked at my watch. Two A.M. I mean, tonight.

Josh was still storming off in front of us. I didn't envy Lydia his foul mood. Perhaps it would have been a good idea for him to go back to his own room this evening. However, it had been quite a while since I'd seen my roommate spend the night alone, and it certainly hadn't happened since Spring Break. I don't know what went on over there in Spain, but whatever it was, it had brought their relationship to a whole new level.

Josh said nothing when we met him at the Prescott gate. I wondered if he felt weird entering my suite with me only a few steps behind—as if not entering by himself was his admission that it was, in fact, still *my* suite. That he was a guest there, not a full-time resident.

Though he'd certainly come in alone often enough when I was inside. Sometimes it felt like I lived inside a sitcom, where your friends felt free to walk inside your house without knocking whenever they wanted.

George stopped at his usual entryway. "See you guys

later," he said, and as the door closed, I noticed he went not up the stairs to his room, but rather cut to the right and headed into the basement.

Huh? These are the things in the basement:

1) The laundry room. Chance that George was washing his whites at 2 A.M.: 0%
2) The Buttery. Hamburgers, pizza bagels, and grape sodas galore, but at this time of night, it was locked up tight.
3) The underground passageway to all the other entryways in the building.

I quickened my pace, took the stairs up to my entryway two at a time, yanked open the door, and sprinted down the basement passageway just in time to see George's fabulous butt disappearing into the corridor toward the sophomore wing.

Huh.

I met a quizzical Josh in front of our suite door on the first floor. "What was that all about?"

"Nothing." I pushed past him and into the common room. Where was George going? At night? In secret? "I thought I'd forgotten to take my clothes out of the dryer earlier."

"But then you remembered?" Josh asked.

Not that I cared what George did. I'd totally moved on. He could have as many two A.M. rendezvous as he wanted with as many sophomores as he cared to. No skin off my back. I had a boyfriend *and* I was over him.

"Yep." I tripped over the laundry bag of obviously dirty Spring Break clothes I'd dragged into the common room that afternoon and then promptly ignored.

"Uh-huh." Josh shook his head. "Night, Bugaboo."

I cringed as he vanished into Lydia's room. "Two dollars," I hissed after him, but I doubt he heard.

Whatever. Like it mattered what Josh thought any more than it mattered what George was doing. If he even was doing what I thought.* Or if he was doing it with a sophomore. Could be anyone. Why should I concern myself anyway? I had Jamie, and that didn't bother *George* one iota. He'd even started to support it. Time to get over yourself, Amy.

In my bedroom, I sat down at my desk and opened the lid on my laptop. A few e-mails, including one from my mom about commencement travel plans—nothing I couldn't wait until tomorrow to answer. The file with my thesis draft was open. I clicked over and stared at the blinking cursor for a few minutes.

An IM window popped up on my screen.

DinkStover: Hey. Wondered when you'd be getting home.

The new window flashed at me, daring me to accept something from this stranger. Whoever Dink Stover was, he knew I wouldn't be back until late. I clicked *Accept.*

DinkStover: How did it go?

I smiled. Oh, he knew, all right.

AmyHaskel: Jamie?
DinkStover: Do I need to provide the secret handshake?
AmyHaskel: Can't be too careful these days.
DinkStover: Good girl.

---

*Who does the confessor think she's kidding? It's George. Of course he's doing what she thinks he is.

I pursed my lips. What, was I a dog?

DinkStover: So how did it go?
AmyHaskel: Fine.

My fingers hovered over the keys. Should I tell him it was
sheer torture? Ask him how in the world he survived it, especially as a voice of dissent? I barely got involved in the
discussion and I was miserable. He must have been the
most wretched person on the planet. Especially since, to
Jamie, Rose & Grave meant everything.

DinkStover: It's okay if you don't want to talk about it.

Long hesitation.

DinkStover: But I'm here if you need a shoulder to lean on.

When I didn't answer, he wrote again.

DinkStover: You still there?
AmyHaskel: Yeah. I'm taking a screenshot for evidence that
there is a Gentle Jamie.

No response.

AmyHaskel: I'm joking.
DinkStover: No you're not.
AmyHaskel: It's harder to tease you when I can't see your
face.
DinkStover: I'm not walking over there at two-thirty in the
morning.
DinkStover: Wait . . . that *was* an invitation, right?

I bit my lip. Was it? I didn't even know anymore.

AmyHaskel: Pretty tired, actually. Class tomorrow.
DinkStover: I understand. So at least tell me how many people you've got on your short list.

I should have figured a die-hard Digger like Jamie wouldn't give up so easy on hearing details about our deliberations.

AmyHaskel: I haven't thought that far ahead yet.
DinkStover: You'd better believe they have.
AmyHaskel: What do you mean?
DinkStover: You were a shoo-in for Quill & Ink last year, right?
AmyHaskel: Until you guys screwed it up.
DinkStover: But you knew it. You were expecting it.
AmyHaskel: Yeah?
DinkStover: Well, this year's shoo-ins for us are expecting it, too.
AmyHaskel: But what does that matter to us? I'm not going to tap someone just because they expect it.
DinkStover: Spoken like Malcolm's true little sib. But don't go the other way, either. Don't *not* tap someone because it's expected.

I frowned at the screen. *Don't lecture me.*

AmyHaskel: This? This right here? It's why I didn't want to talk about it.
DinkStover: Okay. I'll just assume it's the three, then.

The three? The three what? Were we each supposed to start from a list of three and pare down? Josh hadn't mentioned that this evening, but maybe that's because everyone

else knew how it worked. After all, they'd been part of the
whole winnowing-down process. But if that was the case,
why would Malcolm have had to pick me last year? After
the whole debacle with Genevieve, couldn't he have gone
to either of his two backups? Or was I always a backup, and
it was standard procedure to keep us thoroughly in the
dark as to our status? I hesitated, then began to type.

AmyHaskel: Probably going to regret this, but what's "the
three"?
DinkStover: The three people I already know you have on
your short list.
AmyHaskel: And who, pray tell, would they be?
DinkStover: The usual suspects: EIC of the Eli Daily News,
managing ed. of same, and, because it's you, the EIC of the
Lit Mag.
AmyHaskel: Oh. Those.

Of course that was how it would work. Rose & Grave always tried to tap either the editor-in-chief or the managing
editor of the *Daily*. They were probably sitting at home expecting the little white and black envelope to slide under
their door any minute. And though I'd never had a moment's experience in campus journalism, I'd be expected to
tap one of them to replace me. This was the system.

I didn't know the editor-in-chief at all, though I'd read
a few of her columns, and her name was either a point of
envy or a punch line in my suite (depending on how many
Gumdrop Drop shots we'd imbibed): Kalani Leto-Taube.
Her reputation was one of accomplishment and elegance,
and her position ought to belong on the top of any short
list I made. Rose & Grave hadn't gotten the EIC last year.
I could fix that.

The managing editor I knew, to my chagrin. Topher

Cox. He'd drunkenly hit on me in Cambridge at The Game during my junior year. Between the Andover T-shirt and the sloppy leer, I'd been sure he was from Harvard. It was Glenda, my predecessor at the Lit Mag, who'd explained to me that he was the resident golden boy over there at the castle-like headquarters of the *Eli Daily News*.

A son of Eli. One of our own. And if I followed standard Digger M.O., he'd be another of me.

AmyHaskel: I'm supposed to pick a girl.
DinkStover: Is that how you guys are working it? All the girls pick girls?
AmyHaskel: Are you going to keep *bugging* me until I tell you everything?
DinkStover: We have ways of making you talk, Miss Haskel.

I laughed and typed *wish you were here*. But I didn't press *Send*. Some circumspect backspacing later, I typed:

AmyHaskel: You bring up an interesting point. What if our perfect tap is the wrong gender for our assignment?
DinkStover: You have to find a way to work it out. Your perfect tap might be the wrong gender, or might be abroad and unreachable, or might not be interested in joining. We don't all get our perfect taps.
AmyHaskel: True. Malcolm didn't.
DinkStover: Malcolm did okay for himself.
AmyHaskel: Oh, so *now* you're okay with it?
DinkStover: You know I am.

I wondered what Jamie would have done had he drawn a girl marble last year. Actually, wait . . .

AmyHaskel: Who is your little sib? Mara?
DinkStover: No.
AmyHaskel: Who?

There was a long silence. Jamie was probably trying to figure out the best way to scold me for my lack of observance. Maybe if I were a really good Digger, I'd have memorized the line of succession of every knight back to 1832. I'm sure he had. I didn't even know who'd tapped Malcolm, my own big sib. Then again, I'd actively avoided Jamie for the first few months of our acquaintance. It wasn't like I spent much time seeking out the company of either him or the people in the club he'd be most likely to hang out with.

DinkStover: George was my tap, Amy.

I blinked at the screen. I was clearly up too late. That made no sense. They never hung out. They weren't anything alike: Not in background, not in personality, not in interests or majors—the only thing George and Jamie had in common was . . . well, me.

AmyHaskel: I didn't know that.
DinkStover: Now you do.

What was the correct response here? *I'm sorry you tapped someone I later slept with before I started liking, let alone dating you, with whom I have not slept?*

Way to nail the issue, Amy. But still, I had to say something; the silence on the screen was turning fatal. The cursor blinked at me like a ticking time bomb.

AmyHaskel: You don't like him.

Probably never had, not even last spring. George Harrison
Prescott had been born with a silver spoon in his mouth,
then with the triple threat of his looks, his entirely decent
brains, and his significant charm, received the rest of his
life on a matching silver platter. He'd never had to work
for anything. Not Eli, not girls, and not Rose & Grave.
Last spring, Jamie's class had practically forced the tap
upon him. As George was a legacy of one of their most
supportive patriarchs, his membership was an absolute
must. At the meeting, George had mentioned that his big
sib's constant presence "cramped his style." No kidding.
No wonder I hadn't seen them together much. George and
Jamie clearly did not have the same kind of relationship
that I had with Malcolm.

Jamie hadn't yet answered me. Maybe George hadn't
been the only one forced that particular Tap Night. And
maybe this was not the conversation to have over IM.

AmyHaskel: You know, sitting in stony silence loses some
of its punch over IM. I just assume your Internet connection
blinked out.
DinkStover: Curses.
AmyHaskel: I'm going to hit the sack, I think. You coming
tomorrow?
DinkStover: We'll see.
AmyHaskel: I want to see you, either way.

He was quiet, and I pictured him in his lonely apartment
halfway across town, sitting on his couch, shirt off (hey, a
girl can dream) and looking at those words on his screen. I
smiled.

DinkStover: You will. Good night, Amy.
AmyHaskel: Night, Pajamie.

Alone in bed as the garbage trucks and street sweepers heralded the morning in the road beyond the boundaries of Prescott College, I thought about all the times that I'd gone to Malcolm while navigating some of the more confusing elements of society membership. Had George done the same?

Hey, Jamie, I was wondering what you think about this? The other day, Amy and I had quite a lot of sex in the abandoned tomb. We even did it in the Inner Temple. Is that okay?

What had I gotten myself into?

————

The next evening, the club convened to work out the details. At dinner, Soze expressed his fervent wish that yesterday's debate was well and truly behind us, and that the remainder of the tap process would run "smoothly and harmoniously."

Poor, naive little boy.

Though we'd all arrived toting our short lists, as requested in Soze's e-mail that morning, it was anything but the simple, straightforward process our dear secretary had been hoping for.

Recounting in detail may make my brain explode, and I need that to graduate. So here are the lowlights:

1) At least three of the knights already wanted to be released from their marble-mandated gender assignments. Including Thorndike.
2) Some knights' short lists were anything but. For instance, Frodo had placed every pitch of the eleven all-male singing groups on campus (and a healthy handful of talented tenors outside the a capella sphere) on his. "Look at it this way," he'd said by way of explanation, "half of these guys are

going to join the Whizzbangs anyway. So that cuts
the potential to actually get them down a lot."*

3) On the flip side, some lists were deemed too short
(mine, which had only the "three" that Poe had
suggested), or were generally too inappropriate
or too dadaist altogether. Puck's latest attempt
at rebellion was to introduce his list with the
following: "After long consideration, I have
decided that no one currently on campus meets
the proper specifications to take my rightful place
in the society. Therefore, I submit the following
proposal: I desire that the full weight of Digger
influence be deployed to encourage at least one, if
not more, of the following persons to matriculate
to Eli within the next month: Samuel L. Jackson,
Richard Branson, or Hunter S. Thompson."

"Hunter S. Thompson is dead," Bond pointed
out.

"Fine." Puck consulted his alternates. "Prince
Harry of Windsor will do."

I blinked, trying to imagine the list that
contained both deceased gonzo journalists and
tabloid-fodder British royalty. To be perfectly
honest, Harry wasn't a half-bad choice.

4) Worst of all, Poe sat through the whole meeting
and opened his mouth only to take another sip of
coffee. He didn't even look at me while George

---

*The confessor is sad to report that this generated a good fifteen minutes of dis-
cussion, during which Juno postulated that perhaps they'd be more likely to convince a female singer to ditch her slot in the senior class women's group, which
was significantly less prestigious. Then Thorndike wondered—aloud—what it
said about heteronormativity and the devaluation of anything classified primarily
feminine. And Graverobber said that singing was girly from any perspective. And
Soze called for order before all hell broke loose.

made his ridiculous pronouncement about who was worthy of replacing him (though I definitely stared at Poe enough to gauge his reaction: not amused).

His poker face remained firmly in place no matter how heated the debate grew, and he declined to offer advice about any of our lists or suggestions, despite the frequency with which the other Diggers and I looked to him for an opinion—even a tacit one.

I would have called him on it, but a public squabble with my new society-incest boyfriend was hardly going to lessen the tension within the tomb. Besides, I knew enough by now to figure out that when Poe bothered to keep his opinions to himself, it was because he was armed with a weapon of mass destruction. Whatever he said would likely devastate us. "Walk softly and carry a big stick" was practically engraved over his heart.

He must really think we're hopeless.

The only things we'd resolved by the end of the meeting were that we should really try to get a "science tap" to fill Howard's open slot, and that if any two knights so desired, they could "switch marbles" in order to get a tap who may not be of the right gender, but otherwise fit their requirements. This latter move put Topher Cox back into play for me. If anyone wanted a girl, that is.

When the meeting ended, Poe walked me back to Prescott, chattering away about everything but the one subject I was interested in—what he thought of our process. Instead, he talked about whether or not he wanted to apply to the Eli law journal.

"On one hand, it's incredibly prestigious," he was saying.

"Well, that sounds about right for you."

If he picked up on my sarcasm, he didn't show it. Or maybe he simply agreed with me. "But on the other, it's a huge commitment. I might prefer a really good clinic or maybe greater freedom in my schedule. In case something comes up."

I looked away from the path, finally engaging in the conversation. "Like what?"

He shrugged. "I don't know. Other opportunities. A research gig for a professor. A job."

"Then staying flexible seems like a wise choice." I laughed ruefully. "Look at me. I'm the epitome of flexible."

He slipped an arm around my shoulders. "Do you have any idea when you'll be hearing back on those applications? Fellowship or grad school?"

"I've already heard from a few," I admitted, though I was loath to. "A whole mess of 'thanks, but no thanks' so far. Maybe I was kidding myself with the idea that I should veer from my plan. My resume looks great for an assistant at a literary agency or a publishing house. It isn't designed to impress anyone outside of that."

Beside me, Jamie was silent. I figured he knew the truth of that better than anyone—after all, he'd studied my C.V.

"Of course not, Amy," I prompted him. *"Don't be silly. Someone is bound to jump all over your application."*

"And if they don't?" he asked instead, bypassing my comforting-boyfriend script. "Is your alternative no longer desirable? Go to New York, work in publishing?"

"No. I could probably still get a decent job there—could probably start looking even this summer if I wanted. They don't hire in advance like consulting firms. They hire when there's an opening, and people look all the time. But…" But what? It wasn't what I wanted anymore? Or worse, I didn't know what I wanted at all? A hundred thousand dollars in debt for a degree and I had no idea what to do with it. Eli diploma or no, Rose & Grave pin or no, it still spelled failure.

"What you do next isn't your life, Amy," Jamie said.

"Easy perspective to take, 1L at Eli Law. Besides, you were plenty bitter when you wound up landscaping last summer."

"I made the mistake of not having a good Plan B," he said. "It's one I'd like you not to make. There's nothing wrong with Plan B. Play it right, and no one will even know it wasn't your first choice."

Spoken like a true secret-keeper.

"Because it matters so much what people think," I mocked.

"It does," Jamie said. "And you know it. Malcolm runs off to Alaska to go fishing for a year and it sounds romantic and bohemian and earthy. Malcolm runs off to Alaska to go fishing for a year because the stress of losing his family on top of a first-year workload at business school might shatter his spirit—that sounds pathetic. Weak. Not like someone who should be entrusted with your money. Not like a Digger."

He was right, of course. I'd thought of Malcolm's gap year as nothing but a bit of fun before he settled down to the grind, and it was indeed sexy and masculine and adventurous. Thinking of it as his alternative to a public, academically recordable nervous breakdown didn't go over so well.

Jamie said, "And so I ask again: You don't want to go to New York anymore?"

I studied my shoes. Truth was, I wanted to be there more now than I had a month ago, when I'd turned in applications for graduate schools that might take me down south or out west or back to Ohio. Now I had a reason to want to stay within commuter-train distance of Eli. And he was standing right next to me.

Jamie followed me inside the gate and up to the door.

"Want to come inside?" I asked.

He leaned against the doorjamb. "It is late."

"Yeah."

"And it's a long walk home."

"Yeah."

"So if I did come in—"

"You probably should stay," I finished.

"Yeah." He looked at the door for a long moment, then at me. "But—to sleep."

"Ah." I nodded.

"Because it is late."

"Indeed." But that wasn't the problem. The real problem was that it was early. As we crossed the threshold, I marveled that there seemed to be as many rules in a real relationship as in my hook-up dalliance with George or my friends-with-benefits deal with Brandon. The things we'd do, the things we'd *say*—and the things we wouldn't.

Lydia's room was empty, so she was either still at the library or she'd be spending the night with Josh. We were alone. And maybe that thought made me just the slightest bit nervous, despite our stated parameters for this tête-à-tête. Nervous enough to skip the snuggling and fall into old bad habits. I went on the offensive.

"Why didn't you say anything at the meeting tonight?"

"What do you mean?"

An innocent act from Poe? Nice try, bud. Still, I could take the high road. "We're—" I took a breath "—floundering. And you just sat there."

"About that," he said. "I may pass on attending the next few meetings. It's like a combat flashback."

"Great. Right when we need you."

He raised his eyebrows. "Need me? Aww, that's sweet. Disingenuous, but sweet."

"I'm serious. We actually could use your help."

"And yet, I pass."

"Since when do you pass on anything having to do with the society?"

He shook his head. "I did this already. And it was one of the most torturous, thankless, relationship-eroding events of my entire life. I'm not going to make any friends if I step into your deliberations, and I have a vested interest in doing nothing that might endanger the few friends I've got in your club. One in particular."

"Yesterday, you wanted all the info."

"You telling me in private what you're thinking after a long night is different from me dispensing advice to your entire club in the tomb. I'm more than happy to support *you*, my girlfriend, though. I know what a hard time this can be."

"And you could make it easier."

"No, I couldn't." He flopped back on the couch. "Last year's tap was contentious because of me. Debate went on for eighteen, twenty hours at a stretch. I'm hardly a good role model for painless delibs."

"But you've learned your lesson," I argued.

"No," he replied. "If there was an issue I believed in, I'd still fight for it, and I'd advise you to do the same."

"But you were wrong last year!" I said, exasperated.

"No. I wasn't," he said, and my mouth snapped shut. Huh? "What happened to us last spring is exactly what I said would happen. It caused a huge problem, it hurt our members, it hurt the taps, and it damaged both of our clubs' relationships with the patriarchs. It will likely do the same for future clubs, and it may take years for the ripples to settle."

I stared at him in shock. What had happened to my Florida Poe, who'd held me in sunlit waters and protected me from sabotage and treated me as an equal—no, as more than an equal. As something precious. Who was glad to have me in this society. I thought he'd changed. At the very least, I thought he'd changed his mind about the women in the club.

"So yeah," he went on, "I wasn't wrong. It was, is, and will continue to be an issue. But—" He caught my hand and my gaze. "—it's worth it, Amy."

―――――

As a second-semester senior, my course load tended toward the light end. Aside from the credit devoted to working on my senior thesis, I was only taking three classes: a Nabokov seminar I'd been waiting four terms to fit into my schedule, an interdepartmental study of Protofeminist Thought in Victorian Art, Literature, and Performance; and a geology survey course on Atmospheric Change I was taking pass/fail.

This last was a recent addition to the schedule. Right before the conclusion of the drop/add period last month, I'd received notice from the Registrar's Office that I was short one Group IV (Eli-speak for "hard science") distribution requirement. Given the nature of the pranks Dragon's Head had been pulling on me at the time (they'd also hacked the library system to make me responsible for every missing book since 1963), I'd chocked it up as another of their jokes and continued blithely on in the Intro to Renaissance Italy lecture I was taking because the prof seemed cool and liked to meet his students for beer and plague chat at a local pub every Friday afternoon.

But it wasn't sabotage. The next day, the entire class list of my sophomore year anthropology seminar had been called into the dean's office and informed that though the class had originally borne a III/IV designation in the

Course Catalog (owing to one field trip to a bone lab), it could not be used to fulfill a distribution requirement. Apparently, the course as a whole was deemed a little "soft" for the Group IV purists, and they had downgraded it into Group III (where dwelt what my Physics major friend called, disdainfully, "people sciences" like linguistics and sociology).

Bye-bye, Medici.

The only other low level Group IV class I could take pass/fail conflicted with Nabokov. Not an option, as that course was my sin, my soul. So Atmospheric Change it was—even though the Geology department was situated about as far from the heart of the Eli campus as it could get. At least the class only met for fifty minutes twice a week, at eleven-thirty.

Actually, there was supposed to be a weekly section with a T.A., too, but I never went. After all, I was taking the class pass/fail. No choice on the matter really, since I'd started the darn thing more than three weeks in.

This particular morning, before making the trek across campus to the science buildings, I had an appointment with my thesis advisor to discuss my progress on his recommended reading list as well as the actual writing of the paper. It went like this:

Amy says: It's going great! I really appreciate all that analysis you gave me on the *Aeneid*. I'll have a draft to you by the end of next week.
Amy thinks: I'm dead meat.

Leaving Professor Burak's office afterward, I caught sight of Arielle Hallet, my successor as editor of the *Eli Literary Magazine*, and a resident on my short list, sitting on the steps of the building and adjusting her iPod.

"Amy!" she called, popping out her earbuds and smiling up at me. "What's up?"

"Not much." How fortuitous. I'd been meaning to have a little chat with her. I joined her at the base of the steps. "How was your Spring Break?"

"Fab. Went to Cabo with my suite. You?"

"Florida with some friends." I tugged the back of my T-shirt down over my tattoo. "Then spent a week working for Habitat."

"Oh, wow," she gushed. "I've always wanted to do Habitat for Humanity. Did you go with the Eli chapter?"

"No, just a group of friends," I said. A group of Diggers, to own the truth, but I wasn't supposed to do that to a barbarian.

"I should so try that," Arielle said, packing up her iPod. "Maybe next year."

I nodded and checked my watch. Twenty minutes to class.

"You headed up to Atmospheres?" she asked me.

I looked at her quizzically. "Are you in the class, too?"

She giggled. "Pass/fail. I've been skipping a lot."

Well, we clearly had more in common than I'd once thought. Arielle wouldn't have been my first choice last year for editor of the Lit Mag. But she was the only one who'd applied (the previous year, both Brandon and I had vied for the spot). She'd been a diligent sales recruiter since first joining the staff as a freshman, regularly coming up with way more than her quota of ad revenue. That had always been my least favorite part of the job. I'd hated going into coffee shops and stationery stores and asking for money in return for a business card–sized slot on a page of a magazine hardly anyone (except those who appeared on its pages) read. Arielle, however, relished the task.

If only she had relished the part where she picked the

stories. Now, I'm not saying the Lit Mag editor has to be a Lit major, like me. Brandon is Applied Math. Arielle, I think, is History, or maybe American Studies. Something like that. But I'm not sure she really liked literature all that much. She'd never joined in any of the office debates about books or authors, and she didn't seem particularly well read, whether in the world of literary or of popular fiction.

I'd made that argument to Brandon, back when we elevated her to editor. "I'm not sure I like the idea of the Lit Mag editor not knowing what the Booker Prize is."

"It's British," he'd responded. "Be satisfied she knows about the Pulitzer."

So Arielle it was, and if I noticed any decline in the quality of the magazine since her name had started appearing at the top of the masthead, I'd never mentioned it to anyone. And I had put her on my short list for Rose & Grave, if only to make it look a tad less skimpy. After all, Arielle and I were more simpatico than Topher Cox and I would ever be.

Perhaps I had never given her an adequate chance before. She clearly *valued* literature, even if she wasn't a writer herself. That she worked so hard for the Lit Mag without any outward show of literary leanings was a sign of... something, right? Maybe this would be my opportunity to discover what it was. If Rose & Grave could make me friends with Clarissa Cuthbert and James Orcutt, maybe it could do the same with Arielle Hallet and me.

We chatted the whole way up Science Hill, and sat together in the back of the Geology department's enormous lecture hall (dubbed "the Bat Cave" by Geology majors who clearly spent more time with rocks than people). Afterward, she insisted on grabbing a late lunch with me at Commons, and then I had to run to Nabokov, so we parted ways.

Or so I thought. When class ended, I went to the bathroom. As I trailed out of the engineering department annex room where the seminar was held, well behind my classmates, I caught sight of Arielle trudging back toward the main part of campus, head down, iPod earbuds in place, scuffling a bit as she walked.

At lunch, she'd told me she had an afternoon Art History lecture all the way across campus. So what was she doing outside the engineering building?

Had she been waiting for me?

I hereby confess:

The society has changed me.

I'm not sure that's a good thing.

3.

Stalkers

Over the next few days, I noticed Arielle a lot. She was in the coffee shop I frequented, on my walks to and from classes, and she always had a seat saved for me in Atmospheric Change. Not that there weren't plenty of empty ones in the humongous auditorium. I saw more of Arielle that week than I had when we'd worked together in the Lit Mag office.

If she was following me, there was only one reason why. Tap. Like Jamie had warned me, the people on my short list would be thinking about the fact that they *were*. Arielle must have—rightly—assumed she had a shot. Was this sudden friendship with me her attempt to cement the situation? Or remind me that she was out there, just waiting to be tapped? I thought we were the ones who were supposed to suddenly start showing up in *their* lives.

I hoped she understood that I was in Rose & Grave. If she was chasing me around campus for a slot in Quill & Ink, she was bound to be disappointed.

Saturday morning, Arielle sidled up to me in line at the

Prescott College Dining Hall. "Hi there, Amy," she said brightly, and served herself a scoop of scrambled eggs.

"Hi." I ladled syrup over my pancakes and lifted my tray, ready to move on to the drinks station and dessert cart. Arielle was not in Prescott herself, she wasn't in stayed-over-with-a-boy oversized sweatshirt and wet-hair wear, and the chances she was meeting a friend at 8 A.M. were pretty slim.

Sure enough, I'd hardly started my meal when I saw her emerge from the food line, her gaze surveying the dining room before landing on me, visibly brightening, and coming my way.

"Mind if I sit here?" she asked, wedging her tray in between Josh's and Lydia's (the lovebirds were currently cuddling by the coffee cart). This would go over great. They were practically joined at the hip.

"Um, I think those two trays are together..." I began, as she sat down. More Arielle? Nice girl and all, but I was beginning to doubt that proximity would make my heart grow any fonder. She was losing points to Topher Cox, of all people! At this point, Kalani Leto-Taube might win purely by default. I didn't really know anything about her.

Yet. Still on my To Do list, though, if I managed to shake my shadow.

Lydia and Josh returned with their coffee mugs and I did the introductions.

"Nice to meet you," Josh said, sliding his tray across the table and sitting down next to me.

Arielle ignored him (bad move, Hallet) and started in on what I have discovered is her favorite topic: I So Wish My Senior Year Could Go As Great As Yours Seems to Be Going.

Hilarious, right? Perhaps I should tell her about the harassment, the heartbreak, the kidnapping. Heck, even drop some hints about the incident with the projectile vomiting. That would cure her of the Rose & Grave jones right quick.

"If I were you," Lydia said at last, unsuccessfully trying to hide her snicker behind her mug, "I'd do whatever it takes to avoid having a Spring Break like Amy's."

"Did you go on the Habitat trip?" she gushed at Lydia. "Didn't you like it?"

"No, I'm not part of that group," Lydia responded evenly, and took another sip.

Josh rustled his newspaper. "Amy," he said. "Have you seen Topher Cox's new op-ed?"

Arielle shot him eye-daggers. "I didn't care for it," she said quickly. "That guy can't string a sentence together, even in defense of his sexist trash. How he ever scammed his way into the managing editor job I'll never know."

So at least she knew who her competition was.

"Maybe it was pesk—er, persistence?" I suggested. Over Arielle's head, I saw George at the salad bar, and excused myself.

"Hey," I said, meeting him by the dressings. "See that girl at my table?"

He looked. "Yeah. Cute." He went back to spooning out blue cheese.

"I'm not setting you up on a date, George! That's Arielle Hallet."

"Oh." He looked again. "Still cute."

"Well, she's starting to piss me off. Always popping up whenever I think I'm going to get a moment to myself."

George grinned. "So it begins. I had to put up with that from the opposite direction all last spring."

"With Jamie?" I asked, my tone dry.

He made a show of flinching. "Yeah, well...Hey, at least it's not Topher Cox. That guy's a douche."

"Arielle's been telling us so as well."

"Really?" George looked up from the bacon bits. "Give her credit for doing her research as to who else you'd be likely to tap. Very Digger-esque of her. What does she say about the Kalani chick? Because if you ask me, that's her real competition. She's the hottest girl in the junior—" George clammed up as a group of underclassmen jostled around the other side of the bar.

"We don't tap on the basis of hotness, George."

"Speak for yourself," he joked.

I rolled my eyes. "Are you coming over?"

"With that promise of scintillating table talk? Hmmm…"

Back at the table, Josh's frustration at Arielle's ignorance of his own Digger status was beginning to show, and Lydia, amused by the proceedings, was holding up her end of the conversation with comments designed to make the red around his ears grow darker.

This was the inherent design flaw of a secret society. Societies tapped ambitious, brilliant, successful young people with no lack of pride and a more-than-occasional touch of hubris. Their induction was a moment of triumph in their lives—proof that they were, in fact, one of the elect.

Then they weren't allowed to tell anyone.

So Arielle's fawning around me and my best friend only aggravated poor Josh, who should have been a prime candidate for fawning himself. Of course, as soon as I returned, all attention was back onto me, rather than Arielle just asking questions *about* me to Lydia. Josh's mood did not improve.

I listened with half of my attention, and kept my eyes on George. He was spending an awfully long time constructing that salad, wandering over to the other side of the salad bar and insinuating himself into the crowd there. I watched as he exchanged pleasantries with a brunette in a

Prescott College T-shirt and denim skirt. Casual enough.
They might be arguing over who got the last spoonful of
garlic croutons. Then he reached over and flicked her pigtail.

She giggled—who wouldn't, when George Harrison
Prescott flicks your pigtail?—and then hip-checked him.

I paused, fork halfway to my mouth. George flirted as a
matter of course, but a hip check was a little more intimate
than I expected from a salad bar encounter. I looked more
closely at the scene:

1) Body Language: check. Tops of torsos angled away,
   but groins definitely pointed in each other's
   direction. Casual, yet secretly sexy.
2) Teasing Touches: check. Innocent with an
   underlying sense of familiarity.
3) And now he was following her to her table filled
   with—wait for it—sophomores.

I had discovered the identity of George's secret rendezvous. Apparently, secrecy was no longer an issue. He
was having brunch with her. In his own college. In her own
college. In front of all of us.

Had the world gone mad?

"What do you think, Amy?" Arielle was asking me,
about heaven-knew-what.

I thought that perhaps I was jumping to conclusions.
After all, George and I had had brunch together plenty of
times during our affair. But then, we'd known each other
for years, even before we were in the same secret society.
We'd shared plenty of meals, merely by belonging to the
same class and college. He was not friends with this sophomore, and due to her youth, he certainly wasn't courting
her for Rose & Grave.

And not once during the times that George and I had been both sleeping together and having brunch together in front of our friends had I ever once thrown my arm around his shoulder and pressed a kiss to his cheek. As Little Miss Sophomore was doing now.

My mouth went dry. George and I were over, but that didn't make it the slightest bit easier to watch him canoodle with another woman. Was this even remotely how he'd felt when he'd seen Jamie and me making out on Cavador Key? Did George—could George?—have this same lump in his throat when he'd approached me in Louisiana and told me how Jamie had tried to rescue me?

"I gotta go," I mumbled, grabbing my tray. I had to . . . what?

Check out Facebook, for starters. Who *was* this girl?

"Where?" Arielle asked. "I'll walk with you."

"Room . . . study . . . thesis . . ." I faltered with a hand wave as I headed toward the back of the hall to bus my dinnerware.

But I didn't go to my place.

I went to Jamie's.

———

Jamie answered the door in an undershirt and sweatpants. "Hey there!" he said, smiling broadly. "What a pleasant surprise. Have you had breakf—"

I threw myself into his arms and started kissing him.

"Pleasanter surprise," he managed, backing us away from the threshold. There's the idea. I pushed him gently against the wall and started tugging on his shirt.

"About to get even pleasanter," I murmured against his neck as my fingers found the drawstring of his pants. Bad grammar is such a turn-on. I loosened the strings, then dragged the pants down and over his hips. Ooh, nice. He had a bathing-suit tan going on. I trailed my fingers across the line of demarcation on his torso, then lower.

I leaned in, pressing my advantage. I was fully clothed, his pants and boxers now pooled around his ankles. He leaned against the wall of the foyer, practically in view of the street, relaxed and yet utterly alert. "No," I whispered. "I haven't had breakfast."

"Oh," he said as I began to slide to my knees. "Because I'm making waffles."

"Hmmm."

A loud buzzing noise interrupted me. Jamie clunked his head against the wall.

"What's that?" I asked.

"I told you: I'm making waffles."

"Will it go away?"

"Around the time the fire alarm starts up, yes."

I groaned and rocked back on my heels and Jamie hurried to pull up his pants and tend to his burning breakfast.

I stared into the kitchen. "That's a Dining Hall waffle maker." I knew them well. The industrial-sized spinning machines were stationed on tables for student use every brunch.

"I know. Can you believe they were tossing it?" He pulled a golden, fluffy Belgian waffle from the machine and plopped it on a nearby plate. "All it needed was some work on the springs."

"You fished that thing out of the trash and now you're cooking with it?"

"I washed it first. And fixed it, too, I might add. Aren't you impressed with my engineering skills?" He rejoined me at the wall. "Okay. I'm back."

I stood up, lips pursed. The scent of freshly cooked waffle filled the air—sweet, bready, wholesome.

"Or did you want me to bring the syrup?" he asked.

The first time I'd been in this apartment, I'd felt nothing but contempt for the guy standing before me. And every ounce of that contempt had transferred to his belongings—the sagging couch, the old and threadbare clothes, the giant snake. His room hadn't had the same panache as George's jukebox-filled bachelor pad or the comfortable, lived-in look of the suite I shared with Lydia. But Jamie's place had reincarnated waffle makers and half a dozen vegetarian cookbooks and a pet mouse he'd kept and named for my sake. The people in my club didn't know this about him. I hadn't known this about him.

I don't know if anyone did.

"Why don't you have a roommate?" I asked abruptly.

"Huh?"

"It would be cheaper."

"It would also be less private," he hinted. "Now, about that syrup—"

"Do you have any friends at Eli Law?" I pressed.

His eyes narrowed. "Why do you want to know?"

So he didn't. "How about people still in undergrad?"

"A couple. And a few at the law school, too. Some folks from my section."

Study buddies. And undergrads I'd never heard about before. The defensive tone was back as well, threaded through with a shot of frustration. Now I knew what I'd done to him last semester, kicking him out of the tomb, and why it had made his general disdain for me turn into full-on hate.

"I told you last year, Amy. I made Rose & Grave my life. Nothing else mattered. I don't keep in touch with many of my barbarian friends."

Something in the way he said it gave me pause. "How about your ex-girlfriends?"

He sighed and retied the strings on his sweatpants. "Is that what this is really about? I have condoms."

Wow, was that not at all what this was about. It was about knowing him, having the slightest idea of what made up this guy's life outside the tomb.

"Though to be perfectly honest," he continued, "I haven't had sex with anyone in a while."

"How long a while?"

He fixed me with a look I could read clear as day. *Longer than you.*

Because of course he knew all about me. Unfair.

I swallowed. "I think you need to understand a few things about . . . George."

"I promise you I understand everything I care to." He turned and entered the kitchen. "And my waffle is getting cold."

"But this is going to keep coming up." I followed him.

"Whose fault is that?" He ladled more waffle mix into the machine and slammed the top down.

"What did he tell you?"

He shoved a waffle plate in my hands. "Nothing."

I suppose he didn't need to. Everyone knew George's reputation. And Jamie was not stupid. I wondered if he thought I was different, having slept with George. If I expected something special . . . or could do something special.

"You know," I said before I could stop myself, "it's really not George who should bug you. Remember that guy I was upset about right before Spring Break? Brandon?"

"And I thought I couldn't hate this conversation more than I did five seconds ago," he grumbled without looking up from the machine.

"Not that either of them should bother you," I clarified.

"They don't."

"They clearly do."

The buzzer went off. Jamie swatted at it, then righted the machine, pulled out the waffle, and dropped it onto another plate. He grabbed my dish from my hands and brought both over to the coffee table, with the syrup and two forks. As I sat down, I noticed he'd put the older, colder waffle in front of himself.

"What bothers me," he said, pouring on the syrup, "is my girlfriend coming over, making a pretty good show of seducing me in the hallway, then stopping mid-act to talk about her ex-boyfriends. Call me crazy." He shoved a bit of waffle in his mouth.

Reepicheep rustled in her cage. Lord Voldemort, as usual, was asleep in a coil in his tank. Jamie chewed softly. I ate my waffle. He was quite a good cook.

Pretty good show of seducing him, eh? Go, Amy. But the tension hadn't eased one bit from Jamie's end of the couch. Wouldn't either, what with this George-shaped gorilla between us.

"The last time I had sex," I said, "was Halloween."

He nodded slowly. "That was my birthday."

I choked on my waffle. This was getting worse and worse. "No!"

"Why do you think they called me 'Poe'?"

I had always guessed it was because he was morose and taciturn and creepy. "Um...because 'Hotstuff' was taken?"

He snorted. No points there.

"Anything I say will just dig myself in deeper here, won't it?" I asked at last.

"Likely."

Did he have a crush on me way back on Halloween? He

couldn't have. I'd kicked him out of the tomb. He'd hated
me. But then, I'd pretty much figured he'd hated me last
month, when he'd comforted me and took me out for pizza
a few short days before saving my life. He'd liked me then.
And he liked me now, which was the material point.

"I'm sorry about the hallway," I said, after another long
silence.

"Me too," he said. "Way sorrier than you, I imagine."

"Why is that?"

"I wasn't the one who would have been kneeling on
hardwood floors."

————

Jamie and I did not sleep together that day. Or that weekend. We didn't talk any more about George, either. Instead, we hung out, studied together, and discussed my
short list and how best to approach the remaining two people to get a feel for their behavior. Arielle, of course, I had
covered.

"I just don't know if I have the choice I'd like to," I
complained to him. I was lying with my head in his lap,
pretending to read my Geology textbook. "Arielle is fine, I
guess, but she's not the person I want to leave my legacy
to."

"From what you've said, it sounded like you felt that
way about her last year, too." Jamie patted my hair, then
returned to his law books. "So why repeat that disappointment?"

I lifted my shoulders as much as I could against his
thighs and turned a page.

"She doesn't need to be on your list just because she
mirrors your role, Amy. It doesn't need to be that literal.
You were a . . . special case."

"A charity case, you mean."

"Charity for whom?" he asked. "We needed *you*, remember? You would have been perfectly happy in Quill & Ink."

"Who would you have tapped, then?" I asked, sitting up and facing him. "If I'd rejected?"

He shook his head. "Nope. Sorry. You know our deliberations are sealed."

I pounded my fist against the sofa cushion. "I need to know this information. It will help me pick my tap."

"How? The person is a senior. Not eligible for tap anymore."

"*Person?* Not a girl?" Could Malcolm have traded out, too?

He returned his attention to the book.

"You're impossible." I lay back down.

So many secrets. In the tomb and outside of them. He never had answered the question about his ex-girlfriends, I realized. Or about the last time he'd had sex. He spent his time alone in this apartment or alone in class or alone in a tomb filled with people who were not his society brothers. No wonder he got used to keeping things to himself.

"If I don't include Arielle, that makes my preliminary list really small. I've got Topher, whom I'd have to trade for, and whom no one seems to like very much, and then Kalani. So . . . really just Kalani."

"What's wrong with Kalani?"

"Nothing. I hardly know the girl. But I'd like to have some options."

"Maybe it's better not to. Court Kalani. Call it a day. Work on your thesis."

He had a point. These next few weeks would be way easier on me if I just picked a tap and moved on. And Kalani seemed to have it all. A perfect prospective Digger.

But that wouldn't be very true to my legacy either, would it? The perfect Digger, I was not. If anything, I'd been the exact opposite.

———

Kalani Leto-Taube proved difficult to track down. I got her course schedule care of Jenny's access to the registrar, but when the junior wasn't actively in classes, she was usually holed up in her office at the *Eli Daily News*. It got to the point where I wondered if I'd have to book an appointment with her to get a chance to chat.

Fortunately, all that activity needed to be fueled by something, and I finally cornered my quarry at a table in the back of a coffee shop. Even among the mug ring marks, discarded sugar packets and stirring sticks, she looked like a queen. Kalani is some sort of exotic mixture of Cuban, Polish, and Hawaiian—tall, big-boned, with huge dark eyes she kept ringed with kohl, and pouty pink lips. Her hair was pulled back in a tight, ballerina-style ponytail, and she was dressed in a cream-colored skirt suit with a taupe shell that only made her golden skin seem more luminous.

I looked down at my yellow Converse All Stars. Yeah, we had *so* much in common.

"Kalani, right?" I asked. She looked up from her book and I caught a peek at the title. *War and Peace*. Bingo. "I think we've got the Russian Novel class together. I'm Amy Haskel."

"Hi," she said. "I don't know if I've seen you there."

Probably because I took the class last spring. Aced my final, too, thanks to Rose & Grave's backlog of exam questions. "It's a big lecture." I invited myself into the seat beside her. "I guess almost everyone takes it at one time or another."

"I really wanted the Nabokov seminar," she said, "but it was full again this year."

"I'm in that, too," I said. "I love it. Definitely try again next year." Maybe this would work out. We both loved to read, we were taking a lot of the same classes (or wanted to). "Are you a Lit major?" I asked.

"History and Music," she replied. "I know, you think it's strange. Like I should be a Lit major just because I work for the paper."

"You work for the paper?" I asked innocently, eyes wide, and she laughed.

"God, I sound awful," she looked down in her coffee.

And obligingly forthcoming. I smiled. "Nah. I know who you are." And it wasn't that awful. Everyone in school read the *EDN*. We knew who was in charge. "Tell me about Music and History."

"I think History, especially modern history, might even be better for me if I want to be with a newspaper after graduation."

"Do you want to be with a paper after graduation?"

"Yes and no." She eyed me. "You're a Lit major?"

"Yes."

"But you didn't work for any of the campus publications."

"I was the editor of the Lit Mag," I replied.

"Oh." Her face said she'd meant *real* publications. There's a reason hardly any magazine publishes short fiction anymore. "Well, what I mean is that in the old days, if you wanted to be a reporter, you worked a beat at some small local paper, moved up, moved to a bigger paper, moved up, et cetera. Now it's all about getting your MFA and then interning at the *New York Times*."

She sounded as conflicted as I did, which, ironically,

was better and better for my purposes. "Which would you rather?"

"Well, the beat reporter gig is cheaper," she said with a laugh.

"But the *New York Times* is nice." I sipped at my coffee.

Kalani stared into hers. "I think what I'd really like to do is write books."

At that, I froze. I'd made an attempt at a novel, back in the day. Rose & Grave had found it on my computer and waved a copy of its pathetic pages in my face. "Fiction?" I croaked out, cool as the coffee in my fist.

"Oh, no!" She made a face. "Nonfiction. High-concept. My literary agent is shopping around a few proposals right now."

Her. Literary. Agent. "Oh." Probably the one for whom I'd be making photocopies next year. I pictured taking Kalani's calls and confirming her booking on the *Today* show.

"It's social history type of stuff. I've written a few 'this is how our generation feels about XYZ' pieces for *Marie Claire* and *Salon*, so it's sort of an expansion of that." She hunched her shoulders. "Boring, right? Tell me more about the Nabokov class. Promise me I'll like it better than *War and Peace*."

So I couldn't hate her. I could be jealous through the whole conversation and all the way back to my dorm room and as I pounded away at my thesis and as I waited for the phone to ring about *any* of my applications or future plans, but I couldn't actually dislike her for any of it. She had worked for and therefore obtained things that I had not, in fact, worked for (and therefore hadn't obtained).

She was too nice to hate. Also, one shouldn't think bad thoughts about anyone forced to spend time in the vicinity of Topher Cox, as Kalani did every day at the newspaper.

The last person on my short list was easy to find. When he wasn't working at the *EDN* offices, he was training in the Eli gym. Fencing team.

No, really. Fencing.

I always confuse fencing outfits with beekeeper uniforms. Not that I'm personally familiar with either one. But if I were watching a movie about beekeepers, and a bunch of folks turned up in fencing outfits, I probably wouldn't think it was strange. (Unlike watching, say, a Regency-set piece where they're all in Victorian clothing, but then again, I'm a Lit major.)

But both beekeeping and fencing outfits are a lot weirder than period clothing. Unless the period is "future," which, according to Hollywood, features some pretty ridiculous fashion. Topher Cox looked pretty ridiculous in his beekeeping outfit. Fencing outfit. Whatever.

The fencing itself was a little cooler. Or maybe I was just really into all those period movies and liked to watch a good swordfight. Unfortunately, very few of the alien beekeeper pairs out there on the mats were having good swordfights. Mostly they hopped around each other in a complex little dance for an undefined period before moving toward each other and striking. Or I think striking. It was always tough to tell who'd won. It reminded me more of those reflex hand-slap games you play when you're ten.

I didn't have sports like this at my high school. We had basketball, football, track, stuff like that. I'd never even heard of squash until I got to Eli. Topher came from a world with strange sports like polo, squash, and dressage. Not that we needed another athlete in the club, as Ben's tap would likely have that covered. But it didn't hurt.

And there was really no reason to hold it against him, either. After all, my ex-boyfriend Brandon had played badminton, and at the time, I'd found it adorable.

I waited until Topher removed his beekeeping mask and headed over to the bleachers in the rest of his space suit. "Hi, Topher," I said, as he sucked down the contents of his water bottle. "How's it going?"

He looked at me. "Who are you?"

An auspicious beginning, to be sure! "Amy Haskel. We met at The Game in Cambridge a while back?" I stopped myself before I could add, *and you drunkenly hit on me*.

He looked skeptical. "Sorry. Hey, have a nice visit, though." He waved at me and turned to watch the practice.

"I'm not from Harvard," I said, and the pleasant mask slipped just a tad. "I go here. I'm a senior." Perhaps he would catch on.

He turned back around. "Great," he said dryly. *Nope.* "What can I do for you?"

Golly, let's see. You can take my place in the oldest and best secret society on campus, guaranteeing yourself a life of wealth, power, and general fabulosity—or so goes the party line. I wasn't so sure about when exactly that stuff was supposed to kick in for me.

"I wanted to talk about your recent op-ed in the *Daily*. The one that posited a justification for sexual harassment as necessary for the continuation of the species." I don't know why I was bothering. Demetria was certain to blackball him after that vile piece of bullshit had run. But I should at least give everyone on my short list a shot.

"Oh, God, another one? Look, write a letter to the editor, like all the others. They print anything less than 150 words and without bad language."

"Oh, no!" I said, tamping down my urge to strike. He was lucky that

A) Demetria wasn't nearby and
B) his lance was several rows away.

"I was fascinated," I lied. "I'm an editor emeritus at the Lit Mag, and I was thinking that the situation you put forth at the end—your hypothetical employer and receptionist— would be a really great basis for a short story."

Actually, I thought it would make a really great basis for cut-rate porn. Topher's "receptionist" was a slutty tease who secretly wanted it despite her protests to her over-bearing but apparently heroic boss. And it was badly writ-ten, too—I agreed with Arielle on that point.

"Huh."

"You write any fiction?"

"For the Lit Mag?" he scoffed.

Again, with the violent urges. I forced myself to smile sweetly. "Oh, I'm not there anymore. And in a month I'll be graduating and moving on to the publishing scene in New York. I'm fielding offers now, but I'm thinking defi-nitely agency over publisher. Really *work* with the talent."

Inwardly, I gagged. Who was this talking? I sounded like a total sleazeball. Like someone who actually wanted Topher as a replacement. What was the point of pretend-ing to be someone else to impress a person that's supposed to be like me the way I am? Telling Kalani I was currently in her Russian Novel class had been one thing. This felt completely different.

"Which agency?"

Crap. "William Morris."

Interest lit his eyes. Yep, Amy, go for the name recogni-tion.

"I'll just be an assistant, of course, but if I could even pass your stuff on to someone, give it that little extra push..." I raised my hands, palms up. "Maybe we can talk about your ideas more over dinner?"

He checked out my breasts, then agreed.

———

Dinner was the waste of time I thought it would be. Before I entered the Hartford College Dining Hall, I promised myself to keep an open mind. Maybe under all that asshole bluster he was really a sensitive soul. Clarissa hadn't been the rich bitch I'd originally taken her for. Jamie hadn't been the cold, vindictive misogynist I'd pegged him as. Well, maybe just the cold part. If he was mad, he could frost you like a meat locker.

I'd also promised myself to act like myself. After all, I wasn't trying to impress Topher. I was trying to get to know him. I couldn't care less what he thought of me.

Fortunately, I didn't have to act like much. The topic rarely strayed from Why Topher Cox Is Totally Radical. If I'd thought listening to Arielle's flattery was boring, listening to Topher's solipsism was deadly.

"What do you think?" he asked, after finishing his latest spiel on his work, his personal philosophy, his plan for world domination. Who knew anymore?

"Very Bret Easton Ellis," I replied. Which was true.

"Huh?"

"*American Psycho.* You know, except without the social satire bit." I took a bite of my burrito.

"Oh, yeah. Love that movie." Topher nodded vigorously. "I'm totally like Patrick Bateman."

I blinked at him, my mouth full of burrito I dared not try to swallow under the circumstances. Patrick Bateman was the pathetic, envy-poisoned yuppie, the delusional, wannabe serial killer who narrated the book.

"You mean Christian Bale?" I managed, raising my napkin. "The actor who played him? Also played Batman?" It's possible he got the names confused. Bateman/Batman. It could happen.*

"Yeah, whatever. He was so ripped in that film."

It was too late. I was already picturing Tap Night. *By the order of our Order, I dub thee, Topher Cox, Patrick Bateman, Knight of Persephone, Order of Rose & Grave.* Hey, if Josh could cart around Keyser Soze as a society code name for a year, I could stick Topher with Bateman.

Not that I wanted to tap him. Kalani was clearly my girl.

"Hi, Amy." I looked up to see Arielle standing over the table, looking near tears. "Guess you're in my college tonight."

For some strange reason, I felt guilty, as if I'd been caught cheating. "Guess so. Do you know Topher?"

"She does," Topher said. "We're old friends, right, Ari?"

Arielle ignored him. "Can I talk to you for a second, Amy? I need your advice on something."

"Um . . ." I looked at Topher, who seemed even less tolerable with Arielle nearby, offering to take me away.

"It'll only take a minute."

"Okay." Topher looked unconcerned as I left the table and followed Arielle to a quiet nook just beyond the dining hall. We sat in a pair of leather armchairs. Arielle tucked her legs beneath her.

"What's up?" I asked her.

Arielle traced a pattern on the leather armrest. "I was wondering . . . do you think I should join Quill & Ink?"

"I don't know," I said. "Do you want to?"

---

*No, no, it really couldn't happen. The confessor realizes this now.

"They interviewed me today," she said, meeting my eyes now. "Seemed really nice, very enthusiastic."

Was she trying to make me jealous, or honestly looking for advice? I couldn't tell. "Maybe it would be fun," I said.

"But *you* didn't join them."

"No," I admitted. "I didn't."

Arielle nodded, slowly. "So I wanted to know if you think I should."

Oh, I got it now. *Are you going to tap me, Amy, or should I just go ahead and join Quill & Ink?*

She cast a glance back into the dining hall. "He's a real asshole, you know that, right?"

I was quickly figuring it out, yes.

"I just don't want you to get hurt."

"Oh," I said. "I'm not—it's not—I have a boyfriend."

But that wasn't what she meant and we both knew it. I liked Arielle more in this moment than I ever had before. She was the only one on my list of potential taps who I hadn't had to lie to. It was refreshing to play the game this way—innocently, like the way Lydia teased Josh and me. Both Lydia and Arielle were barbarians, but they knew the score.

"I hooked up with him once," she said. "Freshman year. Huge mistake, and he hasn't ever let me live it down."

"I'm sorry." Now, how to say this without breaking my vows? "He doesn't seem like the kind of person I'd trust to know private things about me."

Maybe that would do it.

Arielle raised her eyebrows.

Yep, that did it.

"So," she said again, "do you think I should join Quill & Ink?"

I sighed. Arielle would be a decent choice. She was smart, and fun, and more witty than I'd given her credit for during the week she'd been following me around like a puppy. But if I was really doing right by Rose & Grave, the best choice was Kalani. Kalani was true Digger material. She was the superstar; the student with the best potential for future success and stardom. She would be a feather in the Rose & Grave cap. And it wouldn't be fair to lead Arielle on. Not when she had other opportunities.

"Yes," I said. "I think you should."

I hereby confess:
I thought I had it all figured out.
Boy, was I wrong.

4.
New World Order

I was taking notes on the couch in our common room that evening when the phone rang. Lydia was over at Josh's for the night, Jamie wouldn't be out of his study session for at least an hour. Perhaps it was my mother trying to finalize commencement plans.

I clicked the *Talk* button. "Hello?"

"Amy?" said a voice I knew too well. "It's Darren."

My throat went dry and my hand grew so clammy the phone almost slipped from its grip.

"Darren?" I whispered. "How did you get this number?"

"My dad got it from the caretaker at the tomb," he said. I breathed a bit easier. Of course. "He said I have to call you and ... apologize."

Oh. Apologize for drugging me, kidnapping me, almost drowning me. How does a fourteen-year-old kid even begin to prepare a speech for something like that? "Where are you?"

"Uh..." He hesitated. "I'm not supposed to tell you the name. It's against the rules."

A rehab facility, probably. Troubled teens, delinquents. A place parents could send their children before the law took over. At least Gehry was adhering to that part of the promise.

"My stitches are supposed to be coming out tomorrow," he said. "They had to shave off a lot of my hair."

I glanced down at my wrist, to where the scabs had mostly peeled away, leaving shiny new pink skin. I wondered if it would scar. Darren's injuries definitely would. He'd cut his head open on the boat when it had tipped over. He'd passed out in the water and, like me, had almost drowned.

Well, either those were the stitches he was talking about or the first thing they had done to him was a good old-fashioned prefrontal lobotomy.

I couldn't think of anything to say to him. Did Kurt Gehry really think that his son wanted to chat with his victim? That I wanted to chat with my kidnapper?

"And Dad said—I wanted to... thank you," he said, the words sounding oddly unnatural from his mouth. "For letting me come here instead of jail."

"Okay," I answered, because nothing else seemed to fit. Yes, I'd refused to press charges. I wouldn't call it largesse. I lay down on the couch and curled my knees up to my chest. Where was Lydia when I needed her? Where was Jamie?

"But it kind of sucks," he went on. "It's all these girls with, like, anorexia and stuff."

I doubted they had rehab centers reserved solely for budding sociopaths. I "hmmmmed" into the receiver to keep myself from speaking those words out loud. Though the way I remembered it, Darren Gehry had a good sense of humor. When he wasn't trying to kill me, that was.

"I told him you wouldn't want to talk to me," Darren said. "That you'd be too afraid."

There was a soupçon of pride in his tone. Yes, he'd terrified me. He'd set out to do so, and he'd succeeded. He was doing it now, even from a distance, even imprisoned. I sat up.

"I'm not scared," I said. "I'm angry. I don't like you. I have nothing to say to you. And your repeated declarations that the only reason you're on the phone with me right now is because your father is forcing you isn't really helping the conversation." Darren couldn't hurt me.

On the other end of the line, the teenager was silent. Was he sad? Furious? It would probably be too much to hope that my admonishment had actually made him rethink his attitude. Heck, it had probably shocked the hell out of him that I could stand up for myself. After all, I'd been plenty pliant when I'd been . . .

Begging for my life.

"Darren?" I said into the phone.

But I heard only a click, then a dial tone.

———

"I can't believe he actually called you," said Angel. We were in the tomb, researching initiations of old to get ideas for the upcoming festivities.

"According to him, his father was making him do it," I replied. It was amazing how styles had changed to suit the times. Rites of the seventies included mind-altering substances to really get the initiates in the magical mood. Notes from the eighties were awash in references to cocaine,* and

*At least, the confessor assumes that was the general gist behind a "snow"-themed initiation. After all, it was in May.

the nineties-era clubs had printed all their invitations on recycled paper.

My own initiation into the Order of Rose & Grave had a theme of women and power, to fit with the momentous occasion of tapping women for the very first time. The skits had all been about Cleopatra or the Salem Witch Trials. I'd have to ask Poe about some of the messages behind those skits, as things had not ended well for either Cleopatra or the goodwives of Salem.

He probably had picked those out himself.

"You should have hung up on him immediately," argued Lucky, pulling down another stack of Black Books.

"I don't know," said Lil' Demon, flipping through a scrapbook of early 21st century initiation photos. "Maybe it's part of his therapy. You know, apologize to those whom you have wronged."

"This isn't AA," said Angel. "And it's clearly too soon. A short stint at Delinquents-R-Us and he's suddenly no longer a psycho?"

Lil' Demon shrugged. "It depends on the rehab place. In some, you walk the walk and talk the talk and they pronounce you cured and give you massages and pedicures for a week. In others, it's major lockdown."

"If I know Gehry," said Angel, "it's a matter of getting Darren 'cured' as quickly as possible. That's probably why he called you."

"Yeah, well, Darren's not cured," I said. "I was completely unprepared for his call, and he could tell. Relished it, in fact." I shuddered. If what you liked was scaring people, controlling people—did that ever go away? Even if you got into the major-lockdown-style rehab facility?

And if so, did it matter whether I pressed charges or not? Even if he did get into legal trouble for kidnapping me, his juvenile records would be sealed when he turned eighteen.

Like that girl who'd murdered her mother, then ended up at Harvard. Of course, that was assuming the Gehrys could prevent the story from leaking to the press. The media had been focusing a lot of attention on the ex–Chief of Staff after it had been revealed that the hard-line conservative had employed a household staff composed of mostly illegal immigrants and the whole family had fled Washington, D.C., in disgrace. The likelihood that our case would provoke a media circus had been one of the factors that convinced me to keep the whole matter under wraps. Darren deserved punishment. He didn't deserve tabloid covers.

"What did Poe say?" Lil' Demon asked.

I focused my attention on the book in my hands. "I didn't tell him."

I caught Angel and Lil' Demon exchanging a look.

"What? I didn't tell him! Sue me. What would he do about it?"

"Fix it," said Lucky. "That's what he does. I mean, I'm not crazy about your boyfriend, Bugaboo, but I can admit that he knows how to get stuff done."

"Like what?" I said. "He calls Darren at his undisclosed location?"

"Or he calls Gehry and tells him to get his son to leave you the hell alone," said Angel.

"That's exactly what I need," I said. "Poe's protection from the big, bad fourteen-year-old." Poe's pity. Poe's opinion that I was pathetic. Forget it. If I'd managed fine when I was drugged and tied up on a deserted island, I could manage a stupid phone call. This wasn't *Scream*.

"On the subject of wormy patriarch's spawn we'd rather not spend time with," said Lucky, "I've got some bad news about Topher Cox."

"You're kidding me," I said. Lucky had been in charge of background checks on all our potential taps.

"Turns out, he's the grandson of the illustrious Achilles of D125," Lucky went on. "Lionel Drake, importer/exporter. Homes in Singapore, Paris, and Martha's Vineyard."

"Crap," I said.

"Are we obligated to tap legacies, though?" asked Lil' Demon.

"If we think it could help our standing with the patriarchs," said Angel. "I'm not an idiot. I know one of the reasons I was picked last year is because D176 thought it would smooth things over with my dad if one of those horrible girl taps was, in fact, his own daughter." She pursed her lips. "How little they understood my father."

True. If anything, their choice of Angel, who had always been a disappointment to her father, had only ignited Mr. Cuthbert's belief that women did not belong in the society.

"But I've never heard of this guy," I said. "He's not on the board, the way Angel's dad is. Maybe he couldn't care less if his grandson gets tapped."

"Good point," said Angel. "Usually the concerned patriarchs are pretty vocal about which direction they would like the nepotism to swing. They all know I'm a 'legacy' tap, and I've received no less than four e-mails from patriarchs wondering if their rugrats are on my short list. Most include resumes. One included a video."

Lucky just sat there, arms crossed, waiting for us to finish. I groaned and looked at her. "Don't tell me."

"One month ago, Lionel Drake donated ten thousand dollars to the TTA."

———

Later, Lucky found me up to my elbows in Black Books near the back of the Grand Library. "Everything okay, Bugaboo?"

"Yeah," I said, pulling down another stack. "Fine."

"You don't *have* to tap him," she said. "There's no law."

"Right, because we can afford to lose any more support from patriarchs." I sat back on my heels and sneezed. "Doesn't Hale ever dust back here?"

I'd really been getting excited about the idea of Kalani. She was everything Rose & Grave could possibly want—smart, accomplished, ambitious, focused, driven. She'd more than correct the temporary sidestep on the path toward world domination they'd experienced when Malcolm had tapped me. I understood that Kalani outclassed me completely on paper, but she worked hard, deserved it, and was really sweet, to boot. I wanted her to be in our society, on our team. I wanted to be her big sib. Maybe the support of the Rose & Grave network would help her along her path to superstardom. Maybe, if she was a Digger, she wouldn't forget the little guys like me when she actually became a huge success.

I yanked down another stack of books.

Topher, on the other hand—I dreaded the idea of a guy like him having access to any of our secrets.

"Well, I'd still have to trade for him," I said. "You want a girl tap?" Jenny's marble had been black.

"No, I'm good," she said. "I've got my eye on a Cognitive Science major in Calvin College. We had this great talk the other day. His goal in life is to discover the location of the soul. Right now, he's trying to decide if he wants to do seminary before medical school, or vice versa."

"Convince him to go to seminary first," I said, remembering Howard, the D177 tap who'd dropped out to concentrate on the MCATs and med school applications. "We'll be more likely to get him."

"I'll add that to the list immediately after 'Convince him we're not a bunch of devil worshippers.'" She laughed. "I hear that sometimes people think that."

I grinned and shook my head. Was it only a year ago that Lucky had believed that herself, had joined Rose & Grave with the express purpose of bringing it down from the inside? No wonder she'd volunteered for the job of background checks. Not only was she the most capable, what with her network access, but she had a personal stake in ensuring we didn't make the same mistake with our taps that D176 had with her.

"And...how's everything else?" she asked. "Just as fine?"

"You want to know about the boyfriend you can't stand?"

"I want to know if *you* can stand him," Lucky said, idly flipping through yet another Black Book. "Enough to, you know, talk to him about important events in your life. Or at the very least, about when the guy who kidnapped you calls for a chat."

"I told you," I said. "He'll only get upset."

"We all got upset," she replied. "Why should he be any different?"

I frowned at the shelves. It just was. Only Poe had serious doubts about my ability to handle the issues in my life.

"I want to make sure he's making you happy." Lucky folded her hands in her lap. "I've been there—remember last semester? The impossible boyfriend who asked for everything and gave nothing? Remember how I was willing to hide or change everything I was for him?"

"And now what are you hiding?" I snapped back. "The fact that you *have* a boyfriend?"

She sighed. We'd spent most of Spring Break accusing Lucky that there was something going on between her and fellow knight Tristram Shandy. She always denied it. She did again.

"Poe's not like that," I said. "I don't care what you guys think."

"Right now, I am only thinking that not only is he your boyfriend, he's your society brother. And that's two reasons you shouldn't be keeping secrets from him."

"He keeps plenty of secrets from me," I grumbled, and pulled down another stack of books.

Lucky began organizing and reshelving the ones on the far side of my pile. "Okay, leaving the issue of the boyfriend aside, how's everything else? Between what happened during Spring Break and all this tap stuff, I feel like we haven't talked in forever. How's school? Your thesis? Your job search?"

Sucks (except for Nabokov), sucks, sucks. "Fine."

"Do you know what you're doing next year?"

"No," I admitted.

"Because I've been thinking," she began. "Caritas could kind of use a public relations chair."

I stared at her. "What makes you think I know anything about public relations?"

She stared at me right back. "What have you been doing for us all year long? What about that article you spun for the *Daily* last spring where you single-handedly turned a damaging exposé on the society into an argument for the expanding role of equal rights in the Ivy League? What about all that work you did last semester when I . . . well, when I made that slight error in judgment? You mitigated that little snafu as well. You'd be great in PR."

"Great in PR would require me having contacts. I don't have contacts."

"*I* have contacts, though," Lucky said. "When I sold my program, back in high school, I was on dozens of news shows. They did a whole feature on me in *Wired*. And my Rolodex is your Rolodex."

I raised my eyebrows. "Have you ever even *seen* a Rolodex?"

"Fine. My iPhone. But the bottom line is, I want you for your skills."

"You want me because you're creating an all-Digger corporation."

"No, I'm hiring my brother's girlfriend, too."

"What are you, an employment assistance program?"

"What's wrong with me surrounding myself with a built-in pool of brilliant people I trust?" she asked. "Isn't the whole point of this society to make contacts that will help us later in life? You, and Angel, and Tristram, and everyone else are the best thing about being a Digger. Knowing you, trusting you. I'd hire Soze out of Stanford if I didn't know he wants to go into politics. And in five years, he'll be coming to me for campaign contributions, and I'll be happy to give him what I can, because I know that he'll do great things for our country. Not because we're both Diggers, but because we were Diggers together and I know exactly what he can do, and I want him to do it."

This was what no barbarian really understood about the nature of secret societies. They were suspicious of our bonds, of our tendency to stick together, work together, hire one another, support one another. To outsiders, we were a nepotism network, an old boys' club guaranteed to keep other people out.

But it wasn't that simple. I didn't love and trust every person in my society. I worked hard to even respect some of them, especially those with whom I disagreed on every point. I'd probably never end up keeping in touch with Nikolos or Mara. But the people I'd come to love over my months in Rose & Grave would be people I loved forever. Working for Jenny's company would be an amazing experience. Helping close friends I admire succeed in their dream jobs—what could possibly be wrong or elitist about that?

But Lucky sensed my hesitation. "Well, just keep it in mind," she said at last. "I know you have a lot of pans on the fire right now. I don't expect an answer right away."

"Thank you," I said. "Who knows? I may get into grad school yet."

"I'll pray that you have the best option open to you," she replied, and shelved another stack of books. "And that you and Poe stop keeping secrets from each other. Him I understand—but you? You've never really been the taciturn type. No offense."

"None taken." I opened the book on my lap. The first few pages related plans for the Straggler Initiation of D176—when the members of the club got together at the beginning of the school year to perform the full-on initiation of knights who'd been abroad during the junior year in which they'd been tapped. According to the notes in the book, the Knight Poe had been particularly instrumental in designing the ceremony. Whoever the minute taker had been at that particular meeting, he'd had quite a talent for the poisoned pen. A small sampling:

10:46*: At which point, the Knight Poe recommended procuring *live* chickens for the festivities. The Knight Atlas, having some experience with poultry on his family farm, advised against it. Hale interrupted the meeting with the coffee

*All times are Diggers-time.

         cart and a staunch plea to keep livestock out of
the tomb. Rebuffed, the Knight Poe proceeded
to glower at his assembled brothers for a full
five minutes.

11:15: Chickens again.

11:52: And back to chickens.

12:05: Uncle Tony recognized the Knight Lancelot,
who diffused tensions thusly: "It seems to me
that Poe's argument is for an added element of
chaos in the proceedings. Rather than focusing
on this whole chicken conundrum, perhaps we
can find another way to infuse a dash of
pandemonium?"

         Brainstorming ensues.

12:17: Chickens dropped in favor of strobe lights
and small-scale fireworks. The Knight Poe
mollified. Hale? Not so much.

From the very beginning, it seemed, Poe had been gung-
ho about society life.

    I wondered what else I could find out about him by read-
ing the Black Books. I started flipping through the pages
faster. People reported on their summer vacations, then the
Connubial Bliss reports began. The first one wasn't Poe's,
and neither was the second, though the third, the Puck of
D176, had some rather spicy anecdotes. An orgy? Seriously?
Wow, last year's Puck made even George seem tame.

    I pulled down the next Black Book and started flipping
through that. Not Poe's, not Poe's, not Poe's. George's father, George Prescott, came to talk to the club about
emerging markets in China. More C.B.'s. Ah, here it
was. The Connubial Bliss Report of Poe, Knight of
Persephone, Order of Rose & Grave.

    The book slammed shut in my hands. "Amy!" Lucky

cried, her hands on the binding, and I was so startled I forgot to fine her. "What are you doing?"

"Looking for initiation ideas."

"Not in the December volume you weren't," she said. "I saw what was on that page."

"It's in the Library," I argued. "I can look at it if I want. Any knight can." Besides, he knew everything about me already. It wasn't fair.

"Don't you think if he wanted you to know these things about him, he'd tell you?"

"Don't you think a guy like Poe automatically assumes I've been snooping around behind his back?"

I had a point there, and Lucky knew it. "In that case," she said, "I recommend you take the high road. You shouldn't look at this *because* he doesn't trust you to do anything else."

That made no sense at all, and it sounded especially false coming from Little Miss Computer Hacker.

She wrenched the book from my hands. "I think I'm just going to hold on to this for a little while."

I lunged for it and missed. "No. I can look at anything I want to. What other purpose do these books serve but to let the current knights read them?"

She shook her head at me. "Four years at Eli and you still haven't learned basic research skills. This is what becomes of English majors, you know."

"Lit majors."

"Whatever. The purpose of secondary sources—like these books—is to fill in the blanks when we can't get our information from the primary source."

"I *can't* get my information from the primary source," I argued. "He won't tell me anything."

She pulled it out of reach. "Well, it's dishonest to sneak around behind his back."

I put my hands on my hips. "I'm showing media savvy. Finding ways to get what I need when my contact is being uncooperative. You should be glad I'm so resourceful."

"I'd be gladder if you were honest with your boyfriend," she said, turning to go, with the book still firmly in her grip. "Because more than I want you to work for me, I want you to be happy."

———

Today, I was auditing The Russian Novel. The plan was to find a seat next to Kalani, but the girl was apparently popular on top of all her other positive attributes. Every seat in her row was filled. So instead I sat behind her. While the professor set up the podium, I tapped her on the shoulder. "Hey there."

"Oh, hey, Amy. How's it going?"

"Great." I fished around for a topic of conversation. "I was wondering if you have the notes for the February 15th lecture on *Crime and Punishment*. I missed that one and I wanted to make sure I had everything covered for our paper due next week." Yes, I can search the online syllabus with the best of them.

She flipped back through her binder. "February 15th... hmmm. They might be on my computer back at my suite."

"Oh, no." Oh, yes. "Is there a time I can drop by your suite and pick them up?"

"I can just e-mail them to you. That would probably be easiest."

Yes, it would. Crap. "Great."

Now I just had to sit through fifty minutes of lecture for a class I passed a year ago. As if I have time for any of this with my thesis due and only half-written. We hadn't even hit deliberations yet and already tap period sucked.

It didn't get any better at Atmospheric Change the following morning. Arielle's switch had flipped from *On* to *Off* following our cryptic conversation in her dining hall. Now that she assumed I would be tapping Topher to take my place in Rose & Grave, there was no more saving seats for me in the lecture hall, and a definite dearth of offers to carry my books to and from class and lay down her jacket in any puddles along the way. One never notices how nice it is to be worshipped until one has fallen from grace.

Avoiding the chill emanating from Arielle's turf in the back of the hall, I hoofed it down to the front of the classroom and slid into a seat in the terra incognita of the first row. In my guise as serious student, I flipped open a page of my spiral notebook, uncapped a pen, and prepared to take my first-ever set of copious notes about the fascinating field of greenhouse gases.*

"Excuse me, Amy Haskel?" said a girl two seats to my left.

I looked up. "Yes?"

"I'm Michelle Whitmore."

"Uh, hi." Should I know this girl? She had straight brown hair pulled into a messy upsweep, pale skin with a dash of freckles across her nose, and was dressed in a green scoop-necked shirt that almost, but not quite, made her eyes the same color. "How did you know my name?"

She pointed at my notebook. "Written right there."

Oh. Smooth one.

---

*The confessor is being somewhat less than fair, here, given as atmospheric change and greenhouse gas buildup is a serious issue that deserves attention from everyone, not just Geology majors. And no, she was not coerced into saying that.

"I find it really embarrassing, for both of us, that I have to introduce myself to you."

Wow, ego much? "Excuse me?"

"I've been waiting very patiently for your last problem set. It's a week overdue."

I gawked. "You're my T.A.?" I'd been seeing this chick's green smiley face on top of my homework assignments all semester, but nothing more. As far as I was concerned, this Michelle Whitmore could have been named "Section 4."

She gave me a mock salute. "Which you'd know if you ever showed up to my section."

Ooh, busted.

"You're a senior taking this pass/fail, correct?" When I nodded, she shrugged. "I'd be e-mailing you if you were veering into the fail zone. Class participation is only ten percent of the grade."

"But problem sets are twenty."

"Affirmative. And that means this probably isn't a part you can skip. So . . . when can I expect it?"

"How's after lunch work for you?"

"End of class would be better," she admitted.

I pressed a hand to my heart. "You can't be suggesting I use lecture period to complete the assignment! What kind of graduate student are you?"

"The kind that's secretly an undergrad who spends her History lectures coloring in her lab notebook illustrations. I know the score."

I narrowed my eyes. "Wait, I'm being T.A.'d by an undergrad?"

She rolled her eyes. "Well, firstly, you're not being 'T.A.'d' by anyone at the moment, between not turning in assignments for me to grade and not attending my sections. And, secondly, welcome to the wonderful world of Group IV."

The professor walked over to the lectern and smiled at the audience. Especially the suck-ups in the first three rows. "I can't do my homework in the front row, at the very least."

"True," she conceded. "Do you have a class after this?"

"Lunch."

"Have lunch with me and I'll give you a crash course on everything you've missed in my exhilarating sessions all semester. Maybe I'll even give you some of that credit back. Then turn in your problem set."

"Really?" After I'd basically disrespected her for the last three months? This chick was being way cooler than I'd be if the situation were reversed.

"No, you're right, they aren't that exhilarating. Mostly we draw clouds."

I laughed, and the prof shot us both a dirty look. Cool and funny. Maybe I should have been going to her class all semester. I settled in and listened to the professor tell us all about carbon sinks and ice ages. It was actually pretty fascinating. Shame I have only developed an interest in things outside of my field of study at the end of my college career. I'm sure that when I'm old and gray, I'm going to regret not taking more advantage of the breadth of classes Eli had to offer when I'd had the chance. I could have squeezed in an extra credit here or there.

Maybe then I wouldn't be choosing, my last semester, between Renaissance Italy and climate change.

After class, I started in on the problem set while Michelle spoke to the professor, the other T.A.s, and the more enterprising students from our section.

"You're doing that one all wrong," she said over me as I struggled with number three.

"Good thing I have a chance to fix it before I turn it in," I shot back. I hadn't dealt with balancing equations since high school. This one was supposed to explain to me the theory behind ozone depletion, but I couldn't seem to get the catalyst right.

"I'm going to make you suffer just a little for your credit," she said. I grinned and packed up my stuff.

Lunch options up on Science Hill were pretty slim. Everyone who doesn't hoof it back to Commons on the main campus eats in the dining hall on the top of the Biology Tower. The food there is only decent, but the views are spectacular, and you're more likely to see grad students and professors in that hall than anywhere else on campus.

"You're a senior, too, right?" I asked her during the elevator ride. The indignity of having an undergrad T.A. would only be compounded by discovering she was younger than me.

"A junior," she replied. "I guess that's what I'd be. I went abroad last spring without credit transfer, and then I took another semester off this fall to do research, though I stayed on campus."

"So you matriculated with my class."

"Yeah, and I'm hoping they don't count me being in the neighborhood last fall. They kick us out after eight semesters taking classes here, you know."

I did know that. My friend Carol lived in fear of reaching her eight-semester limit without completing all her credits. Of course, Carol couldn't seem to keep a full course load. She dropped classes every time she landed a juicy role in a campus play—which was pretty much every semester. I don't know if she wanted an Eli degree as much as she wanted the connections that came out of Eli's prestigious drama program. For her, the diploma was superfluous.

"Is that tough for you," I asked Michelle, "knowing

that all your classmates are graduating this semester?" That was one of the issues that had kept me from doing a semester abroad. Unless I picked one of two Eli-managed programs, my credits wouldn't transfer and I'd have to watch my class graduate without me—Lydia and my other friends, all gone.

She shrugged. "It might be if I were still living on campus. I don't notice so much now that I'm not living in Strathmore anymore."

No wonder I'd never met her. Of the twelve residential colleges on campus, only Strathmore and Christopher Bright had freshmen living within their walls. Freshmen from the other ten, including my Prescott, lived together on Old Campus and only moved into our residential colleges sophomore year. Eli administrators claimed the strategy helped us make friends outside our colleges. Strathmore residents, by contrast, tended to be more insular. If there was someone I didn't at least know *of* in my class, they probably belonged to Strathmore or Christopher Bright Colleges. The fact that Jamie had been in Strathmore during undergrad probably didn't do much for his natural isolationist tendencies.

At the top floor, Michelle stepped out into the dining room and scanned the seating area. "Okay, let's eat here."

As if there was anyplace else to sit? I followed her to the buffet line and grabbed a tray.

"As it is," she said, spearing a rice-and-tomato-stuffed bell pepper and adding it to her plate, "I don't really see a lot of my old Strathmore friends much. I'm mostly up here with grad students and other scientists."

I grabbed a pepper stuffed with ground beef and slid my tray alongside hers. "I think the community I've got in Prescott is one of the things I'll miss most when I graduate." Well, that and the community of Rose & Grave. But if I accepted Jenny's offer, I wouldn't really be leaving them, would I?

"Must be nice," she said, and with her face turned away toward the frozen yogurt machine like that, I couldn't tell if she was being sarcastic or bitter. Not everyone at Eli was as attached to their college as I was to Prescott. I knew several students who had even transferred colleges to be closer to their department of study, their significant others, or, in some cases, the gym. But Strathmore and Christopher Bright residents tended to be more into it than others, as a result of their early bonding experiences.

As we sat down, I took a quick survey of her plate. Meatless. "Are you a vegetarian?"

She nodded. "Vegan. That's not going to be a problem, is it?"

I laughed. "I guess I'm beginning to notice stuff like that more often now. My boyfriend is a vegetarian."

"And he hasn't managed to convert you yet?"

"Nope. We still haven't decided how to raise the kids, either." I took a big bite of beef-stuffed pepper and pondered if Jamie would find that joke amusing or not. I mean, kids?

"Meat scares me these days. The hormones, the chemicals, deforestation and resource allocation—and then there's the possibility of widespread quality control issues. The danger of mad cow makes hamburger decidedly less appetizing."

I swallowed with some difficulty. "You're a real killjoy, Michelle."

"Wait until you hear me get into my spiel about ozone depletion and skin cancer."

Proving she wasn't remotely kidding, my Geology T.A. proceeded to scare the crap out of me for the next twenty minutes. The world, in her opinion, was on the verge of coming to an end, thanks to rampant consumerism and industry and pollution by, well, us. Oil was running out, not that we were doing anything about it, soil erosion and depletion were at an all-time high, the global effects of climate change were and would continue to be catastrophic to food production, wild spaces, and of course, there was that pesky severe weather, of which we could only expect more as the global climate became increasingly warmer and more unstable, atmospherically speaking. Superstorms, super-floods—and that was just from the sky. Related to nothing we'd caused (for once) we really needed to rethink the wisdom of building enormous cities on top of fault lines (hello, Los Angeles) or in other geologically unsound regions (hello, Mississippi River Delta). It was... sobering. By the time I attacked my half-melted frozen yogurt, I couldn't help but see a distinct similarity between my bowl of vanilla mush and chocolate jimmies and our beleaguered polar ice caps. Each skinny, sinking jimmie might as well be a starving polar bear falling through the ice.

"So now you know what you're missing by skipping my section every week," she said blithely, spooning herself some vanilla swirl soy-based concoction.

"What... can we do about it all?" I asked, appalled.

She lifted her shoulders. "I dunno. Recycle? Use public transportation? Take classes like this so you know exactly what we're up against, beyond all the political bullshit?"

"I guess I'm doing pretty well, then."

"Stop eating meat," she went on.

Now she sounded like Jamie! "I'm glad we have geologists like you around."

"I'm not a geologist," she said. "I'm a chemist. I'm on

loan to the Geology department this semester. Long story."

"Interesting one?"

"Not really. Now let me show you that equation for the ozone destruction catalyst..." She started doodling on a napkin, then suddenly stiffened. "Actually, I forgot, I have to be back at the Geology building now. Can we finish this there?"

"For what?"

"Um, office hours. I just have to have my butt in the chair. No one will show up. Let's go."

We bussed our trays in record time, then Michelle practically sprinted to the elevator, her messenger bag flapping hard against the back of her jean-encased thighs. In the elevator, she started jamming on the lobby button, as if the elevator would interpret her repeated depression of L as a sign of urgency and descend any faster.

"Do you get in trouble with the professor if you're late?" I asked.

"Heaps." The door closed, and Michelle leaned against the wall. "And I owe him a lot for taking me on, too. I don't want to flake out on him."

But once we left the building, we headed back to the Geology lab at a pace that could only be described as "casual stroll." She took me to the smallish library on the fourth floor, where I wrangled with letters and numbers until the whole thing made sense:

$$CFCl_3 \text{ [pollutant]} + UV \text{ Light} ==> CFCl_2 + Cl$$
$$Cl + O_3 \text{ [ozone]} ==> ClO + O_2$$
$$ClO + O ==> Cl + O_2$$
$$Cl + O_3 ==> ClO + O_2$$
$$ClO + O ==> Cl + O_2$$
$$\text{(And so on...)}$$

I looked at the results. Man, the Earth was screwed.

"You know," she said, as she marked my score in her grade book. "Judging from your mid-term grade, you're going to wind up with a solid B in this class, even without your ten percent participation credit. Your grades must be pretty good to go with pass/fail here."

"I'm a Lit major," I said. "Anything less than an A-minus is an embarrassment."

"They swing a more classic curve in the science departments," she replied. "I have to fight hard for my As."

And yet, she was an undergraduate teaching assistant. Something told me that Michelle Whitmore was simply being modest. I wondered what her true story was. If Jenny weren't up to her ears in background checks for the potential taps, I might even ask her to find out for me. Because what's the use of having the resources of a rich and powerful secret society at your beck and call if you don't take advantage of it to snoop on your teachers?

Now I was the one who sounded like Jamie.

"You're all set." She handed back my completed problem set with her standard green smiley face at the top. "I assume you'll be heading back downhill now, back to the safety of the liberal arts."

"You better believe it."

"Well, it was nice meeting you, Amy Haskel." As I got up to leave, she settled in with a copy of a dense-looking scientific paper. "Oh," she added. "I like your sneakers."

I looked down at my yellow All Stars. "Thanks."

As I hiked back to the main campus, I thought about what a shame it was that Michelle had been in Strathmore, had taken a semester off, had moved off campus, had locked herself away in the labs. She was someone I could have been friends with, had I gotten to know her earlier than a month and a half before commencement. Then again, I had just started dating a guy a month and a half before commencement.

But Jamie was different. He was a knight, he was in my society. We'd have plenty of time together, even after graduation.

Too bad I couldn't tap Michelle.

I hereby confess:
If you're in a dysfunctional
relationship and you know it,
clap your hands.

5.

Feudalism

Dark water, thick as syrup, closed over my head. I thrashed and thrashed, but my legs seemed to be bound to some great weight that pulled me ever downward. I couldn't get free, I couldn't get air, I couldn't stop it from happening.

"Amy! Shhh, it's a dream."

I woke covered in a thin sheen of sweat and blinked up into Jamie's concerned eyes. He was leaning on one elbow, his bare shoulders bathed in moonlight, his face half in shadow. "Drowning again?"

"Yes." I slipped from between the sheets and yanked Jamie's borrowed T-shirt down over the top of my thighs as I padded into his bathroom to splash some cold water on my face.

"Do you notice you only have those dreams here?" He followed me and leaned against the door. I stared, bleary-eyed, at his reflection in the mirror. "Concerned" had a tendency to look like "angry" on Jamie. It always took me a minute to recalibrate my understanding when I saw him like this. It was too easy to imagine he was mad at me.

"No, I have them at home, too," I said, and then slurped a few handfuls of water from the sink. "Just not when you're there."

"We should fix that."

We got back into bed, and I pulled the covers up to my waist. Boys are like little heat engines. I hardly ever need to use a blanket when I sleep with one.

And that was all we'd been doing. Sleeping. Well, that and some seriously heavy make-out sessions. "Petting," my mother would probably call it.

Somehow, without ever discussing it, we'd realized that a late night study-session-turned-sleepover was not the most momentous occasion during which to go all the way. At least, I think that was the reason. It just never seemed right to have first-time sex with Jamie on the couch of his apartment, our textbooks strewn across the coffee table or the floor. It never seemed good enough to do it after he'd brushed his teeth and pulled me into his arms in his bed (full-sized, but still using the dorm-room comforter designed to fit a single bed). It never seemed natural to do it in my bedroom in Prescott College, with Lydia and Josh only a thin wall away.

I wasn't sure when the correct time would be, though. It wasn't as if we could afford a weekend away at a hotel or some romantic upstate bed-and-breakfast. I didn't have the time; Jamie didn't have the money. Besides, I'd never felt the need to make an occasion out of the first time in any of my other relationships. Dorm rooms were always just fine. You're talking to the girl who lost her virginity at an after-prom party in the bedroom of the kid sister of the party-giver.

Of course, that relationship hadn't worked out. None of them had. So maybe it was time to change things up.

"Sleepy?" Jamie's voice floated across the pillows in the darkness.

"No."

"*Not* sleepy?" His hand brushed against my torso, an invitation.

I took a deep breath. "Darren called me last week."

Jamie's hand stilled on my skin. "Oh?"

"His father apparently made him. They chucked him in rehab."

"They have rehab for sociopaths?"

"That's what everyone else has been wondering, too." Jamie was very quiet for a moment. "Everyone else?"

Oh, crap.

"Who?" he asked.

"My club."

"I see." More silence.

"They're my club, Jamie. I took an oath to tell them everything."

"I'm your boyfriend *and* a Digger. Where does that put me on the hierarchy of communication? For curiosity's sake."

Jenny had basically said the same thing. Considering their entirely mutual dislike, I bet they'd both hate the fact that they agreed with each other. And then they'd hate that agreement, too. "How do you feel right now?"

And Jamie, as always, was straightforward. "Trying hard to keep my anger directed at Darren and not you."

"Exactly!" I cried and sat up. "I knew you'd get mad, so I didn't tell you."

"Extraordinary plan." He rolled away from me, his shoulders and back hunched down around the pillow. "You always do come up with the best ones."

Oh, give me a break. What was the purpose of telling him? I knew this script already:

Step One: Jamie would say that Darren should be brought up on charges.

Step Two: I'd reluctantly agree.

Step Three: Jamie would tell me, with the law-student caveat that it was not legal advice, that I could still press charges against Darren if I wanted.

Step Four: I'd consider it, then remember I'd made Kurt Gehry a promise, and from what I could tell, he'd been keeping to his end of it. Darren wouldn't be fixed in a week or two. Let him call me in a year, and we'd see what he'd learned.

Step Five: Jamie would lose another smidgen of respect for me.

"He should be in jail," Jamie grumbled, still facing away from me.

"I know."

"You realize that you can still press charges, right?"

Here we go.

"I don't want to talk about this with you." I flopped back against the pillow.

"Believe me, I'm aware of that." He rolled over. "Perhaps you should consider making a list of forbidden topics for me to reference at times like this."

"Great!" I snapped, facing him. "We can put your past relationships right at the top."

"Are you kidding me with this?" He sat up. "Amy, you don't really want to know."

"I do," I said. "You just don't want me to."

"It's incredibly morbid."

"I thought you were into the morbid topics, *Poe*."

He didn't bother to dignify that with a fine. "Not that morbid."

"Says the man who tried to sit in on my C.B. last fall."
Oops, perhaps it was a bad move to bring up that occasion.

His tone was tight when he replied. Yeah, I'd messed up. "That was different."

"How?"

"Because you weren't my girlfriend then."

"So you didn't care what I did until you decided I was your property? That's nice and healthy."

"You used the word 'property.' I used 'girlfriend,' " Jamie clarified. "And though I'm sure you'd love to hang any misogynistic label you can on me, you're wrong. I don't care that you had sex with other guys, I just don't want to know."

I caught my breath. His voice had dropped, turned husky. His face was shadowed in the orange light filtering in from the street lamps. And what's more, he was telling the truth, about both of us. He didn't have a used-goods complex at all, and I—well, I couldn't stop acting as if he did. Even half in jest, I still treated him like the man I'd thought he was last year. I didn't stand up for him to the other knights in my club—even they had noticed it.

I reached for him in the darkness. "Jamie, I—"

He leaned over me. "I don't want to hear about some other guy who touched you. I don't want to think about how, and where, and whether or not you liked it. And because I'm so sure *I* don't want to hear about *you*, I am positive you don't want to hear about me." He lowered himself over my body as he spoke, and his voice became a whisper against my skin. "You don't want to know if I kissed her neck, like this."

Oh, God. His mouth was hot and moist, and moved over my throat with the most precise, most intoxicating combination of pressure and suction. My hands slid over his arms and across his back, pulling him in closer. My legs parted and his hips fell between them. Through layers of sheets and shorts, I could feel his pelvis pressing the inside of my thighs.

"You don't want to know if we only had sex in the dark, so that I could feel her body, but not see it." His hands slipped beneath my T-shirt and slid it up to my armpits. "You don't want to know how much hotter that made it." His thumbs traced the undersides of my breasts. My lips parted on a gasp. "You don't want to hear if we made love in this bed—"

"Made love?" I giggled. "You're right, I don't want to know that you're secretly fifty."

He collapsed on top of me and laughed into my neck. "Amy, Amy . . ."

"Jamie, Jamie," I replied. But then, involuntarily, a picture arose in my mind of him having sex with another girl right here, just like this, and I shuddered. He was right; I didn't want to know any of it. And despite the way he was touching me, I didn't want to have sex with him at this moment, my head crowded with *her*—her little moans and breaths and her incredibly infuriating way of staring into his gray eyes just so . . .

The sour sting of jealousy washed over me, filled my sinuses, clogged in my throat. "Wait."

"Wait?" He lifted his head.

What was wrong with me? I'd managed to sleep with George Prescott without forcing him to enumerate his legions of lovers. Without ever picturing him with any of them while we were in bed (or in the tomb, or in the Buttery, or any of the other places where we were concurrently in flagrante delicto). I'd never been like this before. I wriggled out from beneath Jamie and stood up.

"I—I need to go."

"You what?" He caught my arm as I went for my jeans. "Go? Absolutely not."

I yanked out of his grip. "Excuse me?"

"I'm not letting you walk through this neighborhood at 4 A.M."

Oh. Good point. I sat down on the bed, jeans in hand. Jamie sat a decent distance away. "I'm sorry," I said, and swallowed. "I think you're right—about not knowing."

"I'd tell you if I thought it would end this . . ." He shook his head, placed his hands on his knees. "I wish you . . ."

"What?"

He said nothing.

"What?" I coaxed. What did he want from me?

"I wish you trusted me."

"I do."

He snorted. "I wish you loved me."

I bit my lip. That's what he meant. In the stillness that followed, I thought I could hear the soil erosion in the front yard. Now would be the perfect time to brave the rough streets and leave. Muggers would be better than this.

"Forget I said that." His words fell into the silence.

"Do you?"

"Forget? Yes."

No. Did he love me? But I was as likely to get an answer out of him about that as I was about his ex-girlfriends.

"You should go to sleep," he said at last. "You have a big week. The party. The interviews." He scooted back over to his side of the bed.

I left my jeans on the floor and scooted, too. Maybe we didn't love each other—maybe we weren't willing to admit that—but we did care for each other. And I did like the way I fit into the crook of his arm. I liked the way the sheets in his house smelled like him. I liked to hear him breathe while he slept.

"Still feeling good about Kalani?"

Way to change the subject. I traced his arm with my fingertips. "Yeah. She's perfect. Everyone's going to love her."

"What are you going to do about Lionel Drake?"

I kissed Jamie's collarbone, then shrugged. "He'll survive."

"Pissing off the patriarchs is a cornerstone of your club's strategy, then."

"I'd rather piss them off than bring Topher Cox into Rose & Grave. I don't want that guy playing in my sandbox." Let's not even get into the fact that he's fond of likening himself to a serial killer. Talk about morbid.

"So you're not even inviting him to the party?"

I looked up at him. "What would be the benefit of that?"

Jamie shifted so I was lying more fully in his arms. "It could go either way. On one hand, inviting him would send a signal to Drake that you are at least considering his grandson as a prospect."

"On the other, it might give them both false hope."

"Exactly."

I frowned and snuggled closer. "So what should I do?"

"No way in hell am I answering that for you."

I pinched him. "You're so mean. Seriously, what would you do?"

"You know what I'd do, Amy, because you know what I *did*. I tapped the legacy, even though I wasn't overly fond of him."

"George is not Topher." And not just because I'd slept with the former.

"I'll give you that. But a society is only as good as its network. If it crumbles due to lack of support, there's no point."

"A society is only as good as its members," I argued back. "If we tap degenerates, we only beggar future generations."

Jamie pulled me close and kissed me hard on the mouth. It was all the response I needed.

———

In the end, I invited Topher to the party. Our next encounter displayed a decided increase in the deference and respect quotient, which made a firm case for someone—most likely Grandpa Drake—having gotten to our boy in the interim. Perversely, I enjoyed Topher's sycophancy, though I'd resented it in Arielle.

Her party invitation was still burning a hole in my backpack. Clarissa had made one for everyone on our stated short lists (except for the celebrities on George's) as a matter of course, but I didn't want to instill any false hope in the poor girl. If I invited Arielle to the party, would she view it as rubbing salt in the wound?

Or maybe I should just frame it as a chance to get free champagne out of us Diggers?

Try as I might, I couldn't think of a low-key way to accidentally bump into Kalani a third time. Her high-powered *EDN* position meant that when she wasn't actively in class, she could usually be found holed away in the Gothic castle of newspaper headquarters. I'd heard a rumor that she occasionally worked out on the elliptical machines at the gym, but the girl clearly wasn't in a fitness frame of mind that week, and her stupid roommate had apparently even offered to pick up her stupid dry cleaning on Monday afternoon, so my stakeout at the campus cleaners was for naught.

Most frustrating.

By Wednesday, I was getting desperate. The party was

the following evening, and I hadn't managed to slip an invite to my chosen tap. I decided to pay another visit to the Russian Novel class. This time, I chose to sneak in at the end of the lecture, in hopes of catching my prey without being forced to listen to fifty minutes on *The Brothers Karamazov.*

The lecture hall was packed as usual, and I scanned the room twice before I spotted her halfway up the rows on the left side of the auditorium. I stationed myself at the end of the last row, adjacent to the door she'd have to take to leave, and tried to think of an innocuous conversation starter.

Why was this so hard? I felt like I was trying to pick her up. *Hey, Kalani. Wanna go with me to a party tomorrow night?* Yeah, real subtle. Besides, who invites a girl they've talked with exactly once to a party? That behavior might fly the first week of freshman year, when no one had any friends and everyone pretended that the people you met crossing the campus were destined to be your future best friends forever. Seniors had grown out of that nonsense. Juniors had as well. She would think I was a total loser to be pulling that move at this stage in my Eli career.

The lecture ended and the room bustled with noise as students rose in a wave, chattering, powering up cell phones, packing away books and notepads and laptops. For a moment I lost sight of Kalani. No, there she was, down in the front, talking to a classmate. I ran through my icebreaking options.

A) Hey, Kalani. Thanks so much for those notes. They sure came in handy. How'd your paper go?

B) Hey, Kalani. Look, here's the thing. I'd like to tap you into Rose & Grave. Game?

C) Hey there, good lookin'. Going my way?

Kalani was ascending the stairs now, headed toward my row. Her fingers fumbled with the clasp of her bag, as her attention was partially focused on the girl climbing the stairs at her side. Think, Amy, think. *Great lecture. Great editorial in last Sunday's opinion column. Great skirt.* Anything. Just get the ball rolling, then invite her to the party.

She was almost to my row now. I opened my mouth. *Hey, Kalani. Hey, Kalani. Hey, Kalani.*

I looked up. She was laughing at whatever her friend was saying. My eyes slid toward said friend.

Felicity Bower. Felicity, of Dragon's Head. Felicity, who was dating my ex-boyfriend Brandon. Felicity, who had done her best to make my life a living hell for the first few months of this semester. Felicity, who would gleefully step over my cold, dead corpse if given half the chance.

I froze. Abort, abort!

"Hey, Kalani," my mouth said, because it has this pesky habit of working independently of my brain.

"Oh, hi, Amy," said Kalani. Felicity stopped, turned toward me, and her mouth condensed into a tiny, irritated moue. "Great lecture, huh?"

"I'm still trying to figure out that whole metaphor with the aqueous globe," my mouth said, heedless of my brain's new strategy. The one that involved me running for my life from the crazy rival society member with the huge, Amy-shaped chip on her shoulder.

"I didn't know you were enrolled in this class, Amy," said Felicity in an even tone. "In fact, I thought you took it last year."

Kalani's brow furrowed. Dammit.

Strike earlier plan. New plan involves sticking a fist through Felicity's smug face.

"Ah, Felicity, always so busy memorizing my schedule."

True. How else would she have been able to track me down when Dragon's Head was pulling all those pranks?

"Exactly," Felicity replied.

"I think you have it mixed up with something else." I smiled through clenched teeth. "But you know me. I can't get enough of Dostoevsky."

It helped, of course, that *The Brothers Karamozov* was thick enough to pass for a lethal weapon if you wielded it just right.

"We were going to check out this new boutique downtown," Kalani said. "Want to come?"

Oh, we were, were we? I looked at Felicity, at her unabashed expression of challenge. Unbelievable. She was after my tap. My. Tap.

Naturally, Dragon's Head would want a girl of Kalani's caliber for themselves, but why would Felicity, of all people, be the one in charge of recruiting her? She wasn't in the journalism scene. Did Dragon's Head have a vastly different M.O. when it came to finding society members? Did she want her because her part-Polynesian background fit into Felicity's idea of an Asian-American tap?

Nah. That would be giving her way too much credit. Dragon's Head wanted Kalani—*Felicity* wanted Kalani—because they knew I was gunning for her.

This was the society's newest volley in our decades-long feud.

"Sure," I said to Kalani, still looking at my nemesis. "I'd love to."

I swiftly discarded the notion that Dragon's Head had, in fact, bugged the Inner Temple. They wouldn't need to think hard to figure out which juniors we were after. Malcolm and Jamie had told me last year that it was commonplace for societies to compete for the top-tier taps, and

Kalani was a golden girl when it came to secret society wish lists.

I wondered how many of the other potential taps were being similarly wooed. My fingers itched to tap out a quick text message to Jenny or Clarissa. *Watch yr backs. DH on the prowl.* But it was tough to type, walk, and remain insinuated into Felicity and Kalani's conversation all at the same time. I decided to concentrate on the latter two.

Right now, unfortunately, they were discussing fashion. My understanding started at "Don't wear white shoes after Labor Day" and ended somewhere around my abject disdain for formal shorts, so I had little to contribute. I settled for the occasional sage nod and "hmmmm."

We were going to a boutique, though. Which meant that if Clarissa's clothes know-how was at all reflected in her childhood friend, Felicity was going to come off looking a lot better than I was. Score a point for Dragon's Head.

Then we came to the boutique. Felicity's nose wrinkled, then smoothed as she smiled at Kalani. "Neat," was all she said.

Neat was clearly the opposite of what she meant. I peered into the windows. It looked like a Renaissance Faire had exploded in there. Corsets and swords, tiaras and gauntlets, velvet capes embroidered with Celtic knots and pillows printed with scenes from the Bayeux Tapestry. The stencil on the glass doorway read: THE SIGN OF THE UNICORN.

We entered, fairy bells tinkling to signal our arrival.

A woman dressed like Stevie Nicks appeared behind the counter. "Blessed be," she said to us, her hands folded serenely before her chin. A row of books at her back proclaimed all manner of spells and herbal remedies.

"Are you Wiccan?" I asked Kalani. Demetria might approve if I brought some non-mainstream religion into the mix.

"No," she said, and wandered down an aisle stuffed with brocaded skirts. "I just like the clothes." News to me, what with her never-ending supply of beige suits.

Felicity was still standing at the entrance, desperately searching around for some fragment of what she thought proper boutique clothing looked like.

"Hey, Felicity," I called, then pointed at a giant bronze dragon in the corner. "Check it." I followed Kalani down the aisle. If she liked costumes, she'd fit right in with Rose & Grave. This was getting better every minute.

Kalani held a dress of green and gold up to her body, then checked out her reflection in the ornate mirror at the end of the row. "It's silly, I know. But my parents were in the Society for Creative Anachronism when I was growing up, so I was always kind of interested. I actually joined the Eli chapter my freshman year, but then I got too busy with . . . other activities to keep it up."

Like the paper. I couldn't imagine how much she had to give up in order to run the *EDN*. Still, she found time to get a literary agent and keep a full course load. I hoped she'd find time for Rose & Grave, though I was beginning to doubt very much that she needed us anywhere near as much as we needed her.

She held the dress in front of me. "You should try on this one. It goes so well with your eyes."

I held out the sleeves, which were shaped like giant wings. "Great, I needed a new frock for the jousting tournament this weekend."

She brightened. "There's a jousting tournament this weekend?"

"I was joking."

"Right." She frowned and picked at a loose thread. "Hey, thanks for tagging along. Felicity's nice and all, but she's been a little clingy lately. Know what I mean?"

Not really. Felicity didn't cling so much as pounce. Usually armed. "What does she want?" I asked. This was good news. Kalani was clearly more annoyed by Felicity's attention than intrigued enough to join Dragon's Head. Like Arielle and me, in reverse.

"Long story," Kalani whispered, then turned back to the clothes racks as Felicity came down the row. "I'm going to try this one on," she said, and pulled out a gown in a pale, tarnished silver brocade. Even in RenFaire getup, Kalani favored beige.

I rubbed one yellow sneaker against the other as Kalani headed toward the dressing room in the back, leaving me alone with Felicity.

"So what do you think?" I asked her blithely, holding the green and gold gown up to my front. "Is it me?"

"Drop dead," Felicity countered, her eyes on the dressing room door.

"She told me you've been bothering her," I went on. "I guess she and I have that in common."

"That's all you'll have in common," Felicity hissed.

"Why don't you step aside," I hissed back. "Don't you know when you're outclassed?"

"Outclassed? Are you kidding? By you?"

I lifted my chin. "By my people."

"Oh, classic, Amy. You've anticipated my 'you and what army' argument."

"If I remember correctly," I said, "it was you who needed the army. Your entire society all rallying to the cause of what, exactly? Right—keeping me away from your boyfriend." I turned to her. "And how is Brandon these days?"

Felicity stood very still, but there was a flicker in her eyes that revealed my barb had struck deep. "You," she said, "are an unbelievable bitch."

"Takes one to know one."

Kalani emerged from the dressing room, swaying her hips so the material in the skirt bloomed out and swirled around her. "Well? What do you think?"

The gown was stunning. She looked like a Hawaiian Queen Elizabeth. "Where are you going to wear it?"

She shrugged. "I don't know. The Silver Slipper Ball, if I have the guts to go in costume instead of just formal."

"That's Eli for you," I said. "A formal dance every week or two, and costume balls you can set your watch by."

"I guess," Kalani said. "But of course I'm going to the Silver Slipper. I just don't know if this is too much. This is only my second one. Last year I just did boring black cocktail. I wanted to go all out this time."

"I've never been," I said. Who could keep track of every formal dance at Eli?

"Oh, you should!" Kalani exclaimed. "Especially since this is your last year. I'll try to snag you an invite."

Felicity stiffened, then looked at her watch. "My goodness, look at the time. I've got a meeting I just have to get to. You don't mind, do you?" She smiled at Kalani.

"No, go ahead." Kalani inspected her sleeves and craned her neck to check out her beige-brocaded hindquarters.

Felicity gave me a smug smile. "Break a leg, Amy." And then she was off.

Um, did I just win? I stared after her in confusion, then turned back to my quarry. Well, that was easy. Guess my comments really hit home.

"So?" Kalani held out her wing-like arms. "Do you think this is too over the top?"

The corset part of the gown cinched Kalani's waist in tight, accenting her wide hips and turning her breasts into a shelf you could practically set drinks on. Above the decolletage, her golden skin glowed and her dark eyes sparkled. She might, in fact, be having a tough time breathing with that thing on, if the blush spreading across her cheeks was any indication.

This beat beekeeper outfits any day of the week. She looked regal and elegant   far more capable like this than she had even in her business suits.

"It's over the top," I agreed. "But in a good way."

Kalani bounced. "I know, it's fabulous. Now all I need is a date."

An opening. "Hey," I said. "A friend of mine is having a party on Thursday night. I bet there will be a lot of cute guys there." George, at least, would be required to show up. Not that I wanted to foist him on Kalani. Or introduce any more society incest into the group. Still, an opening is an opening. "Want to go with me? It'll be fun. She's got this really swank loft, and she always goes all out for her parties. Champagne, caviar—it's extraordinary. Like a modern-day Gatsby."

"Ooh, sounds fun," Kalani said. "Wait, you said it's tomorrow night?"

I nodded. Kalani slumped.

"Darn, I can't."

"Deadline at the newspaper?"

She turned back toward the rack. "No."

Wait, I knew that coy little turn, that refusal to answer direct questions. I knew it because I'd been practicing it since the moment I was tapped into Rose & Grave.

"Then why?" I asked, as my fingernails bit into my palms in fear and anticipation.

"I have society stuff."

She had *what*? No, *we* were society stuff. We were the society she was supposed to have stuff with.

"Yeah, every Thursday and Sunday night. You know how it goes." She shrugged, and the dress shivered all around her.

Yes, I knew exactly how it went, because I had been do-ing the every-Thursday-and-Sunday-night thing all year.

And then it hit me. The Silver Slipper. The formal ball given for the last hundred years by—

"You're in St. Linus Hall?" I fought to make it a ques-tion, though I already knew the answer.

St. Linus Hall was the only three-year society on cam-pus. The only society whose endowment beat Rose & Grave's. The only one who could possibly have stolen my tap from me.

Because they got to her at the beginning of her sopho-more year.

"Yeah," she said. She cast me a hesitant look over her shoulder. "You're not one of those people who think soci-ety members are lunatic, old boys' club, coffin-sleeping, robe-wearing freaks, are you?"

"No," I choked.

"Because the Hall's not like that. We're not like, I don't know, the Diggers or something. Those guys are weird."

"You know?" I managed to say. "I think I will try this on." I grabbed the green and gold dress and sprinted for the changing room. Inside, behind the relative sanctuary of the heavy maroon curtain, I pushed my fist against my mouth and let out a strangled cry.

No! Why? She was perfect, absolutely perfect. It would be the one thing I managed to do right in my whole Digger experience—tap someone better than me. Tap someone who really belonged in the organization. Who would make the patriarchs proud, make them see that Jamie and Malcolm's class hadn't screwed everything up by letting girls in, by letting me in.

But she was already in a society. And worse, she thought we were freaks! And when a girl in a Queen Elizabeth gown she's planning on wearing to a formal dinner dance tells you that *you* are the weird one, you know you're way out there.

I couldn't tap her into Rose & Grave if she was already in St. Linus Hall. That's how it worked. We might make an exception for Phi Beta Kappas like Josh, but that wasn't a real society. It was a pin you wore on graduation day and a lunch with the dean.

No wonder Felicity had split when she heard "The Silver Slipper." I had a hard time keeping track of all the formal events at Eli, but she and her wardrobe filled with Vera Wang must have the damn list memorized. Stupid St. Linus Hall. What had Kalani called it? The Hall. Stupid nickname. What were they, Hollers? They were such a weird entity. Three years, open membership roster. They even had public areas of their tomb where members could invite visitors. They let non-members come hear their speakers, attend their bashes. The Silver Slipper, I remembered now, was supposed to be the best party on campus. Part of me still wanted to go.

But seriously, what was the point of a secret society if nothing was secret?*

I yanked out my cell phone and flipped it open. Text message to Jenny Santos:

---

*The confessor is loath to admit how appealing the St. Linus Hall configuration actually seemed to her at that moment. All the fun of a secret society, but none of the whole "barbarian" nonsense. Imagine having Lydia at one of the Digger parties!

A: U messed up . . . big-time.

The reply came back in seconds:
   J: U OK?

I typed furiously, the gown forgotten.
   A: Y didnt u find out kalani in st linus?
   J: No! Im sorry. Had no idea.

Then, after a few moments:
   J: Leaving lab. Call me.
   A: Cant shes rt here.

"Amy?" Kalani called. "You need a hand with the corset? They can be a little tricky."
   I hoped she attributed my groan of frustration to the clothing and not to my current convo. I typed to my fellow knight:

   A: Now what?

But Jenny appeared to be thinking. Either that or she'd put her phone away and gone back to class.

   J: Now . . . Topher.

"Argh!" I said aloud.
   Kalani peeked her head inside the curtain. "What's with all the yelps of pain? You haven't even taken your pants off."

I hereby confess:
It's not fun for
anyone involved.

6.

The Party

At least I was finally getting somewhere with my thesis. My new mantra: I am a typing fiend.

> So while knowledge of these mysteries remained an exclusively male privilege, the entrance or initiation into this awareness was most often guarded by a female entity. After all, though it is Aeneas who—

Ping.

From: Jennifer.Santos@eli.org
Subject: Really Sorry

> —Aeneas who peers into the underworld, it is the Sybil who shows him the way.

Ping.

From: Lucky-D177@phimalarlico.org
Subject: Really, really sorry.

I cleared my throat and kept typing.

> Dante's homage to this event is echoed in his choice to make <u>Aeneid</u> author Virgil himself the guide for Dante's own trip through both the <u>Inferno</u> and the <u>Purgatorio.</u> However—

My cell phone began to buzz.

ONE NEW TXT FROM
JENNY
SUBJ: Astoundingly Sorry

I turned the phone display-side-down.

> —However, when they arrive at Paradise, the desirable destination, the one that Dante presumably wishes to actually join, his initiation comes care of not only an angelic female gatekeeper, Matelda, but also a female tour guide: his childhood love, Beatrice.

An IM window popped up on my screen, masking my deathless prose.

HelloGorgeous: Why are you ignoring Jenny?

Clarissa. I typed back: *Busy working. Go 'way.*

HelloGorgeous: This isn't the end of the world, you know.
AmyHaskel: You're right. Which is why I don't care and am busy working on something actually important for a

change: women-as-gatekeepers in epic poetry. Tap Topher.
I don't care.
HelloGorgeous: Don't use the imperative mood with me,
young lady! *You* need to tap Topher. Look at it this way: If
you *had* known about Kalani, what would you be doing
differently now?

Taking Arielle more seriously. Not encouraging her to join
Quill & Ink, that was for damn sure.

HelloGorgeous: This is all for the best anyway. It will help
cement our relationships with the patriarchs.
AmyHaskel: Lie back and think of England?

I clicked back over to my thesis window.

> Of course, it remains to be seen whether or not such initi-
> ations are really in the character's best interest.
> Sometimes it's just a major-league annoyance to join
> their stupid club.

I sighed and deleted the latest sentence, then clicked back
to IM.

AmyHaskel: I'd have to trade for him, you know. I got a girl
marble.
HelloGorgeous: Amy, it's Jenny. You can have my boy marble if you want. I'm so sorry.

I remembered Jenny's chosen tap, the engineer in search of
the physical location of the soul.

AmyHaskel: You'd do that for me?
HelloGorgeous: Sure. It was my screwup. I've only gotten

as far as their Eli apps. So far. I should have dug deeper. And besides, you're my Diggirl.

She'd give up the tap she wanted so I could have the tap I didn't. Something about that was deeply twisted.

AmyHaskel: No, Jenny. We'll figure something out.

I just didn't know what.

———

On Thursday morning, I entered the auditorium in the Geology department, walked down the row to Arielle Hallet's desk, and dropped an invitation to the party on top of her notebook.

She looked up. "What's this?"

"What do you think?" I replied, trying not to sound as weary as I felt. "I'd like you to come to a party tonight."

"A party," she repeated, toying with the envelope. As we were still in a theoretically anonymous stage of the tap process, the envelope was a simple, plain white, not the glossy, black-edge, rough-cut stationery we'd be using later to inform our taps of our choice. "With whom?"

"Some friends." This was painful. She knew, I knew she knew, and she knew that as well. "What do you say?"

She focused on the envelope. "I say what took you so long." Then she slipped it into her backpack and resumed taking notes. She did not invite me to sit with her. She did not look at me again.

This did not bode well. The knights were supposed to be the ones with the power, not the taps. Taps were supposed to feel chosen, plucked from obscurity to become one of the elect. But Arielle was no fool. If I'd come to her now, after being so blunt before, she must understand that I needed her.

I wish she'd given me lessons last spring.

Feeling more miserable than ever, I clomped down the stairs and collapsed in a seat four rows from the front.

"Yo, Amy," said Michelle. She turned around and leaned across the rows, grinning. "Why so glum? Is it the existential guilt over the coming environmental crisis?"

I gave her a weak smile. "You know any other tunes?"

"Not in this class." Now she frowned. "I'd thought I'd convinced you to come to section last week." She leaned closer. "You're kinda ruining my rep with the other T.A.s, you know."

"Huh?"

"I'm already on their hit list since I'm young and I'm not really a Geology major. Now I can't even get people to show up for my section?" She raised her eyes to the ceiling. "Forget it. I'm not allowed to join in any of their reindeer games."

"Why do you care what they think?"

"Because someone once told me that reputation is everything at Eli."

That one I knew well. It was practically a Digger creed. "I'm sorry."

"Prove it. Come to section tomorrow."

I gave her a blank look. "On a Friday afternoon? You must be joking."

"I'm not. To sweeten the deal, I'm bringing cupcakes."

I remained skeptical. "Vegan cupcakes?"

"I refuse to answer that on the grounds that it may incriminate me."

Ugh. Vegan cupcakes. They were probably made with wheat germ and carob.

"Come on, Amy," she said, a pleading note in her voice. "The professor's coming, and he did me a real favor, and I want to show him I can do a decent job. My attendance has been way down this semester and I don't want to look like a slob. Fifty minutes of your life and a slide show on acid rain. Please?"

"Do I have to eat the vegan cupcakes?"

"Totally optional." She turned around as the professor reached the podium and greeted the class.

Grinning in spite of myself, I opened my notebook and started jotting down the professor's words. I'd definitely been missing something skipping section for the past few months. Michelle was a riot. I'd never met a more prickly hippie.

Or was that even the term? Her misanthropy seemed to stem from her environmentalism, but she wasn't exactly dressed in hemp and Birkenstocks. If anything, her outfit was a bit on the preppy side. Today, she had on khakis and a faded polo shirt.

I was writing down a list of carbon sinks when a triangle of paper landed on my desk. Passing notes? That was a little high school.

I unfolded the paper football.

IOU1!—M.W.

Apparently you don't owe me complete words, I, ever the Lit major, wrote back, wondering whether or not note-passing lost her more points with the professor than having a poorly attended section did.

I watched her unfold the note. Her shoulders shook with silent laughter, and suddenly I was filled with nostalgia, remembering a class I'd taken second semester freshman year with Lydia. We'd spent the whole time sitting together, writing jokes to each other in the margins of our textbooks. I still had those books, scribbled all over with nonsequiturs, snarky observations about our classmates and professor, and the foundation of a friendship that would last our whole lives. I'd never take a class with Lydia again. I'd never take a new class at Eli again. A few more weeks of sitting in these hallowed halls with a spiral-bound notebook in my lap and that was it.

Michelle, of course, had another year, being a junior.

A junior.

I sat up straight in my seat. Michelle might owe me for visiting her section tomorrow, but Jenny Santos owed me even more, for screwing up the tap research. And we needed another tap, to replace our one instance of attrition, Howard First.

Howard First, the science tap.

We needed someone smart and accomplished, like an undergrad who was already working as a teaching assistant.

Someone passionate and ambitious, like a student who took semesters off, though it meant dropping behind her classmates, in order to do research for causes she believed in.

We'd made a short list for his slot, same as everyone else's, but given the extenuating circumstances I faced, a last-minute addition wouldn't be out of line. I tore off a scrap of paper as quietly as I could and composed another note to Michelle. It wasn't Clarissa's fancy stationery, but it would have to do.

> *Want to go to a party with me tonight?*
> *—A.H.*

———

I was almost skipping by the time I entered my suite that afternoon. My step was light, buoyed by plans and enthusiasm. Ever since I'd found out about Kalani, the entire tap

process had seemed little more than a burden and time
sink. I couldn't see any way to make myself happy with
Topher Cox, and the idea of being his big sib had cast a
gray pall over the entire occasion. I couldn't very well seek
comfort from Jamie; he'd taken one for the team when it
came to tapping George the previous year, and our differ-
ing opinions of—and experiences with—Jamie's little sib
didn't exactly make him a gilded conversation topic.

Jenny's phone had gone to voice mail, so I hadn't been
able to tell her the good news. Clarissa, deep in planning
for the party, wasn't answering her phone, either. That was
fine. I'd inform her of the extra attendant when I went to
help her set up.

Lydia looked up from the couch as I walked through
the door. She had a couple of envelopes in her hand, and an
untouched sandwich and bottle of pop lay on the coffee
table in front of her. "Hi, stranger," she said.

"Hey there." I swept past her toward my room.

"Do you have a minute?"

Not really. I paused by the door. "What's up?" Please
let it be quick.

"I never see you anymore. You're always either doing
stuff at the tomb or over at Jamie's place."

"Or you're at Josh's," I countered. I resisted the urge to
check my watch. How long did I have until Clarissa expected me? And I still needed to hop in the shower, pull
out something decent to wear...

"I feel like I never get a chance to talk to you these days,"
Lydia was saying. "And soon we're going to graduate—
I don't want to lose you, Amy."

I joined her on the couch and threw an arm around her
shoulders. "You're not going to lose me. We're BFFs,
right?"

She rolled her eyes. "I don't know. I haven't taken any oaths, unlike you and your other friends."

"We don't need an oath. We've got something more important."

"Oh yeah? What's that?"

I furrowed my brow. "Give me a minute. I'll come up with something."

She laughed for a moment, then bit her lip and looked down at the papers in her hands. "I need to talk to you. I can't put this off any longer."

Oh my God, she was pregnant. I steeled myself for the news, running through my supportive, best friend lines. *You can still go to law school. You and Josh are in the best situation possible for this news. Which doesn't mean you have to get married or anything, unless you want to. You have a lot of options. You can even give it up for adoption. A baby from two Eli grads? Talk about high demand. What does Josh think?*

"Look." She held out an envelope bearing the Eli Law seal. I looked inside.

Dear Ms. Travinecek,
We are pleased to offer you admission to the Eli College of Law . . .

I didn't get any farther. "Lydia! Holy cow!"

She nodded. "I know. I didn't expect—it was such a long shot—I was on the wait list—"

"Eli Law! You badass, brilliant woman! This is your dream come true!" I hugged her hard.

"I know."

So why wasn't she bouncing around the room? I studied the letter. Wait a minute . . . "Lydia, this acceptance letter is dated three weeks ago."

"I know."

For someone who just got into the top law school in the country, her vocabulary was remarkably limited.

"You've known for three weeks?"

"Since I got back from Spain." Now she looked at me. "Oh, Amy, what am I going to do? I can't tell Josh."

I blinked at her. "Why not?"

"Because we're supposed to go to Stanford together. We're supposed to get an apartment and be a fabulous law school power couple, then a clerking power couple, then a lawyer super-power couple." She looked down at her hands. "There was a plan."

"The plan included you developing super powers?" I asked. "Please tell me it wasn't laser beam vision."

"Amy—"

"I'm sorry, but what you're saying isn't any less ridiculous. Josh is going to be thrilled for you, honey!"

Lydia was quiet.

"Do you think he'll be jealous that he didn't get in?" I asked her.

"Possibly."

Probably, if I knew him.

"I mean, I think he'll be happy for me, but he'll also be disappointed for himself. But I'm afraid that telling him will make me seem like some kind of martyr."

"Why?"

"Because I'm not going to go."

"*What?*" I stared at my friend in shock. "But . . . *Eli Law*!"

"I know, but it's not like Stanford is some schlub institution of learning. I was going to be perfectly happy there three weeks ago. And it has Josh."

I shook my head in disbelief. This didn't happen. We didn't make decisions about where we were going to school based on our boyfriends. Well, there was this one girl from my high school who turned down Georgetown to be a Buckeye with her boyfriend, and then he dumped her by the end of spring semester freshman year. So it was for nothing.

But that was precisely the point. Boyfriends were fleeting, but alma maters were forever. Didn't Lydia get that?

"Josh will understand," I said, though he might not. "And you can still stay together." Though they probably wouldn't. "This is your future."

"*Josh* is my future," Lydia replied. "Every bit as much as the law. I love him. I want to be with him forever. Don't you think that at some point we're going to have to make sacrifices for that? He gets a clerkship in some city so I follow him there? I get a job in another, and he follows me? I recuse myself when I'm a judge and he's a lawyer?"

"Josh isn't going to be a lawyer," I said. Law school was just another check mark on his resume before becoming a politician. Which was another reason he'd be jealous of Lydia at Eli Law. Unlike Stanford, Eli rarely turned out practicing lawyers, just people with law degrees who became professors or politicians or spies.

"Whatever. You know what I mean."

"But that's later!" I said. "That's *later* that you do all that sacrificing stuff. Like, when you're married. Right now we're too young to be so serious. Follow some guy across the country just because you love him? That's stupid."

"We're not too young," Lydia argued. "We're not teenagers anymore. And I'm not just following him blindly. I'm following him to Stanford."

I read the whole letter and shook my head. "If you've decided all this already, then why are you telling me?"

She shrugged. "I don't know. I want you to tell me I'm doing the right thing, I guess."

But I didn't think she was. "No, you wanted me to talk you out of it."

Lydia picked up her sandwich and took a bite. She chewed and swallowed, and still said nothing.

"If it doesn't work out between you and Josh at Stanford, you'll regret this forever."

She took another bite.

"And if you pick Eli, and it doesn't work out between you two, you'll always wonder what would have happened if you'd been at Stanford instead."

She chewed for a moment, thinking, then put down her sandwich. "So you're saying it's the dominant strategy in a prisoner's dilemma. But what you're not taking into account is the marginal utility of the expected value of—"

"Hold up," I said. "I don't speak LSAT."

"You're saying it's better for me to be at Eli whether or not Josh and I stay together. And that since which school I go to is the only variable I control in this scenario..."

I nodded.

She slumped against the back of the couch. "That's the answer I got, too."

And she'd rocked her test. Wow, maybe I missed my calling. Wonder what I'd get on the LSAT. "So why Stanford?"

"Because I think we're more likely to stay together there."

Logic problems never took into account matters of the heart. Either way, I envied her. Two amazing choices: a top school with the love of her life, or a top school—her dream school—without him. I slumped next to her on the couch and together we stared across the room. Lydia munched her sandwich.

"What are you thinking?" she asked me after a minute.

"I'm trying to imagine a circumstance under which I'd

make a choice about my life goals in relation to someone I'm dating," I said. "Every fiber of my being rebels against the idea."

"Hmm," Lydia said. "In your hypothetical, are you in love?"

"How do you know you're in love?" I asked her. "Because if it's determined by how willing you are to give up everything for the other person, I think it's a flawed system."

"On that note," she said, "how's Jamie?"

Now it was my turn to say nothing. But turning the subject to me seemed like an awfully cheap trick.

"I've heard a few things from Josh that have me worried." Lydia busied herself with her food.

"About Jamie?"

"About you and Jamie, yes."

Oh, this ought to be good. Relationship advice from the girl who couldn't even tell her boyfriend she'd gotten into her dream school. "My only problem is that he likes keeping secrets from me and I find it frustrating. Mark that, Miss Eli Law."

"Josh said you two were, like, mortal enemies or something."

I couldn't deny that.

"He told me that everyone"—she waved her hand vaguely into the distance to symbolize the Diggers of D177—"thinks he's kind of a jerk."

"Not kind of," I said. "Full-out jerk."

"Is he?"

"He's . . ." I struggled for a word. "Prickly."

"Huh." She polished off her sandwich. "I wish I knew him better, so I could make my own judgment."

Join the club, sister.

She turned toward me. "That's a hint, Ames."

"Yeah, like I'm going to arrange a double date for you to put him on trial? You don't have those judge's robes yet."

"Okay." She hesitated a moment. "Just reassure me that you're not dating him because things went south with Brandon."

"Is that what Josh said?"

"No." She took a deep breath. "He thinks you're dating him because you're scarred by—what happened to you."

I studied my hands. "We were together before that."

"Yeah." She nodded slowly. "After you fell off the boat on the way to the island and he saved your life."

"No." I snapped my head up to face her. "It's not like that, Lydia."

I braced myself for more arguments. *Then what is it like? Why are you dating him? If he keeps secrets and he's "prickly" and your friends all hate him and you're leaving Eli in a few months anyway? Why are you spending time with him rather than the people you supposedly love?*

But they didn't come.

"Okay." She sighed. "I want you to be happy, Amy. But know that your happiness does not need to come with a boy attached."

I gave her a tiny smile. "Neither does yours."

———

The apartment was decorated, the champagne was chilled, the hors were d'oeuvred, and I was waiting for Michelle on the corner so we could walk to Clarissa's together.

That I'd just left Clarissa's was a fact I intended my T.A. friend to remain ignorant of. But I still hadn't worked out how to reclaim the jeans and T-shirt I'd worn to set up. I'd changed into my current black pencil skirt and boatneck knit top in Clarissa's guest bedroom (yeah, she has a guest bedroom, which even Jenny, who owns a spare apartment in New York City, thought was overkill). The black was a strategic maneuver on the part of the society members. All in black, we'd subtly stand out from the partygoers. We'd look elegant and aloof. In addition, it would be harder to remember us in nondescript clothes.

"Nondescript" was quite the byword in Rose & Grave after a certain yellow sneaker incident at the beginning of the semester. Today, I had on plain black pumps.

I stood in the shadows and watched the potentials arrive. Most came clutching envelopes in their hands, looking about nervously, as if unsure exactly what the evening held in store. I didn't blame them. Legends about our initiation were elaborate and often gory. But we were still miles from Initiation Night. We were still miles from Tap Night, too.

A few came linked with knights, who brushed their chins with their thumbs as they passed me on the street, signifying that their companions were the top choice on their lists of potential taps.

I saw Topher approach the corner, dressed all in black, the pompous ass. He waved at me, smiling broadly. "See you inside?"

I gave him a slight nod. Well, if he knew enough about the proceedings to wear black, maybe he also knew what it meant that I wasn't walking him through that door. Let him ponder that one for a bit.

"Hey there, Amy," Michelle said, popping up next to me as I watched Topher buzz the entrance to Clarissa's building. "I hope you haven't been waiting long. It's kind of a hike to this side of campus."

"No, it's fine," I said, giving her a sly once-over. Good.

Khaki A-line skirt, green sweater, hair freshly done. I looked down at her feet. Green ballet slippers. They'd do. The Diggers would like her. "Want to go in?"

Unfortunately, Topher was still standing in front of the door to the elevator inside the lobby, so we three rode up together. He and Michelle exchanged not a single word, but their mutual glares said plenty. I remembered what Arielle had told me about his way with women—or lack thereof. Was I about to tap two people into a society who already had reasons to hate each other? I'd have to add this to the list of questions I needed Jenny to answer for me.

Too late to do anything about it for the time being. We arrived at Clarissa's door and she answered it, resplendent as usual, in a black shift dress that shimmered like scales whenever she moved. As she had promised me while I helped her set up for the party, she raised not an eyebrow at my last-minute addition to the guest list.

"It's great to meet you!" she hostessed, shaking Michelle's hand in true Upper East Side fashion. "Any friend of Amy's is a friend of mine."

"That's how it works, you know, Shelly," Topher said, and wandered off to the champagne. Michelle lifted her chin.

I spotted Arielle across the room, talking to Demetria and one of her guests, excused myself to Michelle, and headed over.

"Hey, Amy," said Arielle. She was holding a plate piled high with munchies. "I see you brought Topher."

Arielle, apparently, was similarly aware of the inner workings of this event.

"He was in the elevator with me," I replied.

She shrugged and bit into another canapé. The other junior must be Demetria's front-runner, Tamar Adamo, the leader of the Eli Women's Center. She was a tall, thin girl with a very freckled face and a buzz cut.

Demetria, dressed in black silk cargo pants and a black wife-beater, was grinning broadly. "So, we having fun yet?" She surveyed the room. "I think the problem with this party is that at least half of the people here are already acting like they are at their Fortune 500 company's holiday bash."

"Now, why would they be doing that?" Tamar asked in a facetious tone.

Apparently we all knew exactly what we were doing here.

"Do you ever wonder," Demetria said suddenly, "what the purpose is to keeping the existence of a society secret?"

Arielle gasped at her. "Aren't you not supposed to talk about that?"

"Secret societies?" she said. "Why not? I can talk about them all day long."

"In general, of course," I said, shooting her a warning glare. Just because they knew didn't mean we should go about breaking all our oaths. *Just play the game, Demetria.*

But my fellow knight forged ahead. "I don't know if I mentioned this to you earlier, Amy, but I've decided to take a new approach to this whole endeavor."

"No," I said through clenched teeth, "you hadn't mentioned it."

She wrinkled her nose. "Oops. Yeah, probably because I figured that you and our other friends wouldn't be keen on the plan."

"Which is?"

She took a sip from her champagne and smiled serenely. "Glasnost."

I grabbed her arm, almost sloshing champagne on

Arielle. "Excuse us for a second," I said, and pulled Demetria away. "What are you doing?" I hissed to her.

Demetria's back was straight, her expression firm. "Ushering in a new era. I am the bearer of the light and the truth. Old Eli would be proud."

"Old Persephone wouldn't," I said. "Obey your oaths. Stick to the script."

"Bullshit. There's not a person in this room who doesn't know what we're doing here. Why pretend?"

"Because—" I floundered for a reason. "Because that's what we do." I searched around in desperation for someone to back me up. Where was Jamie?

Across the room, talking to . . . Michelle.

"Hold that thought, and don't do anything you'll regret," I hissed to Demetria.

"You mean anything the powers that be will make me regret?" she said in a snide tone as I walked away.

Michelle glanced over as I arrived. "Hi! I never realized the boyfriend you are always talking about was Jamie, here."

"You . . . know each other?" I asked. Jamie was very resolutely not looking at me. I took in his black dress shirt with a subtle black pinstripe and what had to be new black dress pants. Both looked great with his dark hair and gray eyes. Not Johnny Cash but possibly Joaquin Phoenix doing Johnny Cash.

"Sure, from Strathmore," Michelle said.

"Of course." I tried to read Jamie's expression. Nothing.

"I had no idea Amy was bringing you this evening," he said smoothly. Now he looked at me. Yep, pissed. Because I was the one deviating from the established Digger script by bringing a non-vetted guest *not* on my short list to this party.

"What a funny coincidence," Michelle said.

"Hilarious." Jamie took a sip of his champagne. "So, how have you been?" Well, at least he was planning to be polite.

"Oh, you know..." The two of them launched into a conversation about Strathmore College residents I couldn't quite follow, not recognizing half the names. I grabbed a glass of champagne from a passing tray and tried to pretend both interest and comprehension I didn't feel. Here was information I'd been looking for since we'd started dating—Jamie's friends outside the society, Jamie's past. But knowing that he'd once played—rather pathetically, he insisted, but Michelle denied—for the intramural Ultimate Frisbee team wasn't exactly giving me the insight into his character I desired. He made no more sense to me now than he had before.

However, at least he wasn't making any more caustic comments in my direction. If anything, he and Michelle seemed to be getting along great.

Still, Jamie disapproved. Anything that wasn't established Digger behavior rubbed him the wrong way. And I bet I couldn't get his advice on the Demetria problem without prompting a lecture that my behavior was every bit as unorthodox. He probably thought I should just suck it up and tap Topher.

Speaking of, where was the little turd? I surveyed the room and spotted him in a knot of people by the buffet table.

"I'll leave you two to catch up," I said brightly. Jamie's brow furrowed as I flitted off.

My fellow knight Greg Dorian was holding court by the sushi platter with all three of the members of his short list as well as both Arielle and Topher. Greg was a poet and a Linguistics major headed back to his native England after graduation for an advanced degree at Oxford. The knot of people next to the tuna rolls was probably the most concentrated group of literati in the Eli junior class.

I insinuated myself into the conversation, which appeared to be about famous books with scenes at Eli—which were numerous—and whether there should be a course dedicated to the subject.

"Take *Franny and Zoë,* for example," Topher was saying.

"Zooey." Arielle took a sip of her champagne.

Topher glared at her. "It's Zoë. Zooey is not a name."

"You're correct, it's not." Arielle glared back. "It's a nickname for Zachary."

"The chick was Zoë."

"The *chick,*" Arielle drawled, "was Franny. Frances Glass. And you give Lit majors a bad name." She fixed me with a look, as the others whistled and trailed off to refresh their drinks. "Are you kidding me with this shit?" She polished off the glass and handed it to Topher. "See you."

Topher look flummoxed, and for a second I could have kissed Arielle. But she was hightailing it to the door.

"Wait!" I hurried after her, heedless of the stares we were probably getting from a guest list that would never dream of ditching the party, lest it reflect badly on them and decrease their chances of being tapped.

I met her in the hallway. "Please don't leave on account of Topher. He's an ass; we both know that."

"But only one of us seems to care," she said, pressing the elevator button.

"I thought that was a hell of a zinger," I replied.

"Whatever." The elevator door opened.

I blocked it. "How come I've never heard you talk about books that way before?"

She looked away down the hall. "Look, I may not be a

genius like you or Brandon, but I'm not an idiot, either. I'm running the Lit Mag just fine, you know. Ads and circulation are up."

A genius? Me? I almost laughed aloud but it was undercut by the realization that perhaps the more market-minded Arielle had been a better editor than me. Who was the real genius in that case?

"I know you didn't want me as editor, and I know you don't want me here tonight, either." Now she did look at me. "And I think on the latter, your instincts may be right. Now that I've been here, now that I've seen what you people are really like, who you really *would* like—I don't know. I don't know if I want to be part of it." She shook her head as if clearing it. "I've met the Quill class. I like them. I could imagine spending my nights and weekends with them next year. I could not imagine spending them with Topher Cox."

"But—" But what? If I tapped Arielle, she'd never have to spend any time with Topher?

"I think what I'm saying, Amy, is thanks but no thanks. How do you people put it again? Oh, yeah: reject." She pushed past me into the elevator.

I stood there in shock. This was not supposed to happen. Rejected by your safety tap?

Back at the party, things appeared to have deteriorated. Two voices I didn't recognize were locked in the spare bedroom arguing. Kevin had claimed Clarissa's bathroom as a make-out spot with one of the potentials he'd brought. Michelle was engaged in a lively debate about the origin of global warming with all four of Mara's potentials, and Jamie was nowhere to be seen.

I retreated into Clarissa's bedroom and sank down at the foot of the bed, resting my face in my hands.

How could I be screwing up so badly? My first choice to tap wasn't eligible, my safety wasn't interested, my boyfriend thought every move I made was somehow mistaken, I didn't have a job, I couldn't finish my thesis, I kept having nightmares about some fourteen-year-old kid I'd probably never even see again, and now I was sitting on the floor of my friend's bedroom in the middle of a party like it was middle school and I'd just had a fight with my lockermate.

Also, I was getting cat hair on my skirt.

"Amy?" I looked up to see Clarissa standing in the doorway. "You okay?"

I nodded miserably.

She closed the door and came to sit next to me, cat-hairing up her sequined fantasy. "Good, because I totally call dibs on being the hot mess tonight." She beat her head against the duvet.

"Not fair," came a voice from the other side of the bed. "I called dibs long before either of you." Demetria sat up and stared at us over the top of the mattress.

"What's your problem?" Clarissa asked.

"I don't want to submit anyone on my list to their own version of this crap next year. I hate every minute of this and I've decided that friends don't let friends join secret societies."

This again. I put my head back in my hands.

"You're kidding, right?" Clarissa asked. Demetria lay back down. "Perfect," she said. "This is the perfect end to my perfectly disastrous evening."

"What happened to you?" I said into my knees.

"My favorite choice to tap came in, took one look at the assembled guests, and walked back out."

"Oh!" I cried. "One of mine did that, too! Said she'd rather join Quill & Ink."

"In my girl's case, she can't go anywhere near her ex-boyfriend, and he's on Ben's short list."

"More society-incest issues." Demetria's voice floated over. "And you wonder why I feel this way?"

Clarissa shook her head, her expression dark. "No, apparently they had some kind of really bad breakup and now she *literally* can't be in a room with him. Some kind of agreement with the dean—they can't even be in the same classes. Like an Eli restraining order."

"You're kidding!" I gaped at her. "This is something we need to look into. What happened? Was there abuse or anything?"

Clarissa shrugged.

"Anything that would make a breakup that bad—are we sure Ben's list was properly vetted?"

Clarissa shrugged.

"I bet this is another issue they rarely had before they chose to include women," I said. And another issue Jamie would probably love to throw in my face.

"Don't count on it," said Demetria. "We're already headed straight toward sexual harassment territory with Kevin's lineup of boy toys."

There was a knock on the door and Josh stuck his head in. "Ladies?" he said, surveying the impromptu powwow. "Your absence has been noted."

Translation: Get back out here. We all had to participate in the torture together.

So into the fray, enveloped in fascination and accomplishment and privilege and legacy; a golden, candlelit affair suffused with brandy, champagne, puff pastry, and baby corn. Conversations about New England boarding schools and firms on Wall Street. Debates over departments and endowments and the lineup at the Eli Repertory

Theater. A chat about who got a Fulbright for what and whether or not they had begun to hand those things out like candy. All talk aimed directly at impressing the beings who floated through the room in black, nodding politely and listening as the potentials tore one another down in hope of impressing us.

All but a few—those lucky few—who either knew nothing or cared nothing about why they were there. At one end of the room, Michelle was in deep conversation with one of Omar's choices, who, rumor had it, had once been a spy with the Israeli army. Eli was full of ex–Israeli army folks. I knew the majority of them by reputation only. They were older than most of the teens who matriculated, and tended to be a bit disdainful of the other students' immaturity and softness. After all, they knew how to kill men with their pinkies. What did three years on the student council or a stint on the prom committee have to compare to that?

I drifted close enough to eavesdrop. Apparently, since leaving Israel, the guy had been involved in an NGO to create water treatment plants in sub-Saharan Africa. Once they started in about the various types of membrane distillation, I was lost, so I drifted back out and looked for Jamie.

But every time I found him, he managed to slip away a few moments later and wouldn't meet my eyes.

Later, as the festivities—for lack of a better word— wound down, Michelle caught up to me in the kitchen, where Clarissa and I were seriously considering drowning our independent sorrows in the dregs of the crate of champagne.

"There you are. Hey, thanks so much for bringing me!" She smiled at Clarissa. "Your friends are awesome. This was almost like going to a Master's Tea back in Strathmore again."

Clarissa snapped into hostess mode. "I'm so glad you enjoyed yourself." She needed to work a bit to animate her tone.

"Seriously." Michelle's expression turned wistful. "I really miss living on campus sometimes, and this is what I miss about it. Getting to talk with all the other students. I mean, my professors are great, and the department, and all of that, but it's so limiting at times. I feel like I never get a chance to do anything but discuss chemistry."

My stomach began to cramp. Yes, yes, that was it exactly. That was what I liked about Rose & Grave. The varied points of view, the endless discussions and debates with people whose opinions and experiences differed so much from my own. Not this series of obsequious resume-reciting.

Clarissa's voice was much more sincere this time. "Thank you, Michelle."

"And Jamie," Michelle said. "Where did he go?"

"I'm right here." Soft, steady voice at my back. I turned and my field of vision filled with subtle black pinstripe, my nose with his singular scent. His eyes glazed right over me, though. Instead, he turned to Clarissa. "Lovely party. Your dad would be proud."

"That's a shame," she said under her breath.

"So, I'm heading out now." Still not looking at me! Was this his version of good night? Even pissed, it was unacceptable.

"Where do you live?" Michelle asked. "I'm off Orange."

"Me too," Jamie said. "On Danbury. We can walk together."

Clarissa raised her eyebrows at me, but there might as well have been liquid cement in that last glass of champagne. I stood rooted to the kitchen tile.

"Great!" Michelle said, and beamed at me. "Let me grab my jacket." She bounded off. Clarissa looked from Jamie to me, cleared her throat, and vamoosed.

Jamie watched the door.

"Um," I said.

Jamie watched the door.

"Don't be such a baby about this," I snapped at last.

His eyes met mine, as cold and gray as I have ever seen them. "That's rich, coming from you."

I snorted and turned away.

Michelle reappeared, jacket in tow. "You guys ready?" She looked at us, at our crossed-arm stances on opposite sides of the room and uncertainty flashed across her face. "Oh. I'm sorry, I just assumed—"

That I would go home with Jamie.

"I have so much work tonight," we said in unison. I flinched. He bit his lip.

Michelle laughed. "Okay, I get it. I'm, ah, going to head home anyway. Amy, see you in class tomorrow?"

I nodded, trying to decide if I was more miserable about attending classes on a Friday or about the scene I was sure I was about to endure the second Jamie and I were alone.

But when we were, all he said to me was, "Do you need to hang around and help Clarissa clean up?"

I shook my head. That's why God invented caterers, or so Park Avenue had taught my friend.

"Then let's get out of here."

Again, I nodded. We walked in silence down Chapel Street. The bars and restaurants were still open, spilling golden light onto the dark sidewalks. A few people walked the streets, mostly in groups or pairs. A drunk girl careened from side to side on the concrete, tottering in her high heels and giggling. Jamie put his hand on my elbow and drew me out of her path.

His touch broke the dam. "You have no right to be upset, you know."

"Since when do you get to make those decisions for me?" he replied.

"You've been saying this whole time that it's my tap, my choice, and you don't want to be involved. So stop acting like I broke a Commandment or something."

He stopped in the middle of the street. "I can't understand . . . why are you dating me, Amy?"

What?

"I've been trying to figure it out all night. I seem to make you absolutely miserable, and then—tonight. It was like some sort of cruel joke, you going out of your way to hurt me."

Hurt him! Ha! "Of course, everything I do hurts you. The society is so important, the way that you used to do things is so unbelievably *vital* to the *fiber* of your *being* . . . stop taking it all so personally. You disapprove of me, you disapprove of my club, you disapprove of all the ways we do things that aren't the way you'd do things—"

"Now, wait just a minute—"

"And you disapprove of Michelle. Of course you do, though you're sweet as pie to her face."

He blinked at me, struck silent.

Good, let me say my piece. "You disapprove of her because she wasn't properly vetted like the guy we're *supposed* to tap. The good little legacy, the granddaddy's boy with not a single thing to offer us other than a disgusting attitude and a big pile of family money. Michelle is great! She's interesting and smart and passionate and hardworking—"

"Amy, what are you implying—"

"Nothing! I'm implying nothing! I'm saying it straight-out! You refuse to tell anyone anything." My heart was pounding in my chest and the words were coming in a hot rush. "You hoard up your little secrets and then collect them from everyone else, and you refuse to even entertain the idea of doing it any differently. You think it's wrong to bring Michelle, not because of who it's entirely obvious that she is, but because you don't know her secrets. You didn't get an advance list of all her elementary school teachers and summer camp counselors and the names of every person she's ever slept with—"

Jamie was shaking his head, and when he spoke, his voice was lower than ever. "No, Amy, no. You see, I don't need that list. I already know, because I was one of them."

I hereby confess:
For some statements,
there is no response.

7.
Deliberations

"You knew," he said, taking in my stricken expression.

"No," I whispered.

"Come on, Amy, you knew that."

"No," I repeated, slightly more strongly. No. No no no no no.

He studied my face, searching for the lie that wasn't there.

"How in the world would I have known when you've never—" Right. The Black Books. I *so* called that.

Jamie remained baffled. "Then why did you bring her?"

"I liked her!" I said, throwing my hands in the air. "She's my Geology T.A. and I—God, what did you think? That I was shoving her in your face like she was George—Oh, God." I turned around and started walking down the street. I wanted my room. I wanted my bed. I wanted the world to shut down.

"Stop." I didn't, and he caught up to me in a few steps. "Hey," he said softly. "You're apparently not the only one capable of thinking the worst of the other person in this relationship."

I paused and looked at him.

"That was an apology," he said.

"It was a bad one." I started walking again and he fell into step beside me. "When?" I choked out. They had seemed to get along fine at the party, talking easily. Talking alone. She'd even wanted him to walk her home.

Even knowing he was my boyfriend. My throat went dry again.

"My junior year, her sophomore," Poe was saying. "We hung out in Strathmore—ate together, flirted in the courtyard, stuff like that."

"And?"

"And what?"

"You told me you didn't have a girlfriend in college."

"I didn't. How could I, on my microscopic budget? But we might have been moving in that direction. We liked each other, we hooked up a few times. But we never had a conversation about where it was all going."

"So what happened?"

He looked off down the street. "I got tapped. I got busy. I basically disappeared for the rest of the school year. I was so excited. I wanted to spend all my time in the tomb, wanted to hang out only with all my new friends. Then it was exams and summertime. She just fell off my radar." He kicked at the curb. "She had her summer research position, I had my internship—when I got back in the fall, someone told me she had a boyfriend. That it was pretty serious, too. They were engaged or something. I saw her from time to time in the dining hall and stuff, but I was so busy. I had LSATs and the society and law school applications and job applications and interviews, and then she broke up with the guy and went abroad and—" He looked at me. "We moved on. There were no hard feelings."

That had certainly been in evidence tonight.

"There," he said. "Does that satisfy your morbid curiosity?" When I didn't respond, he stopped and took me by the shoulders, turning me gently to face him. "You swear you didn't know?"

"I swear."

"And it was just some coincidence that you brought a girl you have absolutely nothing to do with to this thing?"

"It's a small school, Jamie," I said flatly. "Naturally I'd get T.A.'d by your ex-girlfriend eventually." He didn't laugh, which was good, because I'd only been half joking.

"I believe you." He looked down into my eyes. "Now answer my question."

"What?"

"Why are you dating me?"

I shook him off. What a stupid question!

"Amy."

I started walking.

He followed. "You thought I hated Michelle. You thought I disapproved of her as a potential tap."

"Because you were clearly upset with me," I replied without turning around. "I think we've established that we were both laboring under mistaken impressions. You apparently like Michelle quite a lot."

"I hardly know her anymore. I have no idea whether or not she'd be a good fit for the Diggers. But Michelle isn't the only time you've decided, a priori, that I'm thinking the worst of your choices." We'd arrived at the Prescott gate. I pulled out my ID card, but Jamie put his hand over the sensor. "So my question remains. If this is what I think of you—if I disapprove of everything you are and everything you want—why are you dating me?"

I placed my hand over his. The sensor beeped and the door unlocked. I pulled it open, mind racing. I was dating him because he'd saved my life on the way to the island. I was dating him because he taught me to swim. I was dating him because I was leaving school in a month and he was Eli personified. I was dating him because he challenged my perception of the world and didn't let me give up, even if it was in his best interests. I was dating him because Jamie seemed to like me more than the guys who had dumped me in the past. I was dating him because he helped me last semester and last year even though he knew it would get him in trouble. I was dating him because he kissed like a fiend and made really good waffles.

He stood on the other side of the gate, like he had so many months ago, and looked at me through the bars. He'd liked me back then, in November. I knew that now. He'd liked me, even though I'd thrown him out of the tomb and he'd been secretly undermining my club by helping a few of the boys start the all-male secret society-within-a-society Elysion. He'd liked me, and it killed him that I'd discovered his betrayal.

"Because," he went on, "there's a word for girls who date guys who constantly put them down. And there's a word for those guys, too. And I really don't like the idea that those words describe either of us."

I still held the gate open, but he wouldn't pass through it. If I didn't say something soon, he'd walk away and that would be it. Jamie may like me more than the other boys I'd dated, but it wouldn't be enough. His pride wouldn't let it be, just as it hadn't let him accept me as his secret hookup and nothing more.

"I like Michelle," I said, "because she reminds me of me. Not in any way you can put on a resume or list for the society newsletter. I like her. I think she'd be a good fit for

Rose & Grave. I want to push forward with her in Howard's position. It will make me feel better about Topher. He's not like me, but if we can get Michelle—well, I'd have a real replacement."

His eyes narrowed.

I let out a little laugh. "And to be perfectly honest—after the initial shock—the fact that you were once into her sort of cements that belief. Because I don't think the things you like about me appear on a resume, either. I know this because you saw my resume, and you didn't like it." I closed my fingers around his through the bar, leaned close. "You didn't like me. Not until you got to know me."

He leaned in, too, rested his head against the bars until our skin touched, warm next to the cool brand of the iron gate.

"Why I like you is no more quantifiable." I stroked his fingers and gazed up into his eyes. "I can't explain it to my friends. I can't explain it to you."

He softened. "You need to try to explain, at least to yourself. If this is what you think of me . . ."

He didn't finish. Strange. So many things he was willing to sacrifice to get the success and security he wanted. Things he *had* sacrificed: friends, romance, money, independence. So many things I knew he'd accept at any cost. But not me.

Where did he draw the line? Who was this man?

I tugged on his hand. "Come inside. Come inside and talk to me. I bet the more I get to know you, the more I'll like you, too."

He pulled away. "No. I told you everything there is to know about me and Michelle. I'm not giving you a C.B."

I came around the outside of the gate and put my arms around him. "I don't want one. I want you."

———

"They're ridiculously expensive," Jamie said, twining his fingers around mine and lifting our arms together into the lamplight. We lay curled together in my bed, no clothing removed aside from shoes and jackets. "For a piece of felted wool? It's absurd."

"A friend of mine sewed her own," I said. "Cost about fifteen bucks."

"My father wouldn't sew," Jamie said. He'd told me long ago that his dad was a gardener who struggled to make ends meet after Jamie's mom, a social worker, had died while Jamie was still a child. "But he would save up to get me one. It was my big gift that Christmas. A hundred-dollar scarf."

With Strathmore College colors. Sold in the over-priced JPress store down the street. The college scarves were a major status symbol among the preppy set on campus, harking back to those good old days when everyone wore beaver coats and straw hats and proclaimed school spirit by having their college scarves and their society pins prominently displayed.

"He was so proud of himself for getting it for me, especially since I'd been telling him how much I wanted one for the last three years."

I imagined a teenaged Jamie, after years of being the scholarship kid at his fancy prep school, trying desperately to make up for lost time by lusting after the preppy trappings of Eli life.

"You could see it on his face. His son, the Eli University senior." Jamie took a deep breath and closed his hand around mine so our knuckles interlocked. He brought them down between us, squeezed them to his chest. "I wore it for a few weeks. But we had an early spring that year, remember?"

I nodded.

"And to tell the truth, it's kind of stiff for a scarf. And in law school—"

"You don't want to be seen walking around campus in your undergrad finery?" I smirked at him.

He smirked back. "With my undergrad girlfriend and my stolen undergrad waffle maker? Yes, there's only so much humiliation I can handle."

I poked him. "Hey. No denigrating the waffle maker."

"Anyway, I'd hate it if he knew." Jamie stared up at the ceiling. "He tries so hard to understand this life. Sometimes I worry that one day I'll go home to him and we'll have nothing in common anymore. There will be nothing he can give me that I'll be able to appreciate. Nothing..."

I rolled toward him and put my palm against his cheek. "But he already gave you those things. The things that got you here in the first place. The hard work, the devotion—the sacrifices after your mom died so you could have this education, this chance. It's not a scarf that's important to him."

"I guess." He ran his hand down my side, from my collarbone to my hip. "And your parents? What do they want from you?"

"To call them more often, I think." I cuddled closer. "I don't know. They're pretty independent themselves, and as long as I haven't gotten into trouble, they let me do what I want. They were proud when I got into Eli, of course, but they would have been proud of me at any college. They aren't snobs."

"What would they think of Rose & Grave?"

I wrinkled my nose. "My dad would probably call it elitist bullshit. My mom wouldn't say it, but she'd think it.

Especially if she knew that I was in the first class of women. She doesn't hold truck with sexism."

"This is the same mother who disapproves of your sexual escapades?"

"Oh, she's totally an equal opportunity prude."

"So she probably wouldn't like that I'm doing this." His hand slipped down over my butt.

I smiled. "Unlikely."

"Or this?" He flipped up the hem of my skirt and brushed his fingers over the inside of my thighs.

"Definitely not."

"Hmmmm..." He leaned in to kiss me. "Then I guess this all should be something we keep to ourselves, huh?"

"Yeah," I agreed, and arched in his arms. "Luckily, we've gotten pretty adept at secrets."

————

"Okay, so you're done," Lucky was saying to Puck as I dragged myself into the Grand Library at some godawful hour the following morning. "And thank you," she added to him, "for not pursuing Prince Harry. Because I really don't have the resources to hack Buckingham Palace."

Early meetings with the vetting committee (i.e., Lucky) on top of a Friday morning section were a travesty of college seniority. I was supposed to be utterly free from the end of the Thursday night meeting on through the start of the Sunday night meeting. But tap meant that every hour of every day was filled with obligations to Rose & Grave. After I was done with those, I could squeeze in the nonessentials like showers, toilet breaks, and finishing my thesis.

Then again, I'd had it easy. While I'd been snuggling with my boyfriend, Lucky had been up getting the files on every one of our potential taps in order.

"Hey, Bugaboo," Puck said as I took his place across from Lucky. "You want me to wait around here and we can head back to Prescott together?"

Curious. Puck hadn't shown any interest in hanging lately. "Can't," I admitted. "Got class after this."

"Sucks!" He waved. "I'm going back to bed."

I bit my lip to keep from asking, *Alone?* After all, I hadn't exactly left my bed empty this morning. Jamie had spent the night with me, curled tightly in my single dorm room bed, spooning me close to his body so I wouldn't fall off the edge. I can't imagine sleeping on his side was comfortable, what with those shoulders.

Jamie, however, did not complain.

The morning had been cold and clear. A fresh day, ready for revision. Of my thesis, of my relationship, of the whole tap process. To balance out all that freshness, I didn't take a shower. I didn't want to wash his smell from me. Plus, ten more minutes in Poe's arms was so worth it.

Especially given the gauntlet I was about to run with the vetting committee. I'd already had one irate e-mail from Lucky.

Lucky cleared her throat. "Off with you," she said to Puck. "Your third-generation legacy, straight-A student, chairman-of-his-college-council choice is not my problem today." Interesting, so Puck had gone the traditional route. "I've got a lot of ground to cover with Little Miss Shake-Things-Up, here."

"Me?" I pressed a hand to my chest in innocence. "What about Thorndike and her new theory about declassifying the society?"

"Angel's handling her," Lucky said. "And Soze if she doesn't come to Jesus after that."

" 'Come to Jesus'?" I asked wryly.

"It's an expression!"

"In the Bronx?"

Lucky cleared her throat. "I've been hanging out with my tap a lot. He's southern."

I raised my eyebrows. "How does Tristram feel about that?"

"About the fact that he's southern?" Lucky responded smoothly, straightening the papers on the table in front of her. "Just fine. And don't change the subject, missy! That was quite the bombshell you dropped on us last night, bringing an unvetted guest to the party."

"I did leave you a voice mail," I argued.

Lucky's expression fell neatly into the not-amused camp. "Three hours before the event is not nearly enough time."

The door to the Library opened and in walked Big and Lil' Demon. "Ooh, are we talking about Michelle?" Lil' Demon exclaimed and bounded over, parking herself in the chair on one side of Lucky. "I want to hear."

Big Demon ambled in and took a seat as well. "Anything that takes the focus off Frodo and his public display of tap affection is fine by me." He held up his hands. "I've nothing against alternative lifestyles, but since when did our primary criteria for who we'd like to tap become—"

"Who we'd like to *tap*?" said Juno, popping into the Library before the door closed. "Seriously! Let's not let our standards slip, huh?" She slid into a seat next to me. "Please tell me we're discussing Michelle."

"We're attempting to," Lucky grumbled.

"Good!" Juno smiled, an expression I'd learned to associate with the same anticipation as I would a shark attack. No doubt she disapproved of my untraditional choice as well.

But even Juno had some surprises up her sleeve. "I

really liked her," she said. "I mean, she's a liberal nutbag, but she gave me some great advice about hybrid cars."

"So that makes for good tapping criteria?" Lil' Demon asked.

"Guys, please!" Lucky exclaimed, raking her hands through her short, choppy hair. "I've got a dozen more of these to do and I haven't been to sleep yet."

Everyone settled down.

"Okay." Lucky spread out some papers. "So, leaving aside for a moment your totally uncool springing of this upon me, Bugaboo, let's discuss Michelle because, as I think we've now seen, she made quite the impression last night."

Well, that was nice to hear!

"There's good news and bad news."

Uh-oh.

"First, the good. Here's a copy of her college application. As you can see, she's stellar. Westinghouse scholar, state science fair champ, rocked 5s on her AP Physics, Calculus A and B, Chemistry, Biology, U.S. History, and English exams, and made all-state on her cross-country team."

"Cool!" Big Demon said, tilting the application toward him. "What were her times?"

"She was accepted into Duke, Rice, Berkeley, Bryn Mawr, Bates, and turned down a scholarship at NYU Polytech to come to Eli."

Lucky pulled out a new sheaf of papers. "At Eli, she jumped into the sciences with both feet. Freshman year she took seven classes and three half-credit labs and had a GPA of three-point-five, which is crazy good once you consider that two of those classes were Molecular Biochemistry and its lab."

Lil' Demon looked confused. "Why is that a big thing?"

"It's a weed-out class," Juno explained. "If you break C-plus, you're a superstar."

Lucky cleared her throat and pressed on. "That summer she was a research assistant for a Professor Coudriet, who together with 'et al.' recently published an article on—" Lucky squinted at the printout "—calcium regulated apoptosis pathways—whatever those are—in the journal *Biochemical Pharmacology* and thanked Michelle in the acknowledgments."

"Good thing for LexisNexis," I said.

"Indeed," Lucky said. "Sophomore year was more of the same, plus she began volunteering at a local middle school to tutor children in the sciences and run their science fair. There's an article in the *EDN* about the program she started." She held up another printout. "Looky here: written by Topher Cox."

"Weird!" I said. And yet simultaneously awesome. Michelle, on paper, was working out to be a fabulous choice for science tap. No one would be able to deny her qualifications. Now all I had to do was convince them to tap her for that spot, and then I'd take Topher as my "official" choice to appease the patriarch powers that be. This would work! It had to!

"Now, here's where things start getting wonky."

Crap.

"That summer, she was apparently supposed to work for Professor Coudriet again, but she bailed by July."

"To do what?" I asked.

"Take a class in River Chemistry and Reclamation at the Eli Forestry School. Which she aced."

I pursed my lips. "Well, she is my Geology T.A. Maybe she decided to leave Pharmacology and get into Natural Science?"

"Possibly," said Lucky. "But would one class prevent her from assisting this guy again? I mean, she was on campus anyway. And, because Professor Coudriet has this embarrassing habit of saving e-mail drafts to himself on the Chem department server, I know that in order to entice her back, he offered to add her to the 'et al.' on the list of authors in his latest article."

"Publication credit?" Lil' Demon asked, already wide eyes growing wider. "As an undergrad? And she skipped out on that?"

Juno's eyes narrowed as she scanned the e-mail. "He sounds like he has a crush on her, here. Sketchy."

Everyone's heads went back and Lucky nodded sagely. "There may be another reason that she quit."

Lil' Demon rolled her eyes. "You people and your standards. Put up with the old lech for a few months and get your name on a paper, girl!"

Lucky flipped to a new page in the pile. "Junior year is when we get to the bad news. First of all, her grades went into the toilet. Her GPA dropped to a two-point-three first semester. She quit the mentoring program she'd started. She dropped not one, but two labs. And the semester abroad she supposedly took in the spring? It's a fantasy."

"What!" She had to be kidding.

"Well, she may in fact have gone abroad. I don't know. But she wasn't enrolled in any program, and get this— according to the records I snagged from the Registrar's Office, she *was* signed up for five classes until the end of the drop/add period."

"So what was it?" Big Demon asked. "An incomplete?"

"Since she dropped them in time, technically she wasn't enrolled as a student in Eli at all that semester. But it's clear she'd been planning to be."

I slumped in my seat. Well, that was that. There was no

way Rose & Grave would countenance a 2.3 GPA, even from a science major, unless they were about to quarterback for the NFL.*

"So . . . is she a burnout, then?" Lil' Demon asked.

"It looks that way," said Juno, adding "Liberals" under her breath.

(This had been happening a lot, ever since her Spring Break job put her under the mentorship of one of the world's foremost neocons.)

"Not entirely," Lucky said. "The research project she was doing first semester this year was totally legit, and what's more, it might get published. And despite the poor showing at the beginning of her junior year, she was still invited to T.A. a class her first semester back. Whatever happened to her, she seems to have gotten her act together."

"Maybe she went to rehab," suggested Lil' Demon.

"A drug addict?" Juno said. "Yeah, *that's* who I want in my society."

"Ex–drug addict," Big Demon corrected.

"And she wouldn't be the first," added Lil' Demon.

"At any rate," said Lucky, her tone weary, "that's her story. I'll see what more I can find." She reached her hand across the table and touched my arm. "Look, Bugaboo, I'm not saying you shouldn't pursue this. I'm not even saying that the things we've found are necessarily deal-breakers. But know right now that she's going to have to explain herself at the interview if there's even a chance of us considering her. And the explanation better be a heck of a lot better than 'rehab.' " She shook her head. "You've got an uphill battle ahead of you."

Of course I did. Of course.

---

*Or, the confessor feels the need to add, if they were a legacy, the child of the head of the CIA and/or President, and a sure shot for future President themselves.

To my credit, I did attend my Geology section afterward. Michelle winked at me when I arrived, which caused an involuntary stiffening of my spine.

It was, I admit, not entirely fair to her. After all, if she wasn't going to act any differently after discovering Jamie was my boyfriend, then I shouldn't act any differently after discovering he used to be hers.

Or that she was a potential burnout and possible drug addict who had just complicated my life in a completely different way. I wondered which bit of info I was reacting most strongly to?

The class itself was genuinely interesting. The professor presented slides from his recent trip to Antarctica and the section (of suck-ups, showing up on a Friday without owing favors to the T.A.) paid careful attention. Some even took notes, as if the shots of the professor and his intern trying to digest Meals-Ready-to-Eat would be on the final exam.

Michelle remained rapt throughout the entire lecture. I kept my focus on her. Perhaps I should be taking notes of my own. Why We Should Tap Michelle Whitmore, Reason #335: It would be cool to have a knight at the South Pole.

Would that make up for the lousy GPA?

When class ended, I tried to get Michelle's attention, hoping she'd meet me for lunch, but she was deep in conversation with the professor and eventually I figured it was awkward to stand around any longer. They clearly had plans.

I hiked back to Prescott and found Josh and Lydia snuggled on the couch, flipping through an IKEA catalog. "Amy!" Josh called. "Maybe you can help us end a debate. Birch finishes are too eighties, right?"

Lydia and I exchanged long looks. "I think it's too early to be thinking about furnishing your apartment in Palo Alto," I said.

"Man, you sound like Lydia," said Josh. "Whereas I'd be on Craigslist today if I had my way. She wants to wait until August to move out there. Why don't we just go, you know? After graduation?"

Lydia stared at her hands.

"I'm sure you'll be deciding soon, either way," I said, giving her a meaningful glance she utterly ignored.

Whatever. I had my own issues to deal with. I headed for my room.

"He went home, you know," Josh said, flipping a page in the catalog.

My steps faltered.

"Also, how did the thing go with the thing this morning?"

Michelle's vetting. I turned back to him. "There are a few complications."

"Figures." He flipped another page. "I'd just go with another one."

"The path of least resistance?" I snapped. "I think too many of us are going in that direction lately. Just doing the easy thing for fear of rocking the boat, upsetting the status quo, going against the plan because the better choice comes with a few risks."

Lydia gave me a warning look it was my turn to ignore. "Don't you think so, Lyds?"

"I'm sure I have no idea what you are talking about," she said with a tiny laugh. "Barbarian that I am."

I perched at the edge of the coffee table. "Hey, Josh. Not to change the subject or anything, but what do you think of Eli Law?"

His brow furrowed. "Uh, I think it's the best law school in the country?"

I leaned forward. "And if a promising young student in the field of law had the opportunity to attend that school, don't you think they should take it?"

Josh's expression was one of bafflement. "Is Jamie thinking of dropping out?"

"Yes!" Lydia cut in before I could clear the air. "It's the loans. He can get a scholarship if he transfers to... Rutgers."

Rutgers? I almost laughed. Rutgers was where Lydia had been offered a scholarship. Josh had to know that. I shot her a dirty look, but we were getting to be experts at the ignoring thing by this point.

"That's tough," Josh said thoughtfully. "Law school loans aren't that bad if you're willing to slave in the private sector for a few years." Which Jamie was, by the way. "But if you want to go into public service, or do advanced study...it can get a little overwhelming."

Oh, this was ridiculous. We were so not having a conversation about my boyfriend's ability to pay for his JD.

"I've always gotten the impression that Jamie didn't actually want to be a lawyer," Josh was saying now. "In which case, Eli is perfect for him—right, Lydia?"

"Some people who go to Eli want to be lawyers," she said, her tone defensive.

"Most want to go into government, though, like Jamie."

I shook my head. "No, Jamie wants to go work for big law and make a mint." He'd been very clear about that when we'd spoken on the train last fall. He wanted to make sure he'd never be financially beholden to anyone. He wanted the security his father had been unable to offer as a landscaper.

Josh frowned. "That's not what he's told me."

"But—" I said, Lydia's plight forgotten, and the phone rang.

Lydia answered, then handed it to me. "I think it's..."

"Hello?" I said.

"Hi, Amy," said Darren.

"Darren," I said as my blood ran cold. "I thought I made it clear last time that I don't want to—"

"I'm just calling to tell you that they are letting me go today."

"Already?" I blurted. Damn my tongue!

"Yep." He laughed. "I talked to the guy who's in charge and he says I'm fine."

"That's...nice."

"And he said that he thought you and my dad were overreacting."

"Over—"

"To what was basically a fraternity prank."

"But—"

Darren's tone was smug. "I guess 'boys will be boys' works again, huh?"

I clenched my jaw, uncertain whether to scream or cry.

"So now Dad's taking us all to Disney World."

"Darren," I said, fighting to keep my voice from shaking, "I want to talk to your father. This was not our agreement."

"Well, Dad's not here. I'm calling from the residence hall."

"Look—" I began, and then the phone was ripped from my hands.

"Darren Gehry," Josh said into the receiver, "don't ever call here again." He clicked it off and threw the phone onto the couch.

My mouth fell open. "Why did you do that?"

"Because I'm sick of putting up with this travesty of justice. The Gehrys took advantage of you when you were in a very vulnerable position, and it's not right."

I took a deep breath. "Kurt Gehry swore to me—"

"That's what 'taking advantage' means, Amy." Josh's tone was firm and condescending. "And now we're going to call the police and report what happened."

"You have no right to make that decision for me."

"Amy," Lydia said, "maybe you should think about what Josh is saying."

"He wasn't even there!" I cried. "He's never even met him!"

"I trust his opinion," Lydia argued, "and if he thinks—"

"That's such crap!" I yelled at her. "If you really trusted his opinion you wouldn't be lying to him!"

"What!" Lydia said.

"What?" Josh asked.

"Lydia got into Eli Law," I said. "She's been afraid to tell you." Then I turned and stalked into my bedroom.

———

Two days later, the chill in my suite still hadn't dissipated. At dinner before the Rose & Grave meeting on Sunday night, Soze made a point of pretending I wasn't there, and I calculated the odds of the other knights deciding that my outburst, which *was* in keeping with my oaths to put my society brothers first, outweighed the fact that telling your best friend's secrets to her boyfriend was an astoundingly uncool thing to do.

I still hadn't come to a conclusion on that issue myself. Nor on whether or not I would have spilled the beans had I not been so frazzled by Darren's phone call and Josh's Neanderthal behavior.

And yes, I totally brought it up to Jamie. We're doing the openness thing now.* How did the conversation go?

1) He wondered aloud why it was that catty BFF/suitemate drama of this nature was almost entirely unique to what some—not *him*, mind you—but what *some* antiquated and backward individuals might call "the weaker sex." (I resisted pointing out that he had neither suitemates nor friends with whom to indulge in catty drama, then gave him a playful—but not at all weak—smack.)

2) He agreed that Josh was better off knowing about Lydia's acceptance to Eli, even if it meant an earlier end to their romance than either of them had anticipated. (He remained silent on the issue of whether or not I had any right to be the bearer of the news.)

3) He asked what I was going to do about Michelle now that we knew there were problems in her record. Apparently, the news had surprised him. Back when Jamie had been friends with her, she'd been an academic superstar. (I said we were going to get to the bottom of it, either before the interview or at it.)

4) He admitted that whether or not Michelle ended up being a good choice to tap, bringing her to the party was still a "patently Bugaboo thing to do." (Naturally, I fined him, and tried my best not to wonder if "patently Bugaboo" held a positive or negative connotation.)

*The confessor admits to a strategic omission of the role Darren Gehry may or may not have played in the fiasco. She may be all for openness, but not when it comes to certain cans of worms.

And, as expected, he hadn't attended this meeting, either. All well and good to be involved in the tapping process when it came with free champagne and sushi, but if it was sitting around debating the relative merits of a bunch of twenty-one-year-olds, Poe wanted us to feel independent and in charge. Right.

All I felt was weary as we discussed and debated and deliberated over the pros and cons of the juniors we'd met last week. Should we interview the guy on Big Demon's list, knowing that if we did, we could cross off the girl on Angel's? Their messy breakup precluded either one of them speaking to the other (let alone taking oaths to protect and love each other). Had Thorndike tainted the purity of the process when it came to her list by explaining to each of them what they were being considered for? Had Frodo corrupted his favorite choice by hooking up with him? (Quoth Angel: "The guy? Perhaps. My bath mat? Definitely.")

"And finally, we come to the matter of Bugaboo's list," Soze said, still not acknowledging me directly. "It is my understanding that the knight wishes to make a trade?"

"Yes," I said, rising. "I would like to trade my red marble for the black marble belonging to our missing knight, Number Two. And I would also like to submit a junior for consideration in that knight's slot."

"And who would you like in your slot, Bugaboo?" Soze prompted.

I was going to have to say it out loud? "I propose to tap Topher Cox. He's got all the qualifications we look for in our members. He's the managing editor of the *Eli Daily News*. He's a legacy, as his grandfather was Achilles of D125. And . . ." Nope, I was out.

"Passionate endorsement, Bugaboo," said Thorndike.

"She's saving her passion for the other one," said Frodo.

"We all know who you're saving your passion for," Thorndike snapped at him.

It was getting *very* late.

"Topher Cox has been vetted by the knight Lucky. What does she say?"

Lucky looked skeptical. "*She* says he's a throwback to some old school Diggerdom."

"Great!" said Juno. "We could use some."

"The patriarchs will be pleased, at least," said Angel.

"I don't know," said Puck. "I know his type. He's always going on about himself, but there's nothing there. He's an empty suit."

"Wait," said Juno. "Am I correct that *you*, of all people, are calling him shallow?"

"Yes," said Puck, refusing to take the bait. "And if I do it, he must really be bad."

Bond shook his head. "I still say any person who purports to be a writer and opts not to use a choriambic byline like 'Christopher Cox' has a tin ear."

"An unpardonable sin, to be sure," Graverobber grumbled into the dregs of his espresso.

Tin ear notwithstanding, there were no major objections to at least interviewing him.

"And the suggestion for the slot belonging to Number Two?" Soze asked wearily.

This was the part of being in a secret society that I hated. Why all the bureaucracy? Everyone knew what I was going to say and what the objections to my choice would be. We'd all made these arguments before the meeting, whether in private conversations or on our society e-mail loop. Why did we have to do it again in the Inner Temple, in scratchy old robes that smelled of must and age, in formal language adopted for the benefit of record-keeping in the Black Books? Why indeed were we still keeping notes in the Black Books, a holdover from a pre-digital era, when with relative ease we could now record audio of every moment of every meeting for posterity?

And yet, I ran through the motions, and listened as Lucky ran through hers, repeating for the assembled club the same facts and figures she'd informed me of two days ago, with this addition: "Also, I've reviewed the appointment calendar of the Strathmore College dean for the last two years. Michelle Whitmore had over a dozen appointments at the end of her first junior semester and the start of her second, aborted, junior semester."

"That's in keeping with the fact that she dropped out, isn't it?" asked Lil' Demon.

"Yes," said Lucky. "But what's curious is that the dean had a habit of making notes in her calendar program from most of her meetings. 'Granted student extension of term paper for History 320.' 'Discussed counseling to deal with student's growing substance abuse problem.' 'Provided excused absences for student's extended medical leave.' 'Joint meeting with student and school provost to go over ramifications of disciplinary hearing due to assault of T.A.' Stuff like that."

"What was Michelle meeting her for?" I asked.

"That's the thing," said Lucky. "It didn't say. There are no notes from any of Michelle's meetings. Whatever they discussed, the dean did not want a written record of it."

I hereby confess:
The sand's not always
such a bad place
for your head.

8.
Filibuster

The classroom had been converted into a cave. The windows were covered with blackout curtains, the tables and chairs were shrouded in dark sheets. Before each of our places lay a clipboard with paper for notes and a small booklight to illuminate the pages but not our faces. The knights sat scattered about the room in no discernable order or pattern, a method that was supposed to confuse and disorient the interviewee as well as assist in keeping our identities secret. It was a lot harder to figure out who we were when you couldn't pin down our positions in the black-hole space. We each wore black turtlenecks. From the chair at the front of the room, you couldn't see more than our jawlines.

Mine has never been my best feature.

I remembered this room. I remembered these black drapes, these booklights. A year ago, I'd been the one in the hot seat while the members of Rose & Grave interrogated me about my grades, my ambitions, and my kindergarten teachers. I'd gotten offended, flipped them off as a group, and stormed out.

They'd tapped me anyway. Possibly, I now realized, because my show of sass had at least broken up the monotony of the process. We were ten interviews in, and not a single potential tap had told us anything we didn't already know. A bad grade freshman year? Explained away by a breakup, a death in the family, a bout of mono, or the fact that when they signed up for the class, they hadn't realized how it was way over their heads.

And that was when they weren't indulging us in a round of interview-speak. Their greatest flaws were always "perfectionism," their failures were all minor snafus they transformed into great life lessons about learning to take charge and be leaders when other people didn't cut the mustard. This was the first time I'd heard this pap from the other side of the table, and it made me wonder how any of us—trained as we were in these same turn-your-negatives-into-positives interview techniques—had gotten jobs. Did we all sound so disingenuous and bigheaded? Employers couldn't possibly buy our brand of bullshit any more than I believed these potential taps when they told me that the four words that best described them were "leadership," "loyalty," "intelligence," and "trustworthiness."

Especially when one of the potentials was Topher Cox.

LOWLIGHTS FROM THE ROSE & GRAVE INTERVIEW OF TOPHER COX

1) "My hero? I guess that would be my grandfather, Lionel Drake. He's such a great guy. Always been so supportive of me and my family. Anyone he thinks of as part of his team, really." (Hint frickin' hint.)

2) "I've pretty much had the same group of friends my whole life. We came up through prep school together, me and Sam and Blake and Alan. We'd do anything for one another—have done pretty much everything. Well, no gay shit." (Quoth Kevin: "That's a relief.")

3) "One of the things I think I bring to the table is a strong sense of the significance of financial solvency. Now, nobody wants to admit it, but money? It's important. And I've got it." (Well, at least he had no illusions about why we were tapping him.)

All in all, he did pretty well. No new drawbacks were discovered, and his pros had begun to take prominence over his personality flaws in the eyes of the majority of the club.

"Sellouts," Demetria had grumbled.

I didn't disagree, but I also wasn't protesting the choice. The patriarchs got Topher; I (hopefully) got Michelle. Others before me, like Jamie, had tapped according to the best needs of the society, and they didn't even get the consolation prize of a bonus tap. The benefit an iconoclast like Michelle might bring to the group would end up being far more influential than Topher's same old boys' network attitude, or even his influx of cash. Sometimes, you needed to compromise. Right?

"One day," Demetria had said, when I pointed this out, "you'll look back on how much you've compromised and you won't even recognize yourself. That's what Rose & Grave has taught me."

We worried that she wasn't presenting the most positive portrait of the society to her potential taps.

Michelle was our next subject. We'd found a free spot in her schedule and allowed for the extended time it would take for her to arrive at the interview from her off-campus apartment up near the science buildings. Kevin, who had the best voice modulation in the club, was in charge of making the phone calls. In keeping with society tradition, all the potentials were given surprise invitations to an interview. They only had a few minutes to properly attire themselves and hoof it to our location. I crossed my fingers under the table as he dialed her number. With Michelle, everything was riding on the interview.

"Hello?" Michelle's voice sounded tinny in the cell phone speaker.

"Michelle Anastasia Whitmore?" Kevin's voice rumbled out like God from a burning bush.

"Um, yeah?"

"Your presence is required at 750 College Street, room 400, at three-fifteen in the afternoon."

There was a short pause, one that we were all used to by now. Up next would come the inevitable *Who is this?*

Except that's not what happened. Instead, Michelle gave a strange little laugh and said, "Yeah. Nice try, jerk."

The line went dead. Kevin tried calling back three times. On the first and second attempt, the call went to voice mail. On the third, Michelle picked up again.

"Listen," she hissed before Kevin had a chance to go into his routine. "Call me again and I'll block this number like I blocked the last three, got it?"

The last three? The knights shifted uncomfortably in their seats. Was Michelle, like Kalani, being courted by another society? By Dragon's Head, perhaps?

"This is not without precedent," Josh said, in the odd, formal tone he'd adopted with me ever since I'd dropped the bombshell in our suite. "There have been, upon occasion, practical jokes played on students. People pretend to be calling about a society interview and the hapless junior shows up to find it's all a scam. That must be what's going on here. She thinks we're joking."

Demetria snorted. "This is why just telling them is better. No surprises."

"So what do we do?" I asked.

"Traditionally," said Clarissa, "that's it. They had their opportunity. We call, they get their butts over here. If they don't, they're off the list."

Yeah. I knew that. I just didn't want to have it confirmed. All that time spent convincing the others to give Michelle a chance, to see what reason she had for bombing her classes and dropping out of school. All my hopes that I could get a tap I'd be proud to call mine—all gone.

"Okay, guys," said Josh, checking the readout from the digital clock on the desk. "That's it for the afternoon. We'll reconvene tomorrow afternoon for the remainder of the interviews—barring any more unforeseen circumstances—and hopefully, that will be it. Then Tap Night this weekend. Let's make sure to leave one by one. Don't want anyone to see us."

As everyone left their seats to chat, mill around, or run to the bathroom, I made sure my path to the door caused me to pass by Kevin's desk. I glanced down at the paperwork as I strolled by. Michelle's address. Michelle's phone number.

In the sunlit hallway, I reflected on how fragile the veneer of society secrecy really was. For all the trouble we underwent to ensure that our identities were really unknown in that room, it required total cooperation on the part of the people we interviewed. They had to be willing to play along. How easy would it be for them to flip on the lights? How easy would it be to just sit here and wait for us in the hallway until we left the classroom?

Societies like mine remained "secret" not through our

efforts, but because everyone on campus accepted the eccentricity and indulged us. They spread the stories of awesome power and unlimited influence, and kept their eyes politely averted when we shuffled into the tomb on Thursday and Sunday evenings, a bunch of ordinary students with overdue term papers, tangled love lives, and buttloads of student loans. Eli students bought into the legends without question—I'd done it myself—though our curriculum taught us to question everything else. Societies were a campus tradition, as much as intramural sports or singing groups, Saturday nights spent drinking from silver trophy cups at Tory's or Sunday afternoons in the stadium singing silly songs that made fun of Harvard. Even the campus satire newspapers and tabloids who claimed to want to "expose" us were only adding to the sense of mystique. The existence of the societies as a unique part of the Eli experience was indoctrinated into every student from freshman year, and by the time they were juniors, many of them wanted to take part or at least get a glimpse into our rarified world.

In a way, the society was a natural next step. All those competitive, ambitious high school students, pressing their face up to the college admissions glass and wondering what went on at these "reach schools," what was so different about Eli or Princeton that it was worth the huge price tag, what made it so special compared to Home State U.? Those same students, the ones who made it, were now looking at the giant, imposing tombs on campus and wondering the exact same things. What was so special about a society, and were they special enough to gain admittance?

Back home in Ohio, people thought it was a big deal that I was at Eli. Dropping the "E-bomb" into conversations became a dicey prospect. There were so many folks who assumed that I was a stuck-up snob whenever they heard I went to an Ivy League school, as if my ambition and achievements were somehow designed to insult theirs, as if my matriculation to an elite school made me an elitist.

Perhaps that was the real reason societies had gone underground and classified their membership roster. Not because it enhanced our own experience within the society, but because it protected us from prejudice outside of it.

I'd joked with Jamie that my mother wouldn't be a fan of Rose & Grave. Maybe there were enough people like her for whom the ill will would actually act as a liability.

Maybe that's how Michelle felt.

The other knights were surely gone by now. I pulled out my cell phone and dialed the number I'd swiped from Kevin.

"Hello?" Michelle said, sounding more suspicious than ever.

"Michelle, it's Amy Haskel," I said in as bright a tone as I could muster.

"Oh, hi, Amy," she said. "I was a little worried after last weekend—wait, how did you get this number?"

"Um..." Stole it from Jenny's research. She, in turn, had hacked it from the Registrar's Office. "I looked it up in the Student Directory?"

"I'm unlisted." The suspicion was back, full force. "Where did you find it?"

"To be honest, I can't remember," I lied. "I wrote it down this morning and I've only just had the chance to contact you. Anyway—"

"I really need to know," she interrupted. "Can you do me a huge favor? When you get home tonight, look in your browser history to see where you got it. I'm supposed to be unlisted and I've been getting these strange calls—"

"Yeah?" I said. "About those—"

"Look, Amy, I've got to go deal with this. Please let me know what you find out, okay?"

I pressed on. "I need to talk to you about—"

"I know. And I promise we will. Lunch after class tomorrow? Great. Gotta run."

And then she hung up. Again.

———

There's nothing better for curing frustration than finding a new source, so I went home to incorporate my advisor's most recent set of notes into my thesis. Miraculously, Professor Burak had actually seemed impressed by my draft. At least, that was my opinion judging from the tone of his rather intense notes. There were very few corrections to what I'd already written. Rather, his suggestions all leaned toward taking my research one step further, finding another example to back up my points. At the top of the pages, he'd placed a sticky note reading:

Some truly original thoughts here. Glad you ditched Persephone!

I may have ditched her, but I didn't leave her in the lurch. My final thesis topic, on the repeated trope of women as gatekeepers to the spirit world, owed a lot to my understanding of the Queen of Hades. I wondered if Professor Burak would be happy to learn that we'd decided to incorporate a few of these ideas into the Rose & Grave initiation. Last year, though I hadn't understood it at the time, Jamie had registered his dissident vote by spearheading an initiation ceremony filled with scenes of upstart women throughout history. (Hint: They were mostly killed.) I don't know how well the irony would have played in Peoria; in New Haven, I'd been scared out of my wits. The pro-women portion of the D176 club, on the other hand, thought the anti-feminist symbols presented a truly appropriate house of horrors, an imbalanced world they were toppling by their bold move to tap women for the first time at the end of the tours.

Symbolism: It's never what you think it is.

Our club had decided to ditch that theme and move toward the obvious next step: As the first club to include women, we thought we'd focus on an initiation that showcased the participation of women in arcane and secret rites. A little *Da Vinci Code*, perhaps, but since I'd done a lot of the research for my thesis, it would be relatively easy to pull off.

Which reminded me. I was supposed to call the prop department at the Eli drama school and put in an order for fake blood. I clicked on the phone. No dial tone.

"Lydia!" I called. She didn't answer and I rose from my chair and headed back to the common room. "What did you do to the phone!"

"Unplugged it," she said calmly, turning a page in her book.

"Why!"

"Because the ringing was starting to bother me. You're not the only one with a thesis to write, you know."

"Well, what if I need to use it?"

She looked up from her work and gave me a chilly glare (her new specialty). "Do you, or do you not, have in your possession an item that we in the 21st century refer to as a cellular telephone?"

I rolled my eyes and plugged the phone back in. "I'm *so* looking forward to having my own place next year. What if that was someone calling me about grad school?"

"They don't call. They send letters. Like the one Eli sent to me. You know the one. It contained private correspondence you didn't choose to respect."

The phone began to ring in my hand. Lydia let out a beleaguered sigh.

"Do we need to talk about this?" I asked her. She gave me another glare, with *What do you think?* written all over her face. The phone trilled again.

"Oh, just answer the damn thing," she huffed.

"But Lydia," I said. "If we need to talk—the 21st century has also provided us with a little thing called 'voice mail.' "

"I'm not ready to talk to you," she replied. So I answered the phone.

"Hello?" A woman's voice, a crisp English accent. "May I speak to Amy Haskel?"

"This is she." I furrowed my brow.

"My name is Maya Butler, and I'm with the Rothemere American Institute—"

"The what?"

She chuckled indulgently at the Yankee. "At Oxford."

"Oh." *Oh.* Oxford. On the phone with frickin' *Oxford* and I'd already managed to make myself sound like an idiot.

"I'm organizing a colloquium this summer on behalf of St. Catherine's College about Women and the Classics. Your thesis advisor, Dr. Yousef Burak, submitted to us an abstract of your paper on—er—" she fumbled over the words "—'Chicks with Styx.' "

He had? He hadn't told me that. "I, um, really need a new title." *Great, Amy. Continue to impress.* I'd been so punchy the evening I'd decided that was hilarious.

"Well, yes, we shall have to work on that," she said, her tone indulgent. "We were curious when the paper will be complete."

She was calling me from Great Britain to ask me that? "It's due on the fifth."

"Marvelous! In that case, we'd be delighted to extend an offer for you to present it at our conference."

You what? I caught myself from shouting that into the phone. Lydia was growing silently frantic at my side.

"Hello, Amy? Are you still there?"

"Yes. Sorry. I was just—present my paper? In England?" I gaped at Lydia! So much for her letter theory.

My roommate, to her credit, squealed and bounced to her feet.

"Yes," said Maya Butler. "Now, the conference is at the end of June. As a presenter, your entrance fee and housing at St. Catherine's will be gratis, but unfortunately, we cannot provide airfare, so..."

I listened as she laid out the rest of the offer, but my mind had already started to race way ahead. England. Oxford. An hour from London. The Thames. The Tower. The West End. And England! I could travel around afterward. Stonehenge. Jane Austen's house. Stratford-upon-Avon. Bath!

Amy. Focus. A conference. A weeklong conference. And me... presenting? On classics? But I didn't even speak Latin!

No, I could do this. This was amazing. I was totally going to kill my professor for not giving me a heads-up, but still...

"...I can e-mail you all the other information you'll need."

"And I can e-mail you my thesis," I replied. "Thank you so much!"

When I hung up, Lydia squealed again and hugged me. "Tell me everything. I only got to hear your end and... well, no offense, hon, but you need some speaking practice before you go to England. What are they teaching you in this secret society of yours?"

I squeezed her back. "Shut up, I was never on the debate team." I pulled away. "So does this mean you're done being mad at me?"

"Not even a little," Lydia said with a laugh. "But there's a moratorium. We have to celebrate!"

———

Jamie was in class until six, so I left a message with him to meet us at the Diggers' favorite bar and took off with Lydia, who'd left a similar message with Josh (sans the "Diggers' favorite" part). As it was Monday night, the large, split-level, wood-lined bar was relatively empty. Clarissa and Odile had already commandeered our usual spot, a vast, circular booth of dark leather, and were blowing off post-interview steam by splitting a pitcher of Rose & Grave's signature drink, the 312. They beckoned us over right away, and we'd hardly gotten settled in our seats when Jenny and Harun arrived, together as always. I still didn't know what was going on with those two—they swore up and down that there was nothing between them but no one believed that. However, no one had ever caught even a whiff of un-platonic behavior either, and given my track record, I couldn't start pressing them to define whatever their relationship happened to be.

Not that it deterred others.

"You know what you remind me of," Odile said to them as they scooted into the booth. "Those sneaky co-stars having an on-set affair who are always so careful not to let anyone photograph them together because they don't want the paparazzi to have any material by which to draw inferences."

"You know what you remind me of?" Jenny replied coolly. "The paparazzi."

Odile: "Touché."

Clarissa made a sizzling sound through her teeth and motioned for the bartender in a subtle, fluid motion I could practice in the mirror a hundred times and never get right, that I could use in a hundred bars and never draw the staff with the efficacy she managed.

Then again, Clarissa's tipping was legendary. That might also have something to do with it.

As we gave the man our orders, Lydia turned to Odile and said, "Actually, whatever you're having looks good. What's it called?"

"Um..." Odile demonstrated her weakness as an improv player.

"Oh, let her have one," I said. "Who the hell cares? There's nothing proprietary about the ingredients."

"Whatever you say, *Demetria*," Clarissa mocked, taking a sip of her 312.

Demetria herself showed up halfway through our first round, along with Ben and Greg.

"You people again?" Ben said, as we scooted over to make room. "Man, it's like I can't get away."

"Not at this bar," Harun agreed.

Demetria checked out his pint glass. "Is that Guinness?"

"Root beer. On tap."

"Really?" She waved at the bartender and called, "Same as him. But with SoCo."

"Ew," said Odile. "Sweet much?"

"Yes, I am." Demetria gave a saccharine smile. "As far away as I can get from that stuff." She pointed at the pitcher of 312s.

"Why?" Lydia asked, all innocence, though her mouth was stained with pomegranate.

"I—" She looked at Lydia. "I didn't know this was a barbarian thing. I would have brought Shannon."

"Ooh," said Odile. "Who's Shannon?"

Jenny glared at her. "Would you, for *once*, leave someone's personal life to themselves?" She took a sip of her soda, and her face softened. "Okay, you're right. I want to know who Shannon is, too."

"And how you've managed to keep her secret from us," Clarissa added.

"That's not allowed, is it?" said Lydia, and I kicked her under the table.

"Oh, look," said Demetria, pointing away. "Amy's *boyfriend* is here." She still avoided saying his name whenever she could.

The distraction achieved its intended result, and I slid from the booth to meet Jamie at the stair landing. His book bag was slung across his chest, tugging his black T-shirt and twill jacket tight across his shoulders. He also wore a pair of khakis with a tiny tear on.the right thigh. Strange how his well-worn wardrobe had somehow become one of his more charming attributes.

"Hey, you," I said, grinning as he took the stairs two at a time to reach me.

He slipped his arms around my waist and pulled me in close. "I got your message. *I'm so proud of you*," he whispered against my neck.

"Thanks," I said. "So, that's two weeks down, and only seventy more years I have to create a plan for."

"One step at a time." He looked down at me, and a lock of his dark hair fell into his face. "And the next step is to alert all the places you've still got applications out. This is a huge update—"

"Party pooper," I said. "First things first. We drink."

"I stand corrected." He pulled his bag off his shoulder. "I came here straight from class, so I'm going to run to the restroom for a moment. Order me something?"

"312?"

He looked over my shoulder at the table. "You're drinking those in front of barbarians?"

I smirked at him. "Wanna make something of it?"

He laughed. "What else from D177? By the time you're done with us, I don't think there'll be any secrets left in this society."

"And that's a bad thing?"

He didn't answer. "It may shock you to discover this, but I never actually liked 312s. Get me a gimlet instead?"

"Wow, call the secret society police! What's a gimlet?"

"You've only been to keggers your whole Eli career, haven't you?"

"So not true."

"Don't worry, the waiter will know." Jamie stopped and searched my face. "Everything okay? You don't seem as happy as you should be."

I shrugged. "Michelle skipped her interview, so I'm disappointed."

"Oh, I'm sorry. I know you had high hopes for her."

"And you didn't, I know...."

"What I thought has no bearing on this, Amy."

"Oh, please." I looked away, across the bar.

Then I felt his fingers on my cheek and looked back at him. "It doesn't. You know what I think, what I've thought all along. But I don't expect us to make the same decisions. Have never once expected it, in fact. And honestly, if I'd been making predictions, I should have guessed you'd do something so..." He paused. "Iconoclastic?"

"Heretical, you mean?"

"Yes. Heretical. My little heretic." He kissed me. "Forget Michelle. If she couldn't recognize an offer when she saw it, she doesn't deserve to become one of the elect. You can accept that much Rose & Grave doctrine, can't you?"

"But what if the problem is she didn't know what we were offering? We never say 'Come be a Digger' when we call for an interview."

"If they're smart, they know."

"I didn't," I said.

"You..." *Busted.* "...understood you were auditioning for a society, though."

"Nice save." I pushed his hair back off his brow.

"It was, wasn't it?" His hands went back to my waist. "I can be very, very good under pressure."

"I see that."

Someone cleared his throat behind us. "You're blocking the stairs." Josh. We pulled away from each other and he squeezed by. "I think the phrase I'm looking for is 'Get a room.'"

"With all the PDA going on in my suite?" I asked. "That's a mighty glassy house you're standing in."

Jamie headed toward the men's room and Josh took my place next to Lydia in the booth, scooting in so there would be room for me and Jamie. Odile and Clarissa had wandered off somewhere. The waiter returned and we all ordered another round, including Jamie's gimlet, which turned out to be a subtly green-tinged vodka drink. I took a discreet sip before he got back. Lime. Interesting.

"So what's this news Lydia's been hinting at?" Josh asked, and I launched into my full report.

"...And the best thing about it is that it's this summer. It doesn't cut into anything I might want to do next year," I finished.

"Which is?" Jenny asked.

"Not sure yet," I admitted. Jamie put his arm around my shoulders.

"You really need to get on that," said Ben.

"Sure," I said. "I'll do it in all that spare time I've got."

He held his hands up. "Fine. I'm just saying, what happened to the girl who had her summer internship all lined up the January beforehand last year?"

"I've been a bit busy with other stuff."

"We've all been busy, Amy," said Josh, clearly feeling he owed me no charity after I'd caused a rift between him and Lydia.

And it wasn't fair, either. Those of us who knew what they were doing next year had been more prepared to actually achieve their goals. My grad school applications had been more of a last-minute effort. No wonder they hadn't performed as well. And if I hadn't put as much effort into follow-ups or additional applications since returning from Spring Break, well...

"I've been *really* busy," I said, slightly more forcefully than necessary. "On top of all your stuff, I had that fun extracurricular activity. Remember? The one where I was stalked, harassed, drugged, and kidnapped?"

Everyone got very quiet. Jamie's arm tightened around me.

"Uh, Amy..." Jenny began. "You okay?"

Lydia got a cunning look in her eye. "Wait, don't you all know?"

"Lydia, not tonight," I said, but she was not to be deterred. After all, I'd screwed her over in front of her boyfriend.

"Darren Gehry called last week. He's totally out on the streets."

I hereby confess:
We have more in common
than I'd thought.

9.
Lovers and Other Strangers

I gave my roommate the evil eye, but she ignored me and went on. "What was it he said when he called, Josh? Something about 'boys will be boys'? Sounds like the whole family is taking this 'rehabilitation' thing very seriously indeed."

Jamie dropped his arm and turned to me. "When did this happen?"

"Last Thursday," Lydia informed him. "You must have just left the suite when he called."

I was going to kill her.

"Amy!" Demetria said, on cue. "Why didn't you tell us?"

"Because, like I said, I've been busy." I kept glaring at Lydia, who was about to gold medal in ignoring. "We all have, with—stuff." Society stuff. Now I understood why knights didn't bring barbarians to their events.

"We could have made time to talk about this," Jenny said.

"This is not what we agreed upon, back in Florida."
Demetria was seething. "You need to—"

I cut her off. "I know what I need to do. I need to graduate. I need to fulfill my commitments to my . . . activities
on campus. I do not need to dwell on what happened in
Florida right now. I do not need to go down there and
what—what? Start giving statements? Get in a protracted
fight with the extensive Gehry legal team? Just forget it. I
don't have the time or energy for it. It's over. I'm never going to see that kid again. I just want to move on and concentrate on the stuff that's really important." I cast a glance
around the suddenly dead-sober table. "Come on, guys.
This is supposed to be my night to celebrate."

Jamie hadn't spoken again. I tried to put my hand over
his but he snatched it away and threw back the rest of his
drink. "You know," he said after swallowing, "I have some
reading I have to do for tomorrow. Sorry to cut this short
but I have to run." He grabbed his bag, gave me a quick
peck on the cheek, and scrammed.

If anyone else at the table spoke, I didn't hear it. I was
too busy chasing after my boyfriend.

"Hey." At the top of the stairs.

"Hey!" By the downstairs bar.

"Hey!" As he slipped through the front door into the
New Haven twilight.

He took a few steps down the sidewalk then stopped
and turned around. "What do you want me to do, Amy? I
have two choices. I could sit there with your friends and
explode, thereby justifying their negative opinion of me, or
I could leave."

"And what do you think their opinion is when you split
in the middle of that particular conversation?"

He hissed a breath of air through his teeth. "Okay, you

got me. But what do you want me to do? Darren called you again, and *again* your friends knew before me."

"They were standing in the room with me!" I argued. "Josh practically ripped the phone out of my hands."

He stared at me for a long moment. "None of this signifies. Your friends and me—it's not the point at all. The real question is, what are you going to do about this?"

"How about nothing?"

"How about that doesn't sound remotely like you?"

How about I don't have time! If I get obsessed with punishing Darren, then everything else will slide. What was I going to do about him? Screw that! What was I going to do about Jamie after graduation? What was I going to do about my future? What in the world was I going to do about tap now that I'd lost Michelle? Why couldn't I just have one evening to rest and relax and be happy about the colloquium?

"The Amy I know would never let him get away with this. You made a deal—a stupid deal, but a deal. You'd let the Gehrys handle their son privately, and you wouldn't press charges. But they aren't holding up their end. You don't owe them anything. Again, Kurt Gehry is breaking trust with us, just like he did last year."

"And should we expect any different?" I asked. "A scorpion is a scorpion. And even if he weren't, don't you think your own son comes before anything you might owe your old college secret society?"

"This isn't about the society," Jamie said. "This is about his son hurting you. Really hurting you, beyond any comparison to a society prank or whatever idiotic justification you've created for what Darren did. I don't believe we are to blame for this in any way, no matter what you think Darren learned by spying on us. But now I wonder: Is that what is holding you back from pressing charges? Do you think that going after a patriarch's son would be against your vows to the society?"

"No. I just—I can't deal with anything else right now. With tap, and graduation, and everything else, my plate is way too full." It was true. And it would be true even if I hadn't made sure there was no free time left to spend contemplating what had happened to me.

He folded me into his arms. "But don't you know, there's a dozen people in that bar who will help you? I'll help you. That's what we've been trying to do all along. *That's* where the society vows come in. You made a decision, we submitted to it, no matter how bad of an idea we thought it was. But if you choose to take action, we'll find giving you that kind of help far easier to stomach."

"I just want to put it behind me," I said.

"But you're not," he replied. "You're having nightmares. You know who has put it behind him? Darren."

Darren, who went to Disney World while my life filled up with stress and responsibilities. I buried my face in Jamie's chest.

"I don't know," I mumbled into his shirt. "I have to... think about it."

"Then promise me you'll think about it. Really think."

And then, no doubt, come to the decision he and the rest of my friends advocated. "Think" didn't mean *think*. It meant *realize that our way is best*. But I wasn't the multitasker that some of them were. I'd think about it, all right. After I had my life in order.

I tilted up my chin and met his eyes. "I promise."

He breathed deeply and wound his fingers through my hair to cup my face. "I love you, Amy."

Every cell in my body spun in place. A thousand thousand seconds seemed to pass before I could find my voice.

Jamie leaned his forehead against mine, squeezed his eyes shut. "That was the gimlet talking."

"No, it wasn't."

"No, it wasn't," he agreed. "And now I *do* have to go."

To run away? After that bombshell? Fat chance. "Can I come with you?" My hands went inside his jacket to rest on his hips.

The sound he made was halfway between a laugh and a groan. "No, because I have work. And I—"

"Don't think you could work if I came with you."

"Exactly." He met my eyes again. "But soon." And then he kissed me until my cells started spinning again.

After he was gone, I staggered back toward the bar, wondering if my face was the color of a 312. He *loved* me? *He loved me.*

"Kinda intense, isn't he?" said Odile. She and Clarissa stood by the wall, smoking.

Oh, God. Now my cheeks did burn. I got as near as my lungs and sense of humility would allow.

Odile flicked some ash off the end of her cigarette. "How does that, you know, *translate*? In bed."

"Odile," Clarissa said with a roll of her eyes and a drag on her cigarette.

"Oh, please," said Odile. "We know all the dirty stuff about every single one of us. Amy doesn't get out of sharing time just because her C.B. was early on." She dropped her cigarette on the ground and stamped it out with the pointy toe of her designer boots. "And I have to admit, I've always been kind of curious. Does he like it kinky?"

"Odile!" I said, and looked at Clarissa for support.

But Clarissa's expression had turned thoughtful. "Yeah," she said. "Come to think of it, he kind of screams bondage fetish, doesn't he?"

"Exactly," said Odile.

"Guys!" I cried. "I just had an incredibly romantic moment and you're ruining it. And, for your information, I wouldn't know what kind of fetishes Jamie has, because we haven't slept together."

They blinked at me.

"What are you waiting for?" Clarissa asked.

Odile's mouth formed a perfect little O. "He's not, like, one of those abstinence people, is he?"

"Or gay," Clarissa suggested. "He could be gay."

"He's not gay, and he's not abstinent," I said wearily. "It just hasn't happened yet."

"Huh." Clarissa lifted her cigarette to her lips. "So what was the romantic moment?"

He said he loved me. He said he *loved* me. *He said he loved me.* "That," I replied coyly, "is a secret."

Back inside, the crew had wisely decided to move on to other topics than Darren, and even more wisely had chosen to order food. The nachos and cheese fries had arrived, but Demetria was still waiting on her goat cheese and spinach pizza when George approached the table with his sophomore squeeze in tow.

"Oh," he said, looking around at the group. "I thought this was a barbarian thing—"

"It is," I replied, pointing at Lydia with a cheese fry. "There just aren't many."

"Great." George smiled that devastating grin of his and ushered the sophomore forward. "This is Devon. Devon, meet Amy, from Prescott."

"Oh, hi," the girl said. "I know I've seen you around."

I knew I'd seen her, too. And she was still on George's radar? Interesting. And he'd brought her to our bar? Even more interesting. "Nice to meet you, *at last.*"

George cleared his throat. "Where's Jamie?"

"Working." My tone was even, my expression guileless. George could parade half a dozen conquests around the Diggers tonight. Jamie *loved* me.

"And that's Lydia," George was saying, "Amy's room-mate, and Lydia's boyfriend, Josh. And these are, uh, some other friends. Clarissa, Greg, Demetria, Ben, Jenny, Harun—"

Devon sat down next to me. "I'm sorry. I'm never going to remember all your names."

"Oh, that's okay," said Jenny. "We'll never see you again anyway."

George's face fell and I glared across the table at Jenny.

"I mean, because we're graduating in a month," Jenny amended.

"Yeah," murmured Demetria. "That's the reason." She smiled at Devon. "Want a drink?"

"Yes, please!" answered Devon, though I was almost positive she was underage. "What's that red stuff in the pitcher?"

———

I very nearly didn't have lunch with Michelle. If she couldn't do me the courtesy of joining my secret society while I was making concessions all over the place so that she could, why should I fight for her barbarian friendship? I had work to do, a thesis to edit, a boyfriend—who *loved* me—I'd probably be leaving along with everything else at Eli at the end of the year, college friends to spend some last bits of time with before graduation, a stalker to thwart, and oh, yeah, a whole class of knights to find and tap—a task she'd just made that much harder.

And yet, I couldn't stanch my morbid curiosity. I needed to find out why she was so paranoid about her

phone number. I wanted to know what had really happened to her last year. And—I couldn't help it—I was dy-
ing to hear more about her and Jamie.

Besides, having lunch with Michelle kept me out of my
suite, which meant that Lydia and Josh would not be bur-
dened with my uncomfortable company and I would not
be tempted to throttle my roommate for her indiscretion.
Everyone wins.

The Geology lecture continued the professor's
Antarctic theme from section the week before, and as soon
as class was over, Michelle beelined in my direction.
"Lunch?"

I flipped my notebook closed. "Indubitably."

Since the Biology Tower lunchroom was closed that
day (due to elevator repairs), we hiked down the hill to Eli
Commons for lunch, talking all about atmospheric chemistry and not at all about the other issues on my mind. Cue
chatter about Antarctica. Cue discussion of ice cores and
living arrangements at McMurdo Station. Cue another
vegetarian meal.*

"So," Michelle said as we settled into a table away from
the Commons lunch crowd. "I hope I didn't cause a fight
with Jamie the other night."

"What?" I lied. At last, a real topic. "No!"

She toyed with her spoon. "Because you two looked a
little stormy when I left."

"It's fine." It was a lot more fine than, say, the fact that
she'd flaked on the society interview. And Jamie and I were
so much more than fine. It had taken all my willpower not
to give in and go to his place, all my strength not to booty
call him once I was alone in my room. He said wait, so I'd

---

*No wonder she and Jamie had gotten along so well. They both had an inordi-
nate fondness for soy products.

wait. For a little while. Long enough, at least, to figure out how to respond the next time he dropped the L-word into conversation.

"He, um, told you, right?"

"Yes." Maybe this was a pudding-first kind of day. I dug in, wondering how to steer the conversation to the secret things I knew about her.

"Oh." Michelle dissected her rice, which was already well under bite-sized. "I hope he didn't tell you I was some kind of bitch."

"Why, because you briefly dated him two years ago and had a perfectly friendly conversation with him at a party? We'll live." She wanted to see tangled, meet George. She wanted to know why I was less than happy with her? Well, that part was more complicated, and involved breaking a couple of oaths.

"No, I mean, because of the way I treated him."

I stopped shoveling pudding down my gullet. "Huh?"

Michelle's mouth snapped shut. "Nothing."

"No, not nothing." I pointed my spoon at her like a gun. "Spill."

"I really don't feel comfortable..."

So help me Persephone, if Jamie lied to me about the two of them I'd string him up by the ties on his society robe. "Look, sister, you're going to tell me what you're talking about or things are going to turn very ugly here with the pudding."

Michelle put down her fork and folded her hands in her lap. Her head fell forward, shielding her face with brown hair. "I, um, was kind of seeing two guys that year. And when Jamie found out—he just stopped speaking to me."

Curious. Had he concocted that story about choosing the society over Michelle so I wouldn't know he'd been rejected for another guy? Had he told it to me because he knew that, last year, I'd chosen the society over Brandon and gotten dumped for it?

How many more mysteries did this chick have to unload?

She took in my confused expression. "I know. I almost would have felt better if he'd gotten mad or something. But he never said a word. I hardly even saw him until the following year, and when I did, he acted like nothing had ever happened between us. I guess I should be grateful that he didn't hold a grudge or anything. He's way too good for that."

No, he wasn't. Had she met this man? Jamie was the High King of Grudges. If someone screwed him over, they were toast. Our campaign against Micah Price last semester (after he'd screwed over the Diggers, generally, and Jenny, specifically), or even Felicity's Dragon's Head wrath, was nothing compared with what Poe would have wrought in Rose & Grave. I exhaled in relief. There was no lie. Jamie's version was what he understood. And there was no reason I should disabuse him of his belief.

Michelle bit her lip. "And I gotta tell you, I chose way wrong on that occasion. Looking back, I can't believe how big of a mistake I made. Jamie's a good guy. You should hold on to him." She sighed. "So, now *you* think I'm a bitch, huh?"

Part of me wanted to. Fooling around on my Jamie. Even if she had shown up to the interview, I think this might have been the final nail in her coffin—or the final nail keeping her *out* of the coffin, in this case. It would be contrary to our oaths to tap a person I knew for a fact had done wrong by one of my brothers. Even my fellow knights would agree; they might not be huge fans of Jamie, but he was a Digger, and we were bound to abide by those rules.

"Amy?" Michelle was waving her hand in front of my face. "You do think I'm a bitch, don't you?"

"I'm just curious how you were seeing two guys at once," I said, which was the truth, if not the whole truth.

"Well, Jamie and me—it didn't really go anywhere. He was always off doing something or other. My roommates all joked that he was actually a spy. And I kind of wanted a commitment. The other guy—that's what he offered. Live and learn, right?"

More than she knew. "I'm, uh, kind of the opposite. I wasn't really looking for a relationship, but Jamie..." I trailed off as I noticed Michelle's eyes twitch a little. Perhaps it wasn't a good idea to point out that Jamie had gone out of his way to commit himself to me while he pulled regular disappearing acts on her. "If it helps, I can tell you that he doesn't know about the other guy. He thinks you both just got busy. So there's no hard feelings there."

Her face softened. "That's good, I guess."

"So." Time to change the subject. "What was going on with your phone yesterday?"

She laughed. "Oh, yeah, sorry to get all paranoid on you. I was getting all these weird prank calls, and I had no idea what to make of them. But it turns out they were nothing."

Nothing? "Did you find out who was calling?"

"That's the best part!" Michelle said, leaning forward. "It was some random secret society. They wanted to interview me for membership. Can you believe it? I thought I was past my prime for that kind of thing."

"Wow." I toyed with my spoon. "How did you figure it out?"

"Well, apparently that's how they do it: call you into some

weird impromptu meeting. That's what a friend explained to me anyway. Talk about spies! And now's the time they start tapping juniors, right? I guess, officially, I'm still a junior. I just didn't think they'd be interested in someone like me."

"Why not?"

Michelle shrugged. "I'm just not really the secret society type, you know?"

Yes, I knew that very well. It was precisely why I wanted her. I weighed my next words. Oh, what the hell. "Do I look like the secret society type?"

She blinked at me. "Oh. *Oh.* Amy, I didn't mean—"

I gave her my best innocent face. "Didn't mean what?"

"If you—"

"If I what?" More with the innocence. At this rate, I could pose as the Virgin Mary.

Michelle looked at me for a moment, lips pursed, then started again. "Are you in a secret society?"

I scooped up a spoonful of pudding. "I can't talk about that."

But Michelle hadn't become a Westinghouse Scholar and gotten into Eli and practically published before she was twenty by being a fool.* "Are you, by any chance, in the secret society that was phoning me yesterday?"

"I can't talk about that, either."

Michelle's mouth was open, her eyes wide. "Is that why you're in my class?" she whispered. "Is that why you never show up? So I'd be forced to track you down?"

I blinked. Wow. That was giving me—all of Rose & Grave, really—a lot of credit. I registered for a class and for her section with the express purpose of acting irresponsible

---

*For which the confessor is profoundly relieved, because, seriously? This secrecy thing? Profoundly tiring.

enough to test her scholarly commitment and leadership? "Um…"

"Is that—oh my God—" she clapped a hand over her mouth "—is that what that party was last weekend? Is Jamie in it, too? Are you really—" Her voice dropped again. "Are you really dating him?"

"Yes, I'm dating him," I said, relieved that she'd finally asked a question I could answer. "We're intensely and eagerly dating."

"Okay, TMI." Michelle held up her hand. "But—that other stuff—is it true?"

"I told you, I can neither confirm nor deny—"

"Which one is it?" Michelle asked.

"Are you even listening to me?"

"How can I, when you won't tell me anything?" She bounced a bit in her seat. "Okay, you're not a science major, so it can't be the Prometheus Society."

"Let's not play this game." I tugged on the hem of my shirt, making sure the Rose & Grave pin pushed through my belt loop was sufficiently covered.

"And my grades sure aren't good enough for Book & Key."

"Michelle!" I snapped at her. "Focus." She looked at me. "What you may not realize is that even if there was a society courting you, it's over. You didn't go to the interview. You blew them off."

"Oh." Michelle frowned. "So they don't tell you who they are, then they punish you for not jumping at their command? That's a really stupid system, don't you think?"

Yes. But what I said, like a good little Digger, was: "It's tradition—"

"It's dumb. No offense." She shrugged. "Whatever. I don't like that whole society scene. Keeping secrets, pulling strings? No thank you."

"I imagine it's easier to like when they are pulling strings on your behalf," I said.

"You *imagine*?"

I kept my chin up, though really, what was the point? "Yes."

"Huh." She cocked her head and examined me. "Have you pulled strings on anyone's behalf?"

Aside from Michelle's herself? Yes. Once, with Darren. And it was still sticking in my craw.

"I—need to get more pudding."

As I scurried away, my mind raced. What did that say about Rose & Grave that my only potential tap who actually wanted to join was Topher Cox? Were we really the crack team of future power players we believed ourselves to be? Or were we just the Eli students who weren't offended by centuries-old elitism?

Was a better outfit for us than black robes and hoods beaver coats and straw hats? Were we a relic, no more relevant to current campus life than the clay pipes they traditionally handed out at graduation to a class of ninety percent non-smokers?

"Dammit!" I slammed my hand against the soda machine.

"Now, now, Amy," said a voice at my back. "What did the Sprite ever do to you?"

I turned around. Brandon Weare stood before me, holding his lunch tray and making a "tsking" noise at my outburst.

"Everything okay?" he asked.

"Fine." Last time I'd spoken to Brandon face-to-face, he'd told me he'd dump Felicity and be my boyfriend. Then Felicity had informed me that she and her secret society had been doing everything in their power to mess me up, and that her final achievement was to convince

Brandon that she would pick him over her society (which I had not when I'd been given a similar chance) and that she would leave me alone if he stopped seeing me.

After that, I'd gotten a Dear Jane letter. He didn't even have the balls to tell me in person.

"And you?" I added shortly.

"Trying to figure out what's got you so riled up."

"Well, that's none of your business anymore, now, is it?" I turned on my heel to go.

"Amy," he called to my back. "Felicity and I broke up."

My steps faltered for a split second.

TEMPTING RESPONSES

1) A frosty "How nice for you."
2) Same, but can the frosty.
3) "How ironic. I myself have a boyfriend now."

But I kept walking, perhaps a shade more quickly, until I rejoined Michelle at the table. She looked up, startled, as I sat down.

"Hey."

"Hey," she said. "So, we still friends?"

Friends? Yes. Potential society brothers? Not so much. "Sure."

She looked relieved. "Good, because I have a huge favor to ask you." She leaned over the table and lowered her voice. "See that guy at three o'clock? The one in the blue shirt?"

Though blue shirts were as common at Eli as diamond solitaires in the Junior League, I nodded. The man she meant was impossible to miss. To start with, he was at least 6'5". And then there was the fact that the particular shade of blue in his polo shirt precisely matched the icy hue of his eyes. They stood out like laser beams in his deeply tanned, attractive face.

Also, he was staring at us.

"Mmm." I ate a bite of Spanish rice.

"He's my ex-boyfriend."

"Sheesh, you, too?" I murmured. "I just ran into mine."

"Yeah, well, if I run into mine, we're in big trouble. So will you walk out with me?"

I looked down at my uneaten lunch. "Now?"

"Right now." She suddenly hunched down in her seat. "Too late."

"Shelly." The voice boomed above our heads. I looked up to see Michelle's mountain of an ex standing over the table. Michelle stared down at her plate. "What are you doing in Commons, honey?"

Michelle was silent.

"It's strange to see you down at this end of campus." His voice was perfectly friendly, but if Michelle could have slid under the table, she would have. "Especially on days that you don't have your Art History class." He looked at me. "Who is your friend?" He stuck out his hand. "I don't think I've had the pleasure of meeting you yet."

"I'm Amy Haskel," I said, looking from Michelle and back to him. Something was wrong with this guy's eyes. A shiver passed through me. I did not want to take his hand.

"Amy." He smiled down at Michelle. "Nice to make new friends, isn't it, Shelly?"

He'd positioned himself directly behind her. She couldn't push her chair out with him standing there. Her hands pressed against the edge of the table like she was ready to bolt.

"Please go away, Blake," Michelle said in a small but firm voice.

"Yeah, I bet you have to be getting back to your apartment anyway. It's such a far walk from everything. Sure you don't need me to give you a ride out there? I'd be happy to."

"Please go away, Blake," Michelle repeated.

"Come on, Shelly, I'm just trying to help. Why do you always have to be so difficult—"

"I think she told you to go away," I said.

His eyes shot to me and I froze like a squirrel in the path of a runaway bike. "I don't care what you think," he said, tone calm as ever. "Jesus, Michelle, looks like your taste in friends hasn't improved at all. You still like hanging out with people who think they know what's best for you."

"Can you back away, please?" I asked. "Michelle's trying to push her chair out."

Blake didn't move.

"I think the lady asked you to back up," Brandon said. He was standing in the space between the table rows, tray gripped in both hands, smiling serenely up at the behemoth in our way. "And since you're blocking the aisle, I'd say it was time to move along."

Blake stared daggers at Brandon, whose expression didn't change a bit. Blake had two choices here: cause a scene or back down.

He chose the latter. Michelle shot out of her chair and headed for the doors at the end of the cavernous Commons. I cast a guilty look at our unbussed trays and started to follow.

"Amy," Brandon said. I turned around and he opened his mouth to speak, then waved me off. "Later."

"Agreed." That was the new trend with me and guys: file under "later."

I went after Michelle as she burst into the marble-and-granite memorial hall outside Commons and booked it toward the exit. As always, the sculpted dome and the hundreds of carved-in-all-caps names lining the walls resounded with the thunderous echoes of the students who passed through on their way to and from the science side of campus. Legend had it that the names of Rose & Grave members featured special carvings to tip off their Digger status, but I'd never bothered to confirm it.

"Wait!" I increased my pace to just below a sprint and as my cry bounced around the dome, several students looked up and Michelle slowed to a stop by a column and a metal stand filled with yesterday's copies of the *Eli Daily News*.

"So," she said, folding herself into the space behind the column, "I guess you know now why I should have picked Jamie."

I hereby confess:
the truth, the whole truth,
and nothing but the truth.

10.

Bride of Tap Night

"Thanks for letting me come here," Michelle said as Clarissa handed her a mug of tea.

"Don't even think about it," said my fellow knight, patting Michelle on the shoulder and returning to her seat across the room. She curled her feet up underneath her on the buttery, cream-colored leather love seat, and picked an invisible bit of fluff off her white silk slacks. "As I said last time: Any friend of Amy's is a friend of mine."

Michelle nodded in understanding. "That's how it works, right?"

Clarissa smiled in a much better imitation of the Madonna than I'd ever been able to pull off. "If you like."

"I was just worried that if I went straight home..." Michelle shuddered. "He'd follow me."

"Has he done that before?" I asked.

She nodded. "I had to change apartments once this semester already. This one's got a doorman, but..." She shrugged. "People aren't always militant about making guests sign in, you know?"

"True," Clarissa said, and I imagined the kind of riffraff she had experience keeping out of her Park Avenue place.

"The last time..." Michelle began, then hesitated. "I sound like an idiot whenever I try to explain this. It seems so reasonable at the time, and then afterward, I think I must have brain damage or something." She stood up and crossed to the window.

"What do you mean?" I scooted over and Clarissa started straightening up the bookshelves, as if pretending not to pay attention would help the poor girl relax any more. It was clear she didn't trust either of us enough to tell this story. If she would only sit still. Not even the tea seemed to help. Was she even in the frame anymore?

Michelle played with the tassel on the edge of the cream brocaded curtain. "He's not like that always, you know. Sometimes he cries, and says really sweet, sweet things, and tells me that it's just the way I disappeared, it was so unfair to him, he needs closure, if he just had closure... he'd leave if he just got closure."

Clarissa's hands stilled on a digital picture frame showcasing shots of our Spring Break Habitat for Humanity team. In the current photo, George was grinning as he and Harun wielded their paintbrushes like light sabers.

Michelle laughed mirthlessly. "Do you know how many times he's gotten *closure*?"

I held on to my own mug of tea as if for balance. It's a very, very good thing that Jamie wasn't here. I couldn't imagine him listening to this with anything approaching composure.

"I don't understand," said Clarissa, though we both understood far more than Michelle knew. "Why don't you go to the Strathmore dean? The college deans are supposed to be our advocates."

"The dean was the one who got me into this mess,"

Michelle said, and returned to her seat. Luckily, Clarissa was still by the bookshelves. "I went to her last year. Told her everything that was going on. I told her about the time he wouldn't let me leave my room for a day and a half. I told her about why I'd really failed that Organic Chem lab—how he'd taken my notebook as punishment because I wouldn't drop the class. He was convinced I was having an affair with the professor. I even told her about how my PhysChem T.A. had found his car smashed in the parking lot. And that was *after* I'd switched out of his section and into a female T.A.'s."

"Not that I'm countenancing his behavior in the slightest," Clarissa said, "but why did he always suspect you of cheating on him?"

Michelle and I exchanged glances.

"Because she was," I said, staring resolutely into my tea. "With Jamie."

"Oh." Clarissa's tone was even more clipped and proper than usual. Her pink phone began to buzz on the table. "Excuse me," she said. "That would be my friend Demetria."

I rolled my eyes. Forget Jamie. It was Demetria who wasn't capable of listening to this without going ballistic.

Clarissa read the text message and pursed her lips. "She'd like to, uh, come over. Do you mind, Michelle? It might be good. Demetria's got a lot of experience at the Eli Women's Center and—"

"I'd prefer not to have to talk in front of an audience, if you don't mind," said Michelle, in what had to be the greatest irony since I'd first brought her to the party. "This is hard enough in front of you two. I know I can trust you, Clarissa, because you're Amy's *special friend*, but..." She trailed off, no doubt remembering that Demetria had also been at the party and was therefore also likely a *special friend*. "I just... can we keep this between us?"

"Sure," I said, and raised my eyebrows at Clarissa. *Oh, well. Too late for that.* She shrugged and shut down her phone. "We're great at secrets." *As long as we could share them with the whole club.*

"And it wasn't really cheating," Michelle said. "I want to be clear about that. The end of—whatever I had going on with Jamie sort of overlapped with my relationship with Blake. A little. Not that Blake ever knew. Jamie was a junior who pretty much kept to himself; Blake was a freshman already in charge of half the college activities...I don't think they even knew each other."

Good thing. Otherwise, he'd probably have gone after Jamie as well. "In other words, he was just naturally a jealous lunatic psycho bastard?"

Michelle smiled a bit. "Yeah. He suspected every guy in the Chemistry department of wanting to be with me. I know I sound like a moron for dating someone like that for a year. I mean, I'm smart and modern and independent and all those things. I'm not supposed to be with a guy who tries to control me. I'm supposed to recognize all those warning signs and avoid men like that."

Now my phone went off. Text message from Jenny. Of course.

ITS A LOT HARDER WHEN THEY DONT HIT U.

"So what happened with the dean?" I asked, trying to get back on course before the rest of the Diggers blew this whole thing with their stupid text messages.

"She said she'd help. Planned a disciplinary hearing. Said all this stuff about how Blake was going to have to stop living in Strathmore College, maybe even be rusticated, how he'd have to stay a certain number of feet away from me, how he couldn't take any of the classes I was in . . .

I felt kind of guilty." She picked up her mug again, though the tea was likely cold by now. "I mean, it was his college, too."

I thought of my mother's friends who lost their social circles in their divorces, of my high school buddies whose popularity and lunch table placement were determined entirely on the basis of their boyfriends' status. Why did women let themselves do things like that? Give and give and give. We were withholding our love, at least let them have their turf? Was that a reasonable strategy?

"But at the same time I was relieved. I hadn't come to Eli to be tormented. To be told what classes I was allowed to take, what professors I was allowed to have. Who I was allowed to be friends with..." She took a sip of tea and made a face. Yep, cold. "Every time I think of it, I can't believe I let myself get in that position. Like, I must have been some other person. It couldn't have been me organizing class schedules around the ugliest professors I could get. Me not joining a study group because there was a boy in it."

"Or dropping out of a research project?" Clarissa slipped. I shot her a look.

But Michelle seemed lost in thought. "It couldn't have been me letting some guy trap me in my room. He..." She paused, squeezed her eyes shut for a moment, then went on. "He promised to kill himself if I left. What could I do? I never even had Psych 110. I skipped all those lectures they made us take freshmen year about safe sex and alcoholism and depression and unstable roommates and boyfriends and went with my suite to get fake IDs instead. It seems so crazy, but when I was there, it made perfect sense to listen to him, to do whatever he wanted in order to keep us both safe. Just like it makes perfect sense when he tells me that if I would only have sex with him one more time..."

She took a deep breath and shook herself free. "There was a phone, a window—I could have called for help. I *should* have gone for help as soon as I did get out. But I was so exhausted by that point. I'd missed a mid-term, spent hours crying on the floor with him—I wasn't thinking straight. It *wasn't* me. I was a different person. He made me into a different person. Slowly, but inexorably. By such tiny increments that I hardly even noticed what I was giving up."

The words fell into the lush carpet and rich furnishings, and I absorbed their meaning in silence. I imagined Jenny, who despite her brilliant, logical mind, had let the boy she thought she'd loved talk her into betraying folks she'd known had done no wrong. I imagined Demetria, who couldn't stop expressing her disappointment about her inability to change the fabric of Rose & Grave, and who was more than a little worried that it had changed us instead. She was proof that it wasn't only boys that could seduce you like that. Little by little we'd sold out to the society's archaic value system, placed its need for secrecy, pedigree, and blind loyalty above the things we knew to be right.

Like reporting Darren to the police. Maybe we as a society had screwed up, but did that honestly account for his actions?

Why was I even giving in to the concession of Topher Cox? To keep one patriarch happy out of the hundreds who thought we were the ruination of everything they held dear? Would Topher be enough consolation for them, or would they keep complaining and being disappointed until we were exactly what they wanted us to be? And would we and the clubs that came after us give in, little by little, bit by bit, until the world changed around Rose & Grave so much that the society no longer held any relevance at all?

Had it already happened while we played dress-up with our robes and pins and secret songs?

"I don't understand," Clarissa was prompting Michelle. "*You're* the one who is living off campus now."

"Yeah," Michelle said. "Funny thing. The dean got the *time* of the discipline hearing wrong. Can you believe it? How *silly* of her! We *missed* it. So of course the charges were dropped. And when I went to her to reschedule, it was a whole different tune." Michelle's expression turned sour, as if she was holding back tears. " 'Really, don't you think you're being a bit too dramatic?' 'Sometimes relationships just go wrong, and no one is to blame.' 'Well, I understand if you don't want to live in our college anymore. It's too late to transfer, though. You should consider moving off campus.' " She looked away. "I don't know if there was ever any disciplinary hearing planned. It was... humiliating. I trusted her and it was like all of a sudden I was the one to blame for all of this. She was so closed off. Like someone had gotten to her."

Maybe someone had. We should do more research into Blake... and his family. He'd slipped away from due punishment despite Michelle's attempts to prosecute. It made me wonder: If I did press charges against Darren, would anything really happen to him?

"The college deans are supposed to be our advocates, all right. But the thing is, we're both in Strathmore College. She was obligated to advocate on both our behalfs, and I guess she didn't want the scandal." Michelle bit her lip.

"I was so defeated. I canceled my classes that semester and went home. Personal break, all that. Went stir-crazy after a month and found a job interning at a research lab near my parents'. Once I got my act together, I contacted this professor I'd worked for freshman year. He helped me get a gig assisting a Geochemistry team in the Ring of Fire. I loved it."

"So you switched to the Geology department?" I asked.

"Not right away. I sneaked back to campus last semester and did some more independent research. Just wanted to see if I could be here on the DL before enrolling again. It wasn't perfect, but I really, really wanted to put all that stuff behind me. So I decided to come back to school. I gave it one more shot with Strathmore, but my old dean had left, and it turns out, she'd left no records of our chats at all. Go figure, right? The new dean had nothing to pin on Blake; he was pretty much a model student. Even my old friends in Strathmore were on his side. I had bad grades and left, he stayed and was on the dean's list. Who was the unbalanced one when you looked at it like that? It was the previous year's humiliation all over again."

On paper, Blake would be a more likely candidate for a Rose & Grave tap than Michelle. I wondered if there was another society on campus looking at him.

Michelle went on. "So I did what they said. I moved off campus. I avoided him. Or tried to. I even transferred into the Geology department so I wouldn't have to see him in the Chemistry labs. He's pre-med, you know." She sighed. "But still...I like Geology. And the guy I studied under last fall was really helpful, hooking me up with a professor who needed a new teaching assistant, stuff like that. So it worked out."

"Worked out?" I blurted. "A pariah in your own college? Sneaking around Science Hill because you're worried about running into him? That scene in Commons—"

"How about sleeping with him to get him out of your apartment?" Clarissa added. "I'm pretty sure that's coercion, which means it's rape."

I was pretty sure Demetria was frothing at the mouth

by this point. Clarissa clearly hadn't skipped her freshman orientation sessions. I can't believe the dean of a college at Eli would put reputation above a student's safety. How often did something like that happen on this campus, and no one ever knew?

"What can I do?" Michelle said. "It's his word against mine, and because the old dean screwed me over, it'll just sound like I'm making up stuff that happened over a year ago to excuse my own bad academic record. Who would believe me?"

"We believe you," said Clarissa.

"You can't keep Blake away from me," Michelle said.

"Don't be so sure about that," I said, standing. "There's all kinds of things we've been able to pull off." Of course, they usually leaned in the direction of folks not getting in trouble, but still ...

"No." Michelle shook her head. "I don't want to get into this again. He almost succeeded in ruining my life last time. My grades, my ability to stay with my graduating class, all of it. I can't risk that again. I just want to keep my head down and finish school and get out of here. Get far away, where he won't bother me anymore."

"Antarctica?" I asked.

"If that's what it takes." Michelle hugged her arms around herself and looked out the window again. "I'll take semesters off until he's graduated himself if I need to. He didn't bother me when I went away. Out of sight, out of mind. It's only when he sees me that he gets all ... riled up. Like he can't stand being reminded that I escaped. That I'm not under his control. He keeps showing up, calling, getting in my face. Doing whatever it takes to remind me what he got away with. What he can always get away with if he wants to."

My blood went cold and I couldn't think of a response.

Could barely move, just sat on the couch, dumb as a rock. Like Darren, rubbing Disney World in my face. This is what came of ignoring guys like Darren and hoping they went away. They grew up into Blakes.

It didn't escape Clarissa's notice, either. "I think that he needs to be brought to justice." She didn't specify which *he*. "And I want to help."

But Diggers weren't good with that. No, we specialized in obfuscating justice. We were experts in doing exactly what Blake had managed to do. Cover-ups. Getting our crimes swept under the rug, for the good of the society. *Just forget about it. Youthful indiscretion. He'll grow out of his sociopathic tendencies. You'll see.* Michelle was right in not wanting any part of Rose & Grave.

"I'm fine," Michelle said. "Really. I'm just going to go...catch the bus back to my apartment and do my homework."

"Are you sure?" I asked. "You could always stay with me if you want. I don't like the idea of you being alone." Guys like Blake, they picked on you when you were alone. That's how Darren had gotten to me.

"No," she said. "It's fine."

"Or I could call Jamie, have him meet you at your apartment, make sure everything's cool."

"No," Michelle said, more firmly this time. "I think Blake would throw a fit if he saw me with Jamie. He'd remember him from Strathmore and maybe he'd even put two and two together and then Jamie...I couldn't have that. I'm not even sure what would happen if he saw *you* with Jamie after this. Remember, this was the guy who didn't like me having male T.A.s." She stood up. "Um, can I use your bathroom?"

"Sure," Clarissa said, and pointed the way. As soon as

Michelle had closed the door, we glanced at each other and bolted toward the master bedroom.

Inside, the other twelve members of the Rose & Grave club of D177 sat on the bed and floor, huddled around a TV screen displaying Clarissa's living room through the hidden camera mounted on the bookshelf digital picture frame. It may not be the usual format for an interview, but it worked.

"Well?" I asked them. Everyone nodded.

Josh stood. "Okay. She's in."

The day of Tap Night dawned with a rather disappointing drizzle wholly inappropriate for such a momentous occasion. Good weather would have made it easy for us to run around and deliver our black-lined letters; a thunderstorm would have added an air of Gothic mystery to the event. But there was nothing romantic or convenient about a drizzle. It was an entirely anti-climactic climate in which to choose new knights.

Not that any of us had much time to ruminate on the weather or the metaphorical significance of same. Every knight in the tomb had a task to perform to make sure that Tap Night ran as smoothly as possible, from preparing the letters to cleaning the ceremonial robes to coordinating with the other societies on campus to make sure that no one on our lists overlapped, or, if they did, that we could all come to a mutually satisfactory compromise.* Fortunately, I was spared that detail, and only had to listen throughout the day as my fellow knights reported back to headquarters (the tomb's Grand Library) on their findings.

---

*Historically, this meant Rose & Grave telling the other society to back the hell off. Given the perceived weakness of the Diggers this year, the knights feared it might get more complicated than that.

"There's no one on the Book & Key list," Juno announced to us around noon. "Does that mean we're tapping a class of dummies?" It was rumored that Book & Key had more simultaneous Phi Beta Kappa members than any secret society on campus.

"It means we're tapping people who have more going for them than book smarts," said Lil' Demon, dripping hot wax onto yet another finished Tap Letter.

"No one on our list at Serpent, either," said Bond a little later. "But you'll never guess who they do have on their list!"

"Who?"

"That fellow Big Demon had on his short list—Andrew Cortland."

"Good for them," said Big Demon. "I knew someone would snatch him up. He's a great guy."

"He's an asshole, if you listen to Meredith," Angel said, naming her tap. "She told us he cheated on her with her best friend."

"If cheating on a college girlfriend or boyfriend were an offense for which we did not tap, half our club would be out on their ears," Lucky said. She was highlighting maps with our route around campus. "I listened to the C.B.s."

"And that had nothing to do with it. We couldn't have them both, so I compromised," Big Demon said.

"For which I still owe you one," said Angel.

"And for which I still plan to collect." Big Demon stood, stretched, and walked over to her table. "You can start by folding these stupid envelopes. I was never any good at origami."

Angel frowned at the stack of paper he'd dumped on her. "Is it too late to get that Andrew guy back from Serpent?"

"No one else we know?" I asked Bond.

"Not Blake Varnham, if that's what you're asking," Bond said. Good. The last thing I wanted was for the villainy of Michelle's ex to earn him a spot in any society.

The morning passed with few surprises. There was a small snafu when Jenny's chosen tap turned out to be on the list for the Prometheus Society, but apparently the negotiations with the Prometheans were relatively swift and easy.

"They know about my company," was all Lucky would explain. "The tech world's not that big."

At noon, Soze stomped in, his expression far stormier than the indifferent weather outside. "You would not believe the stunt Dragon's Head just pulled!"

"I thought you weren't able to get in touch with their secretary," Angel said.

"What?" I asked him, though my mind was already running through the possibilities. "Did they steal our list? I knew they'd pull something like this. The Inner Temple was bugged all along, wasn't it?"

"*They already tapped their class!*" Soze paced around the room, fists and jaws clenched. "Neatly avoiding any negotiations at all! And they won't release a list. Every society on campus is livid."

"You're kidding." Juno put down her book. "That's—"

"Unheard of?" Soze said. "Unfair? Intolerable?"

"All of the above," I said. "Can they do that?"

"There are no guidelines for our behavior here," Soze said. "This isn't the Hellenic society that can mete out punishment and make everyone adhere to a standard. All we have is a gentlemen's agreement. We agree when to have Tap Night. We agree to compete for our taps on equal footing."

"And *we're* the society class that's breaking all the rules?" Big Demon scoffed. "The patriarchs are lucky they don't have to deal with Dragon's Head."

"But they aren't pissing off *their* patriarchs if they sneak in and steal all the good taps," argued Angel. "Their alums are probably happy about this."

"If they score points on us once again—" Juno said.

"How can we get their list?" Frodo asked. "We have to be able to get it somehow!"

Everyone looked at Lucky, who shrugged. "Do I look like a miracle worker to you people?"

"If we attempt to tap members who have already accepted at Dragon's Head, what happens?" asked Tristram. "On a practical level, I mean. We're tapping people tonight, they accept or reject, and then we leave them be until initiation. What's to stop another society from coming in after us and trying to tap the same person all the time? All it means is they reject."

"We're not supposed to be coming *after* anyone," Soze said, still pacing. "That's why we arrange to coordinate our taps with the other groups on campus. Potential taps aren't supposed to be *choosing* between us and some other, lesser society. It's bad PR. If we come on Tap Night, we're supposed to be the only ones who come. We're the secret society equivalent of Early Decision."

"Not this year." I laughed. "Dragon's Head is. They got us. There's no denying that." And what was the big deal anyway? This wasn't the unprecedented event Josh was making it out to be. After all, the Kalanis of the world had picked another society a year and a half before we'd even considered tapping them. Arielle had chosen Quill & Ink. Even Michelle had to be convinced.

"And if we go out there tonight, and it turns out they did steal our list?" Soze whirled on me. "What happens then? How do we survive that humiliation? How do we get a new class, knowing that half of our leftovers are about to join other societies tonight, and that we have negotiated with our other rivals to allow it? What if this was Dragon's Head's plan all along?"

He collapsed into the nearest chair and buried his face in his hands. "We'll be ruined. We won't be able to concoct a decent tap class out of thin air. Not one the patriarchs will be proud of. Not one that will keep our tradition. And one bad club—that's all it takes. It would take years to build ourselves out of that slump. They've been arguing all year long that *we* are that bad club. Tapping a great club to replace us was our only means of proving them wrong."

The room was silent and sober as everyone contemplated his words. But they still made no sense to me.

"When I joined Rose & Grave," I said, "I had no idea who was in the club that tapped me. I didn't meet Lancelot until after I accepted the tap, didn't meet the others until Tap Night. So that part is false. Most people don't join a society because of the people in the year immediately above them. They join because of the people ten or twenty years before them. Because of what they accomplished, what they created. That's not going to go away because of one bad club."

"But what if we can't get anyone at all?" Angel asked. "You said it yourself. What if Dragon's Head stole our taps?"

I considered this. "Honestly? I don't think it happened. They really would have had to hustle to not only find out who on our short list were the ones we eventually decided upon, but also interview them, tap them, and have them accept."

"Call the presses," Thorndike said, her tone incredulous. "Bugaboo doesn't buy into the conspiracy theory."

"But you're the one who saw that Dragon's Head knight going after Kalani," Lucky said.

"That was personal. Felicity hates me and would relish the thought of screwing with my tap plans. Besides, she didn't know Kalani was in St. Linus Hall either—she ran off as soon as she found out—which means she hadn't done her own research. I don't think it was a well-formed strategy on her part. She didn't want to steal a Digger tap. She just wanted to screw with me. And think about it. Think about our taps. Thorndike's tap, Tamar, already knows exactly who is coming for her tonight. Has known for some time. With this new openness, don't you think she'd give Thorndike a heads-up if she was suddenly planning to pick a different society?"

"True," said Thorndike.

"And then, think about my tap. Topher has been very clear about his family connection and his eagerness to accept. I know he wants to be a Digger."

"But they didn't all know," argued Soze. "What if they thought this whole time that they were being courted by Dragon's Head?"

I rubbed my eyes, momentarily weary with the whole endeavor. "Then we get two taps: Topher and Tamar."

"Three," said Kismet. "My guy knows we're coming, too." He hunched his shoulders. "I slipped."

"Four," said Lucky. "I wanted to make sure there were no . . . misconceptions." Misconceptions like she herself had had, thinking we were a bunch of Satan-worshipping loons.

Juno snorted. "Do *none* of you know the concept of discretion?"

"Would it have helped us in this situation?" I asked her. "Secrecy may be all well and good when everyone plays by the rules, but here, telling the truth may be the thing that saves us."

"Bugaboo's right," Puck said. "And what's more, sitting around and waiting won't help us. We need to figure out where our taps stand without the help of Dragon's Head. We can visit them, maybe—"

"But they'll have been instructed to keep their tap a secret," Angel said.

"Yes," said Puck, "but we've been courting them all month. They've gone to our party. If they think we're the ones who tapped them last night, why would they be keeping a secret from *us*?"

Yet another good point. Puck winked at me and I couldn't help but smile. Yeah, boy, we all know there are some brains behind that gorgeous face.

"Okay," said Soze. "Let's mobilize. Call your taps for coffee, relationship advice, your horoscope. Whatever works. Those of you who are reasonably sure you've got yours locked in can handle the preparations. We've got three hours, guys."

Topher was a lock. Michelle wasn't being courted by anyone else, of that I could be sure. I looked at the stacks of invite envelopes. "Should I make more of these, just in case we need extra alternates?"

Josh scowled. "If we need extra alternates, we're in real trouble."

———

In the end, only two of our taps were affected by Dragon's Head's pre-emptive strike: Samantha March, the chosen tap of Greg Dorian (luckily, his alternate did not appear on Quill & Ink's tap list—though I was happy to see that Arielle did), and Brianna Patterson, who was Mara

Taserati's choice. But Mara got lucky—when she met Brianna at the coffee shop, the conversation went something like this:

Brianna: (looking guilty) I was kind of surprised you wanted to meet today.
Mara: Really? But I adore spending time with you. (She's such a pro.)
Brianna: Well, after last night, I mean.
Mara: Last night? Whatever do you mean?
Brianna: Oh, I see. Fine, we'll keep playing the game. I just hope there are no hard feelings.
Mara: My dear girl, I haven't the foggiest clue of what you speak.
Brianna: I mean, you've been great. And your... friends. They're very nice, too. It's just... I really wanted to join Rose & Grave, now that they let in girls.
Mara: (chokes on her coffee) Huh?
Brianna: I know it's a long shot, but... well, that's why I rejected.
Mara: Brianna, my darling, I must be off. Toodle-loo!*

As the drizzly dusk settled over campus, we reconvened at the tomb to dress and dole out supplies. With the addition of Poe, we'd split into three teams of five so as to tap as efficiently as possible, and as we gathered matches, black candles, and robes, anticipation hung more heavily than the warm spring fog outside. This was it. Our Tap Night. The culmination of D177's year as the Knights of Rose & Grave.

We mingled about the Grand Library, checking maps and routes and making last minute adjustments to procedures and costumes. Lucky's robe needed the hem repaired.

---

*It's entirely possible that Mara's speech was less Mary Poppins than related here.

Thorndike's magenta dreadlocks kept slipping out from under her hood, so we needed to procure a black bandanna to tie them back. Lil' Demon needed to be informed that spike-heeled patent leather boots were not appropriate footwear for racing about slippery New Haven streets.

Poe came over and tugged my cape. "You look cute in a hood."

"That's not a line that works with many women, is it?"

"I don't try to use it on many women." His own hood was already in place, shadowing his eyes and leaving little more than his checkbones and jawline exposed.

I raised myself on my tiptoes and kissed said jaw. "It's not like you haven't seen me like this dozens of times."

"And you look cute every time." Ah, now, up close, I could see his eyes, gray and filled with the same excitement as all the other knights. Or was it the same? His gaze sent tingles all the way down my thighs. He was thinking of what he'd said outside the bar the other night. And so was I.

I dropped back on my heels and played it light. "Great. A cute Grim Reaper."

"The better to lure you toward death," Poe replied in his best Vincent Price. Yes, this is what passed for flirtation in his world. It's what happens when your boyfriend is born on Halloween and given free rein to live out his fantasy life in a crumbling, tomb-like mansion filled with human skeletons and spooky costumes. Maybe Lil' Demon had a point about the kink.

I swatted him and went back to packing extra matches. My anticipation had taken on an entirely new object. Kink or no, I was going to find out what was going on underneath that man's robe.

The grandfather clock in the Grand Library struck eight o'clock while we knights stood in a circle, reciting

our oaths. Each clang of the bell buzzed through my body
like an engine being revved. I could feel it all around, every
knight tugging tightly against an invisible tether, ready to
bolt the second we were able. By the time the echo of the
final chime had reverberated through the room and its oc-
cupants, we were all holding our breath.

"Okay, knights," said Soze, the evening's Uncle Tony.
"Go get 'em."

And off we ran.

Our first target to tap was Omar's choice: the Israeli engineer Tal Yitzchach. To own the truth, I was mildly nervous about how this would go down. Society tradition
dictated that we were to burst into his room, fully robed,
carry him bodily to an undisclosed, pitch-black location (in
this case, the broom closet down the hall from his apartment), and ask him if he wanted in. All well and good, until you considered that Tal was ex-military and an expert at
the art of krav maga. If we caught him by surprise, he
might break all our necks.

Perhaps it was a good thing Omar had slipped up on
the secrecy thing.

Still, I wanted to grab the most non-lethal body part
when it came time to carry Tal out of his studio.

We slipped into his apartment building and up to Tal's
floor. Jenny, the smallest knight in our group and therefore
relegated to candle patrol, shoved brooms and mops out of
the way in the closet, and set up the altar while the rest of
us gathered outside his apartment door.

Omar knocked and we all forced our bodies into stillness. We heard the sound of a chain being released, and all
I could picture was what a funny sight it must be to see
through one's peephole four black-robed, hooded figures
gathered in a narrow hallway under a fluorescent light.
And then the door opened.

We grabbed him, and he lay passive in our arms as we shuffled him into the closet and gathered in a circle. By the light of the candle, I could see a big grin on his face. Omar bent over the altar, the candle flickering strangely on the planes of his hooded face.

"Rose & Grave," he intoned in a rumbling voice. "Accept or Reject?"

Tal grinned even wider. "Accept."

Omar blew out the candle and we were off.

"Hey!" I heard Tal call as we sprinted away. I cast a quick look over my shoulder. He had started after us, then stopped when he saw the black-lined envelope we'd left behind. It contained instructions for his initiation and told him, quite firmly, that he was to stay put for now.*

One down, four to go.

Then we tapped Jenny's Cognitive Science major, Paul Raymond, who, like Tal, lived off campus. Easy peasy. Even easier was Kevin's tenor tap, who had some experience with the process after going through it with his singing group three years earlier.

Topher Cox was next on our hit list. I felt my heart pounding as we approached his entryway. Our robes had grown damp by this point and stuck to our ankles as we walked, rendering our steps graceless rather than menacingly swirly. Students braving the crummy weather in the courtyard stared at us as we swept by, black-robed and silent. Some even followed us. We entered, and Omar blocked the door, keeping prying eyes out. Jamie took a similar stance on the stair landing and Jenny made sure the bathroom was clear and the light was out as I swiftly lit my candle.

*The confessor had insisted upon this addition after her own confusion last spring.

"Who you tapping?" called one of the sophomores on the stoop.

"Yeah, who is it?" asked another. Omar looked resolutely ahead.

"Hey, Topher!" shouted a third, and banged on the window next to the entryway door. "They're here for you!"

"He's been holed up in his room all night," I heard a girl say. "Waiting. Isn't it weird?"

"I don't know," said another girl. "I want to be in one senior year. They're weird, but fun, you know?"

Topher opened the door and peeked out.

"Go!" Jamie cried, leaping down from the stairs, his cape flapping like a comic book superhero. He pinned Topher's arms and lifted him off the ground as Omar slammed the entryway door shut and hurried over to help. Kevin made a grab for Topher's other leg and they shoved him, humble-jumble, into the bathroom. I swiped the candle out of the way, and Jenny tripped over her mended hem.

"Sloppy," Topher said. Jenny was holding her wet cape together with one hand, struggling with the other to conceal her face beneath the hood. The candle, miraculously, stayed lit.

"Shut up, barbarian," Jamie growled, and I felt it in my toes. He whipped his head toward me. "Go."

Go? He'd just insulted us! I stood poised over the black candle and stared at Topher Cox, who stared back, unfazed and entitled, surrounded by a semi-circle of knights I knew and loved.

Just tap him. Just say the words. This was the deal you made. This was what you agreed to. So do it.

Do it.

My teeth seemed to swallow my lips, and I couldn't speak.

"Go." I felt Jamie's hand on mine, his gray eyes like ice beneath the hood of his robe. Even in the stillness of the bathroom, his whisper barely reached me. "It'll be okay, I promise."

I looked across the candle. Topher's smug expression had waned, replaced by a flash of—what? Doubt?

"Rose & Grave," I blurted. "Accept or Reject?"

"Accept!" he rushed to say, as if afraid I'd take it back.

I almost laughed. But instead, I followed the script: Blow out the candle, throw an envelope at his feet, and run.

In the courtyard, Jamie caught up to me. "You all right?"

"Yeah," I puffed, and kept up the pace. Michelle's apartment was across town, so we were running to Jenny's parking garage to pick up her car.

"I was afraid you'd bugged out back there."

"I'm fine." Into the parking garage we ran, black and hooded beneath the sodium lights like a band of Dementors out of a Harry Potter movie. The student garage employee inside the glass box at the entrance was paying attention to her linear algebra homework, as usual. Omar jumped into the passenger seat and Kevin scrambled into the back, leaving the door open for us.

"Amy." Jamie stopped me before I climbed inside. "You didn't sell out."

Was I so easy to read, even hooded? "Then why does it feel like I did?"

"It's compromise. It's mature."

"It sucks."

He laughed. "*Very* mature. Now let's go get your Michelle."

I turned, grabbed him and kissed him. "Thank you," I said. "For giving me all of this. I wouldn't have had it any other way."

"Come on, you lovebirds!" Kevin cried, beckoning us into the car. "We've got tapping to do."

We piled in, scooping up handfuls of our damp, tangled capes to make sure they weren't caught in the door. My legs were thrown across Jamie's lap in the tiny backseat, and I held on to his neck to keep from crushing Kevin. The windows steamed up with moisture as we drove, breathless with exertion and excitement, up Science Hill.

At Michelle's apartment, I approached the doorman as the others hung back. I shoved wet locks of hair off my cheeks and smiled at him. "Hi, I'm here to see Michelle Whitmore?"

He gave me an up-down, then tipped his chin at my companions. "All y'all? Because we have to sign guests in."

"We can't do that," Jenny said. "Can't you just let us in?"

"Afraid not," the doorman said. "Ms. Whitmore has been very specific..."

"Can you call her?" I asked. "She's expecting us, I promise."

The doorman's expression was skeptical, but he picked up his phone. "Ms. Whitmore? There are some people here for you, but they won't identify themselves. They're in costume. Um, about five of them. Really? Okay, but this goes against our policy...Okay, then." He turned to us. "You can go up, and I'll sign you in as a delivery, but if you aren't back out here in five minutes—"

"We will be!" and we raced for the elevator.

Michelle answered the second I knocked on her door. Instantly, half a dozen hands reached for her and she reeled back, her eyes going wide.

"Don't be afraid," I hissed at her as we carried her to the stairwell, which we'd darkened for this purpose. Jamie stood at our makeshift altar, and the black candle burned straight and true.

"Rose & Grave," he declared in a voice that echoed up and down the floors. "Accept or Reject?"

Michelle stood stock-still, hands clenched to her sides. Her lips parted in shock. "Rose and . . . Grave?"

She leaned forward slightly, as if trying to get a better look at Jamie.

He tilted his face farther into shadow against the flame. "Accept or Reject?" he repeated.

She turned in a slow circle, taking in the hooded knights who surrounded her on all sides, their faces obscured and unknown. Then she stopped and stared straight at me. I raised my chin toward the circle of light and winked.

Michelle looked back to Jamie. "I accept."

I hereby confess:
What better way
to celebrate?

11.

Nevermore

"Are we done?" I asked Jamie as soon as we left Michelle's building.

"We need to powwow with the other groups and make sure they've got their taps in order—"

I pressed my body against his. *"Are we done?"*

He looked down at me. "Don't I wish." He cocked his head back at Michelle's. "That was a bit of a cheat back there, wasn't it?"

Even mid-tap, he hadn't been paying attention to Michelle. Only to me. "Yes. And I don't care. If she hadn't seen my face, she wouldn't have believed it. Just like I didn't last year."

Jamie shook his head. "I don't get it. You both got notes with our seal on it."

"Could be a prank. I know that's what Michelle has been thinking all afternoon. She needed to see me to believe it. I thought the same thing last year. *Rose & Grave, tapping me?*"

He squeezed my hands. "I don't know what Rose & Grave would have done without you this year."

"Probably gone on in its merry, misogynist way."

"And me?"

"Same." I giggled.

Jenny came running up to us, cell phone in hand. "That was Harun. The groups on the main campus are finished—we got every one!"

"Yes!" I pumped my fist in the air. "So we're done?" I wagged my eyebrows suggestively at Jamie.

"Not hardly," Jenny said. "Initiation's this weekend. We have so much stuff left to do!"

"Jenny."

"And Harun says a bunch of people are getting together for pizza—"

"Jenny."

"—back at the tomb to celebrate. Don't you want to party?"

"*Jenny.*"

She looked from me to Jamie and back again. "Oh. I . . . see." Her hands clasped together in front of her. "Um, it's pizza from Sally's? Best pizza in New Haven?"

"Rain check?" I said.

She grimaced. "Ooo-kay. Do you guys need me to give you a ride to . . . wherever?"

"We'll walk," Jamie said with a definitive nod.

"In this weather?"

"Yeah," I said, and slipped my hand around his waist.

Kevin and Omar were already in the car. Jenny just waved back at us and hopped behind the wheel. Jamie watched until the brake lights turned the corner, then pulled me into his arms.

———

The walk back to Jamie's apartment took longer than expected; we stopped every few steps to kiss. The drizzle had intensified during Tap Night, drenching our clothes and hair and ceremonial robes. We ran hand in hand up his front porch, and I shivered as he fumbled for his keys in the wet pockets of his jeans, scooting closer to him until I was inside the warm, humid cocoon of his cape.

He wrapped an arm around me and opened the door with the other, half pushing, half carrying me inside. As soon as we crossed the threshold, he spun me around and pressed me against the door. Our wet cloaks hung heavily from our shoulders, their flaps sticking to our arms as we reached for each other in the darkness. Underneath his robe, his T-shirt stuck to his skin and his throat was slick with rain and sweat.

"You know," I said to him as he started undoing the buttons on my blouse. "I could actually go for some pizza right about now."

"Tough luck."

I reached for his belt and my knuckles brushed against his navel and the spattering of coarse hair there. "Melted cheese, spicy tomato sauce, crust with that signature Sally's blackened bottom—"

"Later," he groaned, pushing my sleeves down my arms so my blouse pooled at my feet. My robe instantly melded to the skin of my back and arms. "I promise I'll buy you a dozen pizzas."

"A dozen?" I laughed in the back of my throat and pulled the tongue of his belt through the loops. "That law school stipend *is* a generous one."

His palms trailed up my sides and he moved closer to me until the edges of our robes furled together. His fingers were cold from the rain, but his body was all wet heat. "Is this your version of sexy talk? Financial aid?"

"No," I said, opening the fly on his jeans. "Pizza is." I reached inside and he buried his face in the hollow of my shoulder, breathing hard. "It was our first date, remember?"

"I don't remember it being a date," he managed, in between attempts to unhook my sodden bra. "If I recall, you were a little broken up about some other guy."

"It was our *only* date." There went my bra. I was fairly certain what remained was not a Digger-approved wardrobe.

"Not true." He slid his hands to the front to work the button on my pants. "In Florida, I made a picnic and took you on a hike. That's a classic top-ten date."

"You seduced me on a sandbar, yes," I conceded, and shoved his jeans down.

He yanked me to him by my waistband. "*You* seduced *me*."

I wrapped my arms around his neck. "Stop splitting hairs."

"Stop revising history."

I curled my fingers around the nape of his neck and pulled his head toward mine. "Stop talking."

For a long time we just kissed, half-naked, our robes tangled and clinging to thighs, chests, shoulders. And then I pulled away and grabbed the hem of his T-shirt, lifting it and carefully threading the material beneath the tie that held his cloak around his neck.

"So we're committing to this?" Jamie asked with a laugh as I pulled the last of his T-shirt through the robe and slipped it off over his head. His wet hair lay in dark whips across his brow, and the rain had left slim, shiny tracks on his temples. "Keeping our robes on?"

I tossed his T-shirt onto the floor, then wiggled out of my pants. "Guess so."

He grinned and squeezed me tight. "God, I love you."

"I love you, too."

His arms tightened just a fraction, and then he became very, very still.

I touched his shoulder. "Jamie?"

"I didn't expect you to say that." He still had me in his grip; I couldn't pull back and look him in the eyes. I *had* expected to say it; had been feeling it ballooning inside me all day, ready to burst with the slightest provocation. I was afraid the entire club would read it on my face; was half hoping he'd know before I ever spoke the words.

I'd wanted to tell him in the tomb, while we sprinted from dorm to dorm, after he'd bolstered me through Topher's tap, as we stood in the rain outside Michelle's. I'd wanted to tell him once for every pizza he was going to buy me. I'd wanted to confess it to him spontaneously, in the clear, not as some response to his own declaration. But he'd beaten me to the punch.

"Then why do you say it?" I asked. "It's not like you to give up a trump card like that." Neither, I realized with some chagrin, was it like me.

Go figure, Amy. You're more emotionally unavailable than James Orcutt.

"I told you," he said. "I can't keep secrets from you."

And then we were kissing again, and touching each other all over. The air grew heavy around us, and my body blazed with heat, sensitive nerve endings sizzling every time the rough fabric of our robes rasped against my flesh. Every place they touched me stung, until Jamie's cool, tender fingers came along and his caresses soothed my skin. When he knelt before me I threaded my fingers through his damp hair, still slightly chilly, holding on to him for balance.

"This seems familiar."

"Unlike some people I can mention," he murmured, as little puffs of air tickled my thighs, "I will not stop in the middle."

When I couldn't take the sensations anymore I balled my fists up into the folds of his hood and tried my best to keep my footing.

He steadied his palms against the front of my thighs. "Okay?"

"Yeah," I panted. "You? Hardwood floors treating you well?"

I could hear his smile through the darkness, though saw little more than pale skin in the frame of his robe. "Get down here."

He reached for his discarded jeans, grabbed his wallet, and drew out a condom, then sat back on the floor, his back against the arm of the couch.

After he was ready, I sank to the ground, straddling him, shifting until our robes were both hopelessly mangled, our legs tangled, fighting for purchase as we pushed into each other, the soles of my feet braced against his thighs as I moved on top of him, the ties of my robe tugging against my throat with every thrust, his hands supporting me at the small of my back and between my shoulder blades as I arched in his arms.

Once he was fully inside me, I paused and leaned up to look in his face, barely visible in the glare of distant street-lights through the window. His eyes were shut, his head lolling back, his lips slightly parted. All the pride and insolence that usually characterized his features were gone. His sharp cheekbones and angled jaw, the long, dark locks on his forehead that slashed across his eyebrows suddenly fell into different, softer patterns. Was this the true face of Poe? The man he'd be if he hadn't lost his mother, hadn't fought his whole life to convince himself and others he was worth the things he was capable of achieving, wasn't struggling even now with how to reconcile his past with the elite world of Eli and Rose & Grave? Was this the man I loved?

I leaned forward and brushed noses. His eyes shot open and bored into mine as if he had read every last one of my thoughts.

"Hey," I said. "I love you."

Jamie could hardly kiss me for smiling.

———

After the floor there was the shower, cool tile and thick steam taking the place of robes and rain, and then we adjourned to his bed, still dripping with water and lust, wrapped ourselves up in each other and his ragged bedspread, and dozed. I woke sometime later to feel reverent kisses against the small of my back—no, against the Rose & Grave tattoo placed there—and I smiled sleepily.

"Odile was right," I mumbled.

"About what?"

"You do have a kink. A fetish for Diggers."

"Hmmm . . ." He traced the outline of the hexagon with his tongue. "Lucky you."

I fell asleep again, and the next time I woke, I was alone. The bathroom light was off, so I grabbed one of Poe's discarded T-shirts, tugged it down to cover my ass, and tiptoed out of the bedroom.

The living room was dark as well. Poe sat at his desk, illuminated in blue light from his computer screen. I inched closer. Checking e-mail in the middle of the night?

"Holy shit," I heard him whisper.

I swallowed, feeling suddenly intrusive, and began to back away. I saw him straighten, and start to turn his head, and I ducked back behind the bedroom door. Did he see me? Should I reveal myself?

A few moments passed, and he didn't come in, so I went back to bed, but I fell asleep again before he returned.

I awoke to morning light and the scent of waffles. I padded back out into the living room. Poe was in sweatpants and no shirt, bustling around the kitchen.

"Hi," I said.

"You stole my T-shirt." He got out the syrup. "I was hoping to bring this to you in bed, but, uh, I don't really have a tray."

"It's fine. Waffles anywhere are good." I leaned against the counter and yawned. I bet my hair was a disaster, all dried in tangles. Jamie's hair was mussed, too, and there were shadows beneath his eyes. "How long have you been up?"

"Pretty long," he admitted, and handed me a plate. "You have class?"

"Yeah, at eleven-thirty. What time is it?"

"Eight-thirty."

I gaped at him and put down my fork. "I'm going back to bed."

He grabbed me around the waist. "No, you don't. Welcome to the post-grad world, Miss Second Semester Senior. I've got a study group in half an hour."

What the hell kind of study group met at the crack of dawn? "Are you kicking me out?"

"Amy, if you want to spend the day naked in my bed, it'll be a great fantasy to sustain me through ConLaw. But either way, I have to go."

I pouted. "Ditch school."

"Can't." His expression sobered. "What are you doing tonight? I want to take you to dinner. Something nice, since you claim we have been lacking in real dates."

"Jamie, you don't have to do that."

"I want to. I want you in a dress, and candlelight, and tablecloths, and appetizers."

I tilted my head. "You want me in appetizers?"

"And dessert."

"Dessert sounds *really* good." I kissed him.

He groaned. "And a table between us so I can concentrate for five minutes and talk to you."

"Talk about what?" I narrowed my eyes. Since when did "we need to talk"?

"Just talk." He checked his watch. "I have to hurry. I hate that I need to run, but I do. Look," he kissed me, "I had an amazing time last night. Drop me an e-mail when you know where you want to go for dinner. Stay as long as you want, borrow my clothes if yours are still wet, the door locks automatically." He started to walk away then came back and scooped me into his arms. "Love you."

"You too," I whispered. He bolted out of the kitchen, stopped by Reepicheep's tank to drop some food into her dish and give her a pat on her head, then rushed on.

Talk about what?

———

The rest of the morning passed in a cloud of "I got laid" euphoria. No, that's not right, either. After all, I'd been in that state quite a bit last semester, and this felt way different. More like...I got loved.

And in this admittedly disgustingly cheesy state, I floated. I floated, unashamed, to my Nabokov class in Poe's clothes. I floated, gleeful, into a quick conference with my thesis advisor about preparing for both final drafts and England. (I decided not to admonish him for not telling me about the colloquium, and Professor Burak, bless his heart, decided to ignore my obvious walk-of-shame attire.)

I floated, smug, back to my suite to smirk at Lydia's messages on our white board:

A: Your mom called. I told her you
were off being naughty.—L

The phone rang as I floated out of the shower and back to my bedroom. Probably my mother in a paroxysm of parental woe.

"Hello?" I said dreamily, pushing for the full effect.

"Amy," said Michelle. "I'm confused."

Crash. "You got the envelope, right?" I said.

"Uh, yeah? But . . ."

"Follow the directions." Seriously, I was not going to hold her hand through every step of the initiation. I'd already moved heaven and earth for this girl. Was I this whiny when I'd been tapped? I must remind myself to ask Malcolm next time I saw him.*

"Okay, yeah, fine, but what about the flowers?"

I adjusted my towel. "What flowers?"

"The dead roses. On my doorstep this morning?"

"Uh . . ."

"There was a note, with your—um, the, uh, symbol on it?"

Huh? That wasn't us.

"So I'm just wondering which set of directions I should follow."

"What did this note say?" I asked, baffled.

Michelle hesitated for a second. *"Coming to get you."*

———

*The confessor reports that she has had her memory jogged. She was, in fact, very, very whiny.

"But what doesn't make any sense," I said, "is that he had to know, somehow, that we were tapping her. I mean, dead roses and a note with *the seal*? Left somehow in the middle of the night after we tapped her?"

"Hmm," said Jamie, and took a sip of his wine. He was back in the black pinstripes from the night of the party. I'd borrowed one of Lydia's springy, flowered dresses she'd bought for Spain. The restaurant was everything Jamie had requested: candles, tablecloths, romance.

"So how did Blake know?" I went on. "And how did he even get into her place? You saw that doorman. He was like a frickin' security guard."

"But we got in."

"After we called up to her," I pointed out. "Don't you think if someone called up and then didn't actually come into her place that she would have remembered it?"

"Maybe he dressed up in a robe and pretended to be one of us, saying he'd forgotten something in her apartment, and the guy had no idea, because of our costumes," Jamie said.

That was a possibility. "So you're saying that he'd been watching us all along, and just happened to have a copy of our seal, a spare black robe, and a bunch of dead roses for her?" Sounded a bit far-fetched.

My boyfriend* shrugged. "Assuming that it was, in fact, Blake who left those flowers."

"Who else has been terrorizing her?"

"Not *her*, Amy." Jamie lifted his wineglass and eyed me over the rim.

And then it clicked. "Dragon's Head?"

"Or another society. Yesterday, you were worried that

---

*Darling? Sweetheart? *Luvah*? Okay, okay, the confessor will stop. Eventually.

Dragon's Head was going to steal your tap list. What if they just planned to mess with them, make sure the initiation was a disaster by delivering conflicting instructions to all your taps?"

"And since they tapped their class the previous evening, they weren't busy last night," I added. Of course! Well, that would be a relief to Michelle. Not Blake, but a whole new hassle. *Welcome to secret societies, kiddo!* "Unlike the rest of the societies on campus, they could have easily followed us around and pulled this trick. Do you think that's it?"

"I think it's a possibility." Poe consulted his menu. "And one that's much more in keeping with standard society pranks than stalker ex-boyfriends."

"You're right," I said. "That makes so much more sense. It's a good thing I have you around to explain these arcane society ways." I smiled coyly and, under the table, ran the toe of my pump along his instep.

"Are you ready to order?" he asked abruptly. I saw the waiter approaching the table. I picked the risotto; Jamie, the ravioli. As soon as the server was out of earshot, Jamie spoke again.

"So I have . . . some news."

"Good news?" I asked, and took a long drink from my wineglass. Mmm, Prosecco. I wished every night could be fancy date night with the man I loved.

"Yes and no."

I placed the glass back on the tablecloth.

"I've been offered a job."

I shook my head. "You already have a job. You're working for that firm this summer in Manhattan, the one with the ridiculous name."

"Not a summer associate job," Poe said. "A real job. A full-time job."

"Can you do that while you're a full-time student?" I asked.

"No." Jamie was watching me very carefully.

"But—" My forehead probably had more wrinkles than a pug. "You mean, drop out of Eli?"

"Defer my studies here, yes."

"Why? What kind of job is this?" I asked, puzzled.

Poe cleared his throat. "That's the part I can't talk about."

I blinked at him. "Can't talk about?"

"Yes."

"To *your girlfriend*?" I said, and my voice went up a few octaves. "*To your fellow knight?*"

"To anyone," he replied. "It's a security-clearance thing."

Oh. *Oh.*

Except, no. "I don't understand. You were going to go work for a big firm, make your money back. That's what you told me last fall. Now all of a sudden there's some sort of government job on the table I knew nothing about? One you're going to drop out of school for?"

Jamie reached out to me. "It's complicated—a long story. I wanted this job last year, but I didn't know if I was going to get it. Eli Law was my backup plan."

"Your—" I croaked. "Your backup plan?" Lydia and Josh were going to break up over her dream school, and to Jamie it was little more than a *backup plan*? And then I remembered what he'd said to me right after Spring Break. *Play your cards right and no one will ever know it's a backup plan.* Just another of his many secrets.

He took in my expression. "I'm saying that wrong."

"You bet your ass you are."

He sighed in frustration. "You have to understand, I always figured that Eli was the reality. This was such a long shot. I couldn't depend on it. I mean, Kurt Gehry was supposed to help me, but—"

"But you screwed him over," I finished. "You lost your summer job at the White House and . . . whatever this was." A picture was beginning to take focus in my brain. This was no ordinary government job, like my friends who interned at the FBI or the NSA.

"Exactly." He sat back in his chair. "But now, with Gehry disgraced, things started moving again."

"I see." I took another sip of my wine and swirled it around my mouth, but the bitter flavor rising in my throat wouldn't go away. "Are you going to be a spy?"

"Amy—"

"What? Just last night you were telling me how bad you are at keeping secrets from me. And I'm a marshmallow. I don't own a waterboard. I don't even own a skateboard."

"That's not funny."

"It's not meant to be."

Our plates arrived, relieving us both. For the next five minutes, I kept my mouth filled with risotto and wine, and reflected on the fact that a fancy public restaurant was a shitty place to break news like this to the girl you just spent half the night having incredibly tender sex with.

"So," I said slowly, "what does this mean for us?"

He swallowed a piece of ravioli and spoke. "That's what I wanted to talk about. We've been very good, up until now, about not discussing the future."

"Because we don't know what that is," I said. I refilled my glass of wine to the very top. I was going to need it. "I don't know where I'll be. And now, well, I don't know where you'll be. What's different?"

"The time line," Jamie said. "Back then, we didn't need to make any decisions for another month or two. But I have exams next week, and then, if I . . . do this, I'll be gone."

I choked on my wine. "Next week?"

"And by gone, I don't mean that I'm going to England for a few weeks and can call you every night. It doesn't mean I'm moving to Boston or D.C. or Palo Alto. Amy, I'll be gone." Jamie held my eyes. "Do you understand what I'm saying?"

Of course I did. Rumors of this were as prevalent on the Eli campus as legends about Rose & Grave. Students who vanished in the middle of their final exams and never showed up to graduation exercises. Never showed up anywhere, until forty years later, when they came back to Eli to tell their old secret societies or singing groups about their decades in Moscow or Nicaragua or Iran. Not that they could ever tell the students who heard the stories too much—classified. State secrets. You know the drill.

How many heads of the CIA had been in Rose & Grave? How many students whose names appeared in the Black Books had suddenly disappeared off the face of the planet? Having gone through their trial by fire as Knights of Persephone, how many graduated to even bigger secrets?

"Then don't do it," I whispered. "It sounds horrible. Leaving everyone you love—" *Oh, wow. This is a new record for you, Amy Haskel, both in speed and severity of abandonment. One night with you and Jamie's ready to go into hiding.* "When did you know about this?"

"Last night," he said. "After we...I got an e-mail sometime during Tap Night preparations. And then this morning I had to meet them."

"You didn't have a study group," I realized aloud.

"No."

I wondered if we were being watched right now, and for a split second, my mind concocted several desperate plans to get Poe's offer—whatever it was—withdrawn.

DESPERATE PLANS

1) The Plame Approach: Stand up and shout, "This man is a secret government operative working for the NCS."
2) The Narcotics Strategy: "Why, darling, do you think that's wise, given your ongoing and debilitating addiction to heroin/crack cocaine/crystal meth?" (Note: Quickly find way to spike wine with drugs.)
3) The Madonna Gambit: "But what about our *baby*?"

Sadly none of these would achieve the desired result of a continued relationship with Jamie. I didn't even know if I had the power to screw him over like that. Only someone like Kurt Gehry could submarine Jamie's chances. But Gehry was no longer in a position to do anything either, and hadn't been for several months.

Another thought came to me. "That night, in January, when I caught you in the tomb with all those old files? What were you doing?"

He hesitated before answering, not once looking me in the face. "What I had to."

"And what was that? Contacting other Diggers who could help you?"

"Sort of."

Because what could other Diggers—even ones in the CIA—do if Kurt Gehry had tabled Jamie's application? If he were hired, Gehry would know, and he was *not* above making the guilty parties pay, just like he'd made Jamie pay for helping D177 last spring. No, Gehry had to be brought down before there'd be any movement for my boyfriend.

"You did it," I said in a voice little more than a breath. "The Gehry scandal, his resignation."

Now Jamie raised his gaze to meet mine. "Yes."

"You " My throat had gone dry. "How did you—"

"I talk to servants, Amy," he said. "Cooks, maids, butlers, *gardeners*. They're who I am, and they've always been the ones with the dirt. When I visited Gehry for my White House interview last year, I talked to his. And it paid off. I contacted a few Diggers who had their own grudges against Gehry, and they took it from there."

I stared at him in disbelief.

"You think they offered me this job because of my fashion sense?" The sardonic glint was back in his eyes. "Now, take the next step." His tone was cold, manipulative. At this moment, he was the Poe who'd put me in the coffin. The one who'd played the Grim Reaper. "You know you want to."

The risotto began to churn in my stomach and I took a deep breath. "Darren was right. Gehry *did* have Rose & Grave to blame for his humiliation. But it wasn't D177. It wasn't me."

"No," said Jamie. "It was me."

I fell against the back of my chair, speechless, breathless.

"You okay?" he said, and pushed my glass toward me. "Have some water."

"I've had quite enough *water*, I think," I snapped. "You know all that stuff you said about not being able to keep secrets from me is bullshit, right?"

"Well, you know them all now," he said. "And I was afraid to tell you that one. Way more afraid than I was to tell you that I loved you. I knew if I did, if you thought I was at fault for what happened to you, you'd leave me."

"And you're not afraid I'll leave you now?" I said, much more harshly than I'd intended.

Jamie was silent.

Last night, I'd told him that I loved him, too. Whatever series of events led to my kidnapping, he couldn't have known. It wasn't Jamie's fault that Darren was a psychotic little snot. It was an accidental consequence, and one that someone who loved him as I did couldn't possibly hold against him. All this time, I thought his guilt about Darren had the same genesis as all my friends': He hadn't been there when Darren had found me. But it went deeper than that.

"I'm not afraid of it," he said sadly. "I know it's going to happen. Not because of Gehry. Because I'm taking the job."

"No!"

"Amy," he said, "what are you imagining for us? Pretend it's not me. Pretend it's Lydia. She's been with Josh for months and months, and you're still urging her not to make life decisions based on her boyfriend. I wouldn't want you to make decisions based on me, and I can't make decisions based on you, either."

I bit my lip and my eyes began to burn. It was true. Every word.

He sighed. "I hate saying that."

And I hated admitting he was right.

"But this isn't like Lydia and Josh," I said, failing to keep the sob from my voice. "They would still try to make it work, long distance."

"They also have nine months behind them. We have one."

I stared down at the risotto, now swimming in a sea of tablecloth and candlelight. My eyes were watering and I was relieved we weren't at a usual Eli hangout—a corner Thai or pizza place where everyone I knew could see me sobbing into my food. Jamie had at least granted me that.

"Amy?" His hand came across the table to cover mine.

"If I'd known—if I'd honestly thought I'd had a chance with this job, I would not have let things with us—"

"But you didn't think you had a chance with me, either," I said, and took a deep, shuddering breath.

I'd known this was coming, and sooner, rather than later. Jamie and I had no real future. Not with me leaving New Haven. But there was a huge difference between the expectation of me leaving in a month and him leaving in— when? A week? A few days? And disappearing, like a ghost?

I'd been right last night. Maturity sucked. But it was the only rational choice. If I loved him as I claimed, who was I to get in the way of his dream? Who was I, even if we'd been together for months? To have a shape to your ambition, to hold it in the palm of your hand—wasn't that what I longed for? And here was Jamie's, bright and beautiful, and the only sacrifice required was the one we'd both been planning on anyway.

So there. That was it. Simpler, even, than tapping Topher, when you really sat down and thought about it. And it wouldn't even hurt. Not really. Not like it would if we'd let it drag out to graduation and beyond, let it turn ugly, as long-distance relationships—no matter what I'd led Lydia to believe—inevitably did. If we parted now, respectfully, maturely, like adults who realized that the world was bigger than our bedroom, it could be easy.

Easier, at least. We could still be friends. Society brothers. We could remember each other fondly, at any rate.

So why this deep, sucking wound in my chest?

"No matter which one of us ended up leaving first," I said bitterly, "this relationship was always term-limited. So why did we bother at all?"

His eyes looked silvery and shining, but for all I knew, it was a trick of the candlelight. "I know why I did."

I knew, too. But I also knew my capacity for mistakes.

I hereby confess:
The secret to surviving
heartbreak is finding
more pressing drama.

12.

Goners

I'd love to say that Jamie and I made the most of the time we had left, but that isn't the case. We didn't even spend the night together after our dinner. After all, I had a thesis to complete, homework to do, an initiation to plan. Jamie had to prepare for his finals. I wasn't sure why he even intended to bother, since his leave of absence from Eli would be indefinite—but Jamie was the kind of guy who liked to finish what he started. Usually.

So imagine my surprise when I went by his place the following day, in response to a message he'd left on my phone about a study break, and found . . . nothing.

Okay, not nothing. The door was propped open, the couch remained, and Reepicheep's tank still sat in the corner with the following note taped to the glass:

Amy,
I thought you'd want Reepicheep. I gave Voldemort to a
friend of mine in the Forestry School, Ray Velasquez,

*who says he's more than happy to take Reepicheep if you
don't want to. He promises not to feed her to Voldie.*
I love you.
Pajamie

P.S. The waffle maker's for you, too.

When Jenny came by with her car, she found me curled up
on the porch with both tank and waffle iron at my feet,
holding the note in my hand and crying profusely.

"I'm glad you called," she said, standing over me with
her hands on her hips. "You need more than a ride." She
plopped down next to me and pulled out a bag of candy.
"Gummy Life Savers?"

This only made me cry harder.

"Come on, Amy," she said. "You can't let this get to
you. Remember how you coached me through Micah last
fall?"

"Jamie," I hissed through the tears, "is not Micah
Price."

"Oh, no?" asked Jenny. "Well, I loved Micah, and he
was a jerk, and everyone else already knew it."

"Not the same."

"Explain why not."

Oh, God, where to start? Micah was the guy who spit in
my face, and Jamie was the guy who punched him out for
it? "Because Micah didn't love you back. Because Jamie is
not a jerk. Because Micah changed you, and if anything,
Jamie changed *for* me. I know at times he could seem cruel
or harsh or—"

"Manipulative?" Jenny suggested. "Deceptive?"

"Only with good cause!" Everyone had their faults.
Besides, for the Diggers, qualities like those were viewed as

virtues. "Look, I know you don't like him. But please cease with the suggestions that our relationship was a bad one."

"Fine," said Jenny. "And I guess I can admit that he was okay. I mean, he liked small animals. And he taught you to swim."

"And he read the Bible."

"He's Episcopalian," Jenny scoffed.

"What? They're like Catholics; except no pope."

Jenny just rolled her eyes.

I sighed. "Well, I love him, and he's gone. And though I sat there and made the most mature, rational, grown-up decision I could about it, it still hurts like hell."

"Now I'm on familiar ground," Jenny said, and folded her hands in her lap.

I sniffled. "How so?"

She took a deep breath. "Harun."

"Yeah," I said, careful to keep any tone of *I knew it* from my voice.

"We're not together, Amy, no matter what you all think. We can't ever be together. There are too many issues. Religion, for one. I mean, apparently, a Christian woman is okay or something, according to the Qu'ran, but that doesn't mean the opposite works for me. And his mom would apparently flip if she saw me, which isn't anything compared to what my dad would do if I brought Harun home."

She'd certainly thought about this a lot.

"And then there's Rose & Grave. We have this bond that exists outside of anything else, and that doesn't go away when we graduate. We're in this society for life. So it's not worth it unless we plan to go the distance. And maybe not even then, when you consider all the other hurdles."

"Jenny, why didn't you talk to us about this?"

She shrugged. "And put up with even more teasing? More rumblings about 'society incest'? No thank you. I don't know how you've dealt with it all this time."

"Mostly," I said, "I haven't noticed it."

"Really? Since you've been dating Jamie, it's been brutal."

I raised my eyebrows. *Brutal?* I really *hadn't* noticed it, then.

"Harun and I talked about the situation. We came to a decision. That was all we needed."

"What was your decision?"

"That love exists in many forms, and that it's limiting and unimaginative and...immature to assume that the only way a man and a woman can love each other is in a romantic sense."

There was that word again. *Mature.* Was this what maturity was? Giving up on the things we wanted because we knew we'd never get them?

"I want the best for him in his life, and if I can help him achieve it, I will. I love him, but without expectation, without possession."

The tears began to well up again. "That's it," I said. "That's exactly it."

Jenny put her arm around me and hugged me. "There's even a word for this kind: 'agape.' It's a sacred love, a tender love, and it's separate from desire."

"But what if you want all the kinds of love?" I sobbed.

"It's easier said than done," Jenny went on. "I want to be with him all the time. When something bad happens, he's the person I want to run to. When something good happens, he's the person I want to tell first. For instance, after I'm through convincing you to come work for me, I'm going to call him up and tell him about my killer hiring skills."

I gave her a weak laugh and pulled away. "It's not that I don't appreciate your offer, Jenny—"

"Oh, so I'm good enough to be your taxi service, but not your boss?"

I smiled. "Yes, and that's precisely how I was going to put it, too." I folded up Jamie's note and stuck it in my bag. "Shall we get out of here?"

"Sure. I have to drop off a few of these amendments on the way home." As a result of Michelle's dead-flower experience, we were sending out altered instructions to counteract any possible Dragon's Head sabotage.

I picked up Reepicheep's tank. "Can you get the waffle maker?"

"You're actually going to take that thing?" Jenny asked.

"Yes," I said. "What else do I have to remember him by?"

———

Lydia, it must be said, was not overly fond of our new rodent suitemate.

"You know people pay to have these things *removed* from their dwellings, right, Amy?" she asked, peering fearfully at the little white mouse, who now held a place of honor on our bookshelf. (I hadn't figured out where we would put the microwave, but since we'd be moving out of the suite in a month, I suppose it didn't matter too much.)

"They also feed them to snakes," I replied.

"Great idea! Where do I get another live creature to put in my dorm room?" She clapped her hands together. "What's next in the menagerie? A ferret? A goat?"

I spun the hamster wheel and fitted the top back on the tank. Reepicheep seemed to have survived the move, though she was currently huddled in a nest of cedar chips, trembling all over. I knew how the poor thing felt.

"No more," I promised Lydia, "but brace yourself: I need you to take care of her for a day or two."

"What?"

"You know that thing keeping Josh so busy right now?"

"His term paper?"

I snorted. "Right. The same term paper I have." Meaningfully.

Lydia shook her head. "Why do you guys even bother with the cover stories anymore?"

Honestly? I had no idea.

"Fine," she said in resignation. "I'll feed your stupid rat."

"Mouse."

"Sewer dweller, carrier of plague, whatever." She tapped the tank. "Well, it's probably better that I have some time alone to think this weekend."

I cocked my head at her.

"Law school, Ames. I have to choose."

"I thought you had."

"Yeah, well . . ." She hunched her shoulders. "Not yet. Now that Josh knows, he's been giving me all this grief about self-sacrifice. And I went to talk to some professors at the law school the other day and now I'm all confused."

"Do you want to talk about it?" I asked.

"No," she said. "I've been talking about it. I've talked to you, I've talked to Josh, I've talked to professors, my advisors, my parents. My letter to Dear Abby should be published any day now."

"I hope you're kidding."

She turned to me. "I'm just saying that I've got all the advice I can take. What I need is to talk to myself for a little while. Maybe it's good you two are going to be unreachable this weekend. I'll get the other voices out of my head and just . . . I don't know. Find a solution."

I took her hands in mine. "You know what the real problem is?"

"Enlighten me."

"No matter what you decide, you won't be with *me* next year."

Her laugh sounded more like a cry. "I know. I have no idea how either of us will survive. Who will have Gumdrop Drops with me?"

"Who will trash our suite with feathers and raw hamburger?" I asked.

"Who will pound on the wall when my boyfriend and I get rowdy?"

"Who will despair of me ever finding a boyfriend?"

Lydia bit her lip in contrition. "That actually reminds me. You had a phone call while you were out."

"Jamie?" I exclaimed in hope.

"No," said Lydia. "Brandon."

———

Brandon and I met at our favorite coffee shop. He was waiting for me with my usual order, iced mocha with whipped cream and shaved cocoa toppings.

"You remembered," I said when he handed it to me.

"Of course." He smiled, and his melted-chocolate eyes went right through me, as always. "Want to sit down, or walk?"

"Walk, I think," I said. "I can't get enough of looking at the campus these days."

"Me neither." We exited into the late-April sunshine and started down the street, sipping our drinks and enjoying the interplay of new wet leaves and old Gothic architecture. "Remember the first time you saw this place?"

I did. I'd been on a college tour with my parents and was utterly bowled over by the buildings, by the groups of students quoting Shakespeare and playing Frisbee. It was a picture postcard of American college life and I wanted in.

"Hard to believe we're leaving," he said. We passed into Old Campus and started down one of the paths that crisscrossed through the green. "I always figured I'd have more time here."

"Pretty easy to visit, though," I said. "With you in New York."

"Yeah," he mumbled. "Not the same."

"No," I agreed.

We reached a relatively dry bench and sat, facing out over the campus.

"I'm glad you called," I said to him. "I didn't want things to end the way they did, between us."

"I didn't, either," he said. "And I felt like I owed you an explanation about Felicity."

I busied myself with my mocha. In the church hall nearby, the Russian Chorus was doing warm-up exercises, their harmonized voices wafting through the spring breeze. I kicked at the mulch beneath my feet. Perhaps Brandon was waiting for a response, but I wasn't about to give one. The Diggers had taught me the power of silence.

Brandon broke first. *Watch out, Jamie, I'll become a spy next.*

"When I found out she was in Dragon's Head," he said, "I thought all my hesitance, all my distance from her had been justified. After all, I'd already been burned by you and Rose & Grave last spring. You were supposed to be my girlfriend, but when something bad happened to you, who did you tell? Some people you'd known for a few days, people who wore silly costumes. Not me. I thought I'd learned my lesson after that. Do not get involved with society girls, you know? They'll always put their societies first."

And still, I stayed quiet. There was no denial. I not only chose the society over Brandon, I chose George, my society brother, over him, too.

"But then—she shocked me. She admitted that she'd been behind those attacks on you, confessed like I was a priest or something. Is that what they teach you people?"

"I can't tell you that," I recited.

"Whatever. Anyway, she told me that she'd halt the whole thing if I wanted. She told me she'd do whatever it took, that I was the thing that was most important to her—"

"Stop," I whispered, hit with the weight of the sacrifice that came with Felicity's triumph. If Dragon's Head was anything like Rose & Grave, she'd lost major capital within her society the moment she chose barbarian matters over them. And more than that, she'd done it for something as inconsistent as love. She hadn't let me see it last February, but she had been the one to make the choice that none of us were able to. Not Jamie or me, not Lydia or Josh, not Harun or Jenny. For Felicity alone did love conquer all.

Yet Felicity, like the rest of us, was left with no one.

No wonder she had called me a bitch back in that Sign of the Unicorn shop. I was the cynic, the one willing to weigh love on a scorecard. Had she interpreted my asking after Brandon as rubbing salt in the wound? I'd meant to hurt her, to reference the fact that she'd bound Brandon to her through bribery and blackmail. But what if all I'd really done was remind her that her efforts had been in vain?

"Yeah," he said. "We were together for Spring Break, and it was beautiful. We went down to the Golden Isles, stayed in some haunted B&B in Savannah, soaked up the South. It was like last summer in Hong Kong. But as soon as we got back to campus, we realized that it was make-believe. What was broken between us last February—it wasn't what Felicity had done. It was what I did."

"She dumped you."

"Yeah." He was staring down at his coffee.

"I'm sorry, Brandon."

"Maybe it was broken all along," he said. "That's why we worked on vacation, but not in the real world." He cast me a sidelong glance. "Heard you got together with someone over Spring Break."

"I did." A sip of mocha and a firm resolution not to burst into tears.

"Is it working out?"

"No." Firm resolution. Firm resolution.

"Thought not."

Ouch. Though I suppose I deserved that. After all, the girl Brandon knew had been terrified by the idea of commitment.

"I'm beginning to think the whole system is flawed," he went on. "Boyfriends and girlfriends. You had the right idea all along."

What? I turned to him, sure he was joking, but Brandon's expression was closed, his face reflecting only bitterness.

"It's the underlying inequality. Someone is always the one who loves more, and it eventually drives the other— the less loving one—away. Just the pressure of it."

"Been reading your Auden, I see."

"Huh?" he said, furrowing his brow. "Oh, right. 'If equal affection cannot be / Let the more loving one be me.' " He took another sip of his coffee, then made a face. "I don't know if W.H. was right about that. I've been both. And I prefer guilt to humiliation."

I swallowed with some difficulty. Who was this guy? He wasn't the Brandon I'd known junior year. It was me; I had been the one to do this to him. Felicity was right to blame me. Brandon had loved me without reservation, without fear, and I'd broken his heart. Broken it so that he couldn't let Felicity in, no matter what she tried. He, in turn, had broken her heart. Was this some never-ending chain?

"No," I said softly. "It doesn't have to be that way."

"I don't believe that," said Brandon. "Not anymore."

I hunched into my coffee drink. Brandon might claim to prefer the guilt, but he had no compunction about handing it off to me.

"Which role did you play with that guy from Spring Break?" he asked abruptly.

I straightened. "I have no idea. That's not what happened." Sometimes you met someone that changed the pattern, who wormed their way past the cracks in your heart, caulked them up, sealed themselves in, and stayed there. Sometimes they did it by insisting you meet them at every step, as Jamie had done to me. Sometimes they did it without even knowing, as I had done to Jamie long before.

But how could I explain that to Brandon? He'd asked the same things of me that Jamie had. He'd been as forthright with his feelings—even more so. And yet, I hadn't loved him. I'd loved Jamie. Brandon's method was not at fault. Pursue a girl who could love you that way, and it would be bound to succeed. Had I killed that possibility? Had I destroyed him for future girls, the same way I had for Felicity?

No, I realized. That hypothetical loving girl would come, and Brandon would forget his bitterness. He'd forget what I'd done, and he'd think only of her, as right this second, I could think only of Jamie.

"Really?" Brandon asked. "You'll forgive me if I find that hard to believe."

Of course he did. After all, it was me. And to explain what happened—to tell him that Jamie and I loved each

other, but had chosen certain ambition over uncertain fu-
tures—well, wouldn't that sound like commitment issues
in disguise? It was more than Josh and Lydia's conundrum.
Choosing the life he did meant Jamie had to give me up.
To give it all up.

"I'll forgive you." I looked at him. "If you'll forgive
me."

Brandon said nothing.

I gave him a weak smile. "Not yet, huh?"

"Not yet." He didn't meet my gaze. "Not when you can
sit there and act like you're in love."

"For all the good it's doing me."

He snorted and stared out over the quad. Whatever
he'd been hoping for from this interview, it hadn't happened. If anything, I'd probably made it worse.

*I'm sorry for breaking you, Brandon. I'm sorry you weren't
the one for me, and that we hurt each other the way we did. But
you'll be okay. You'll be better than okay. At NYU, you'll meet
someone. She'll be pretty and smart and fun and funny, and
she'll love you beyond all reason, and what's more, you'll love her
back. I promise.*

But I couldn't say that to him, so I just joined him in
observing the students on the grass.

Which is when I saw him. Even from across the quad,
his eyes burned like laser beams. And those beams were focused right at me. Blake Varnham.

How long had he been standing there, staring?

"Brandon, see that guy?"

It took him less than a second. "The one from Commons?"

"Yeah."

"What a creep." He smirked, and for a second, I got a
flash of the old Brandon. "Let's wave at him."

We waved. Blake put his hands in his pockets, but did not break his gaze.

"Okay," said Brandon. "Now he's just pissing me off."

"Me too." Across the lawn, someone called Blake's name, and he dragged his attention away from us at last as the newcomer met him on the walk. His back was to us. They spoke, and then Blake pointed in our direction. The newcomer swiveled to follow Blake's finger, and his face fell as our eyes met.

Topher Cox.

"Read it!" I hissed at the neophyte from beneath my mask of roses. The clamor rose around me, knights and patriarchs shouting and banging copper pots as they whirled in a circle around us.

"Read it!" they echoed in their best scary voices. "Read it!"

The neophyte ducked his head and peered at the parchment.

"*I, Christopher Lionel Cox, Barbarian-So-Called, most solemnly pledge and avow my love and affection, everlasting loyalty and undying fealty. By the Flame of Life and the Shadow of Death, I swear to cleave wholly unto the principles of this ancient order, to further its friends and plight its enemies, and place above all others the causes of the Order of Rose & Grave.*"

We all howled. Four knights grabbed him, lifted him above their heads, and paraded around the room, screaming like banshees.

Initiation Night was in full swing. I'd thought the event was a whirlwind as a neophyte, but it was nothing compared to the maelstrom of actually running the show. We'd all been moving non-stop since daybreak, making sure everything was ready, hosting an alumni tea to greet the patriarchs, briefing them about the taps we'd be welcoming into the fold, and ensuring that they understood their roles. Even Lionel Drake had attended, like a proud papa bear, though he regretfully informed us that his bad leg would keep him from participating in the tap that evening.

George Prescott the elder came as well, as did Malcolm, and over a dozen other patriarchs, so we had a good-sized cast, though both Odile and Demetria had complained that there were hardly enough women to fulfill the allotted roles.

Topher was carried around the room twice more, then deposited in front of George's father, who was dressed as Don Quixote, in a rusted-out suit of armor, with long gray whiskers. He held a long sword aimed at Topher's heart, then shifted and smacked him hard on the shoulder.

"From this moment on, you are no longer Barbarian-So-Called Christopher Lionel Cox. By the order of our Order, I dub thee Achilles, Knight of Persephone, Order of Rose & Grave."*

Well, that was it. He was a Digger now. Maybe we'd be able to convince him to drop such loathsome friends as Blake Varnham. After I'd seen them together in the quad the previous day, I'd done a little digging of my own. Topher and Blake had gone to prep school together. No wonder Topher had known Michelle at the party—and no wonder Michelle hadn't shown any interest in talking to him! I hoped that, now that they were about to be society

---

*The confessor had voted for "Bateman," but she was overruled. Apparently, Lionel would be immensely pleased if his grandson followed in his footsteps. Oh, well. It was fitting. Spoiled rotten rich kid who thought the world of himself and constantly needed more august family members to make him allowances? Sure.

brothers, they could each look past their history, as I had when Clarissa and I had joined Rose & Grave.

Topher was shuffled out the door, and I ripped off my rose mask and handed it to Lil' Demon.

"Everything going well?" I asked, flipping up the hood on my robe.

"Like demonic clockwork," she replied, slipping the mask over her famous features. "We had a bit of a problem with the sixth level of hell about fifteen minutes ago. One of the flaming tombs actually caught fire. Damaged the wall, but no one was hurt."

"Who was the heretic inside?" I asked. According to Dante, the sixth level of hell housed heretics in coffins of fire.

Lil' Demon shrugged. "I can't keep all the patriarchs straight, especially when they're in costume."

"True." I shoved my hair inside my robe. "Okay, I'm off to play Beatrice."

Beatrice was the final step on the initiate's path before she reached the Inner Temple—our "heaven." In the *Divine Comedy*, she makes Dante drink from the river of forgetfulness. For our purposes, initiates were instructed to drink "blood" from a human skull fashioned into a cere-monial goblet—an event I still wished I could forget.

The next neophyte had yet to arrive, so I decided to take a quick spin around the tomb to bask in the initiation in all its flash and chaos. With two taps to oversee, I'd hardly gotten a chance to observe the proceedings at large.

Which reminded me, where was Michelle? If all went according to plan, she should be just entering the ninth level of hell, which was guarded by our tallest participants, garbed as fallen angels. At the moment, it was Big Demon and one of the older patriarchs. On the ground floor, Angel and Lucky flitted about in voluminous organza wraps that appeared lit from within, thanks to a collection of carefully arranged glowsticks. Threads of smoke wafted from the Firefly Room, and the staircase down into the kitchen (as well as the secret entrance to the barrel vault) had been turned into a slide ramp approximating Dante's ride down the Cliffs of Malebolge on the back of the winged monster Geryon. Other patriarchs, in robes, guided blindfolded neophytes up and down the stairs between these two zones. On the landing, Puck and Lancelot, dressed as minor devils, were leading Juno's tap, Brianna, in a trust fall from the landing to the ground, where a host of other patriarchs waited to catch her with a blanket.

I shuddered, remembering my own terror during initiation. Poe hadn't held anything back in his attempts to scare the taps: Over the course of the evening, I'd been threatened with suffocation, poisoning, drowning, and—let's not forget—rape. He'd made up some crazy story about an in-house prostitute called "the Digger Whore" before dumping me off the landing into the pile of blankets. By the time the other guys had caught me, I'd been positive I was being attacked.

I almost laughed aloud. From the inside, none of this had the same sense of menace I'd imagined as a neophyte. I could understand Poe's desire to spice it up, to bring it to a level beyond your average house of horrors. *Poe.* I took a deep breath. What was I doing? Right, looking for Michelle.

I spotted her then, heading blindfolded into a room on the third floor, being led by the hand by a patriarch in a shimmering purple robe. Between the destruction of the Tap Night rain (and, um, other activities) wreaked on a lot of our robes, and the large patriarch turnout at initiation, we were scraping the bottom of the barrel when it came to costume choices.

"Yo, Bugaboo," Puck called to me, and pointed at Brianna. "You're up."

"That's Beatrice to you," I said with a wink and hurried down to meet the neophyte at the base of the stairs.

"See thou before me, Neophyte?" I paraphrased at Brianna. "I am none other than Beatrice. Through many trials hast thou come to this mountain, where all men—and women—are made happy."

"Great!" Brianna said with a sigh of relief. "I thought this would never end."

"Impatience, Neophyte," I went on, "will not serve you well this night. A few tests remain, before thou mayst enter into our most sacred mysteries."

I guided Brianna through the next step of her initiation, leading her back up the stairs, then watched as she drank from the skull and ushered her into the Inner Temple for the end of the ceremony.

Duties accomplished, I went back down the stairs to peek in at the after-party shaping up in the Grand Library. More than half of our taps were now fully initiated and in the midst of getting to know one another over bowls of punch and in view of some of the more elderly (read: can't get 'em into costumes these days) patriarchs. As I watched, Topher—pardon, Achilles, D178—went over to pay his respects to Grandpa.

Good. We had about five more taps to initiate, and then the knights of D177 would gather one last time in the Inner Temple to pay our respects to Persephone and take our leave. Then we'd join the new initiates en masse in the Grand Library, and the party would truly begin.

After that, I played Beatrice to Paul Raymond, Jenny's

tap. Poor boy, he'd also inherited the society name Lucky. Though it had sounded cute on her, on a boy, it made me think of a farmhand from *Oklahoma!* I headed back downstairs to await the next neophyte.

I reached the bottom step as a scream rent the air. An *unscripted* scream. Everyone paused in their bustle and turned their faces up to the third floor, where a door banged open and out swept the purple-robed patriarch with a struggling bundle in his arms. Michelle.

"Let me go, you psychopath!" she shouted, and he tightened his grip around her throat. She flailed with both arms and knocked his hood from his face.

That was no patriarch. It was Blake Varnham.

For a moment, everyone stood frozen. The neophytes didn't seem to know whether or not this was part of the act, and a few of the patriarchs looked similarly confused. My fellow knights were all in shock. How had this barbarian breached our tomb? How long had he been here?

"Stop, Shelly," Blake said in the calmest voice imaginable. "Don't make me ... don't make me ..." I saw the glint of a knife in his hand. Michelle's eyes widened and her body went limp in his arms. He pointed the knife at her face and brought it close, but before I even had time to gasp, I saw that it was aimed not at Michelle, but at his own chest.

Michelle's eyes were saucers now, her focus trained on the knife, which rested inches from her cheek.

"My God, look what you make me do," he went on. "I'm just trying to save you from these people. Don't you know what they're like?"

"Blake, please, please ..." Michelle cried. Around them, I saw patriarchs inching closer.

Blake whirled on them. "Come an inch closer and I'll plunge this straight into my chest." He looked at Michelle. "Look at them threatening me, honey. You see that, right?"

"Blake, please . . ."

"Shelly, do you think I want this? But what can I do? I can't let them make you their whore. I couldn't survive that. I'd rather see you dead. I'd rather be dead myself." He cast one more warning look at the patriarchs arrayed on the upper level.

Puck leapt at him.

The knife clattered down the stairs, bounced once on the landing, then plummeted to the stones at my feet. I saw Michelle sliding from Blake's arms, and a short, swift struggle, a billow of shimmering purple fabric, then both Puck and Blake pitched over the side.

A forever fall, it seemed, before the crunch.

"George!" I shouted.

He was on top, at an impossible angle, his face contorted with pain, shifting feebly. The tomb seemed to come to life again, but when the screaming started, it was not directed at my ex-lover, my friend, my society brother.

Michelle leaned over the landing, her face white, her mouth open in an endless cry.

Blake had fallen on his knife.

I hereby confess:
Everything happened
very quickly.

13.
Turncoat

"Call 911!" Demetria materialized by my side. "This man needs a hospital!"

George was trying to push himself off Blake's body, but there was something wrong with his arm. As the others tended to Blake, I pulled George off.

Blake wasn't moving. His eyes were open and his hands flittered, feebly, over his torso. His robe was twisted around his body, blood collecting in its folds.

"Blake!" Michelle shrieked. "Dear God, someone call 911!"

"Stop!" yelled a patriarch. "We can't have the police in here."

"Drop dead," said Demetria. All around her, cell phones were lighting up. Malcolm gently turned Blake over, balling up the robe to press against the wound. I couldn't see well enough to determine how serious it was. From the blood, though, I had a pretty good idea.

I turned to George. "You okay?"

He was cradling his left arm with his right. "I can't move my arm, but...yeah. Mostly just scared."

I shook my head at him. "You know you've kind of got a hero complex, right?"

George winced. "Don't you find it charming?"

The doors to the Grand Library opened and I could see initiates and patriarchs poking their heads out to look. One pushed his way past the threshold. "Blake!" Topher shouted, then joined us in the hall. "Oh, man. Oh, shit. Blake, man, what are you doing?"

Blake opened his mouth and coughed up blood. I bit my lip.

As Michelle joined Topher by Blake's side, Topher said, "Shelly, what did you do?"

"Nothing!" she cried. "He threatened me. Like *always*."

There was a knock on the door. A knock. On the door of the Rose & Grave tomb. "Police," came the voice from the other side. For a moment, everyone froze.

Demetria strode toward the tomb doors and flung them wide.

———

Four hours later, I sat with a rather loopy George in his hospital room. He'd broken his collarbone and his arm in two places, and a bruise the size and shape of a Labrador retriever was blooming over the right half of his body. I was also plotting to kill whoever saw fit to give him painkillers.

"The doctor says I won't be able to walk tomorrow," he said, a dreamy smile crossing his features. "You know what that means, don't you, Amy?"

I sighed. "Sponge baths?"

"Sponge baths!" He pumped his uninjured arm in the air. "Ow."

The joke was funnier the first two times. "I do not envy Devon."

"Devon." George furrowed his brow. "I should probably call and tell her what happened to me, huh?"

"Why?" I picked up his cup of half-melted ice chips and took a sip.

"She's my girlfriend."

I dropped the cup. "Your *what*?"

George's mouth snapped shut. "Oh, fuck."

"George," I said. "Did you just use the G-word? *And* the F-word?"

He remained mute.

"George—"

"Don't, Amy. Please, I can't take this from you."

"Take what?" I asked. "The ridicule I'm going to heap on you once you come down off whatever crazy-ass drugs they've got you on?" I laughed. "That must be some really excellent shit, George Harrison Prescott. Girlfriend. Ha!"

He didn't respond.

I blinked in disbelief. "You're serious. You're with her."

He nodded.

"Why?" I blurted.

He thought about this for a minute. "Why are you with Jamie?"

Past tense, I almost said. "But you don't believe in relationships."

"Please, Amy. Don't start in with any 'why wasn't it me' stuff." George laid his head back against the pillow. "I can't take that tonight."

" 'Why wasn't it me?' " I repeated, baffled. "Did you forget the part where I ditched you last fall?"

He seemed to think about that for a moment. Those drugs must have him foggy after all. "Besides," he said at last, "it's so early. I have no idea where it's going."

"Welcome to a committed relationship," I said.

"And when I graduate..." He tried to shrug, then grimaced in pain. "Did I tell you?"

"That you're going to graduate? I figured."

"No, did I tell you what I'm doing?" he slurred.

I shook my head and tucked in the edge of his blanket. "No."

"Teach for America."

I blinked at him. He was high as a kite. First a girlfriend, then bailing on Wall Street to be a teacher? Yeah, we'd laugh about this tomorrow.

"My mom will be...proud," he murmured.

Hmm. Maybe he was serious.

"Amy?" George asked. His eyes were drifting closed.

"Yeah?"

"Don't tell anyone." His mouth went slack.

I smiled in spite of myself. "Don't worry, George," I said, and brushed the hair off his brow. "Your reputation's safe with me."

As George fell asleep, I stifled a yawn, then caught sight of my blood-spattered sleeve and frowned. What a mess. Back at the tomb, the authorities had rushed the profusely bleeding Blake into an ambulance and left the rest of us standing in puddles of blood, answering questions for almost an hour while the pain in George's arm grew progressively worse. Finally, the police let Jenny take him to the hospital.

Michelle had spent the whole time huddled in a corner, her hands clasped before her, eyes as wide as if Blake's body remained on the hall floor.

I knew exactly how she felt. I'd knelt in front of her then. "What happened?"

She'd squeezed her eyes shut. "I thought—you told me the initiation would scare me. So when there was a guy who talked like Blake—who put me in a room and talked like Blake—I thought that was part of the game. You guys know so many other things about me. Why couldn't you know this?"

I caught my breath. "What kind of sick bastards do you think we are? My God, Michelle—"

"He's what scares me," she said. "Being trapped in a room with him is my idea of hell, not flaming tombs or winged monsters. Blake."

"How did you realize what was going on?" I asked softly.

She'd ducked her head even farther into her chest. "He, um, wanted me to do something." Something sexual, from her tone. "And at first, I couldn't tell—I thought maybe this was just supposed to scare me more."

Sure, why not? Jamie had tried to scare me in a similar way.

"Then I realized that this guy—this society guy, I thought—was dead serious. You know the stories you hear about Rose & Grave...they make you think all kinds of horrible things are happening inside." She looked up. "But then I thought about you and Jamie...I've only known you for a little while, but I trust you. I can't imagine you being a part of anything sick like that. I started to get a very bad feeling. Not fun scared or even scared scared. Just—"

"I know." There was a special brand of terror reserved for people who found themselves alone and in the power of someone who wished only to hurt them. I'd felt it on the island. Michelle had been feeling it at regular intervals ever since her friends and her dean had turned their backs on her.

"So I pulled off his hood. I had to know, for sure. And when I saw it was Blake, I tried to run. I thought—Amy, I thought he was there *on purpose*." She started crying anew.

I tried to put my arms around her, but whatever comfort existed in my hug did not seem to transfer to Michelle.

———

Demetria and Jenny waited for me in the hall outside George's hospital room. "Blake's out of surgery," Demetria reported to me. "The way he hit the knife—it didn't go straight in, just sliced his back wide open. He had sixty-five stitches."

I pressed my fist against my mouth. "I don't understand. He was coughing up blood. I thought for sure—"

Demetria snorted. "Turns out he bit his lip pretty hard when he landed. That blood was from his mouth."

"The main problem was the blood loss," said Jenny. "But they gave him a transfusion, so he's doing better now."

"I've been at the police station with Michelle," Demetria went on, "so she could file the battery charges. Hale came with us: One of the lawyer patriarchs said we should try to get Blake on burglary, too. When George gets out tomorrow, he needs to speak to the Prescott dean and to the police. We should expect Blake to file charges against him."

"But George was trying to save Michelle," I said.

Demetria shrugged. "And Blake ended up stabbed in the back. I'm not saying they'll stick, but George should be prepared."

Actually, we all should have been ready.

———

The hammer fell the following morning. The phone rang at 10 A.M.—only five short hours from the moment I'd passed out in bed—calling me into the Prescott College dean's office. When I arrived, the dean's dour secretary gave me a once-over.

"Where's George Prescott?" she asked.

"In—in the hospital," I stuttered. "He had an accident last night."

The secretary harrumphed, then picked up her phone to let the dean know I'd arrived.

Dean Oliver De La Roche beckoned to me from the door of his office. "Amy, come in."

I entered, already formulating theories about what was happening:

1) Having been informed of last night's debacle, the dean required a standard debriefing.
2) He wanted to know exactly what was going on with George's arm.
3) I'd won some kind of award.

"I'll be quick about this," Dean De La Roche said.

He was a young man, a junior professor in the Music department. He lived with his partner, a budding violinist, in the dean's apartment in Prescott and was known mostly for the fact that he liked to serve sushi at finals parties. College deans, for the most part, were judged by the student body on the basis of how hard it was to worm "dean's excuses"—extensions and excused absences—out of them. De La Roche was middle of the pack where dean's excuses were concerned.

"There's an emergency disciplinary hearing scheduled for noon at the office of the Dean of Student Affairs, and since I'm to be acting as your advocate, I need to know your side of the story before I go."

"What?" I said, confused. "You mean George, right?"

"Yes, I'll be advocating for both of you. You're the only Prescott students involved."

I held out my hand, palm up. "Wait, why do I need an advocate? I was only a witness to what happened."

Dean De La Roche consulted his notes. "You appear here on the list of Rose & Grave members."

"I—" I reflexively reached down to cover the pin in my belt loop.

"It's okay, Amy. I have an official list right here." He held it up. A photocopy, but our official society roster. "It says you've been a member since spring of last year and that your society code name is Bugaboo. Is that correct?"

I can't tell you that. "Yes."

"And you participated in the initiation ceremony at the Rose & Grave tomb on High Street last night? You were inducting new members?"

I have to leave the room. I'm not allowed to talk about this. "Yes."

"And you are aware, I hope, that hazing is expressly prohibited in the Eli Undergraduate Regulations for General Conduct and Discipline?"

"*Hazing?*" I spluttered. "We didn't haze anyone! Everyone participating in the initiation knew exactly what they were doing..."

"According to the Connecticut hazing laws, implied or even explicit consent is not a defense against accusations of hazing, Amy."

I had no idea what the Connecticut hazing laws were. I had no idea how to respond. I had no idea what part of the initiation could be considered hazing. Was it the part where we carried them around? The part where we made them drink the 312 out of the skull? The part where we shut them up in coffins? Oh, God. All of it. I bet it was all of it.

But *everyone* did this—everyone had, for years. The

whole campus knew what society initiations were like. If the university had turned a blind eye for this long, what was making them persecute us now? Was it that they couldn't ignore the existence of Initiation Night when the words appeared in a police report?

"I don't understand," I said. "I thought you called me in here to talk about what happened with George and Blake Varnham."

"Precisely," said the dean. "Amy, don't you know? On top of the assault charges, Blake Varnham is prosecuting your entire society for hazing him during his Rose & Grave initiation."

"Wait," I repeated. "*His* initiation?"

"The hearing will determine whether or not the Eli Executive Committee must convene to have you all expelled."

From: Bugaboo_D177@phimalarlico.org
To: Poe_D176@phimalarlico.org
Subject: Need You

I don't know if you're checking e-mail, and if you are, I'm sure you've seen the explosion on the Phimalarlico lists, and already know what's going on. I don't know what to do. I'm so scared, Poe. Can they really expel fourteen of the most successful seniors in the graduating class a month before commencement?

Please advise.
Love you.

While the Dean of Student Affairs held an emergency disciplinary meeting with the college deans and the Varnham family lawyer, the Diggers of D177 convened at Clarissa's apartment.

"How can he possibly have prepared a statement?" Josh

asked, digging into the bag of bagels. "Hasn't he been under anesthesia for the past few hours?"

"Why aren't you more concerned about this?" I asked Josh. "My dean says Blake's trying to get all of us expelled!"

Josh rolled his eyes. "Have you read the Connecticut statutes on hazing? I have, and let me tell you, he's got an uphill job trying to prove that we were doing anything remotely like that. No one at the tomb even knew he was there until he openly assaulted Michelle in front of a dozen witnesses. This isn't going anywhere."

"But my dean said it, too," Jenny piped up.

"The only thing he's got going for him is a battery charge against George." We all turned to look at George, who was fast asleep on the couch, his cast-encased arm sticking up like a flag on a mailbox. "And that's going to fall under 'defense of others' pretty neatly."

"What about Michelle?" I asked.

"She was at the Strathmore dean's office this morning," said Greg, another Strathmore resident. "I didn't really get to talk to her. I was too concerned about the possibility of my Fulbright being revoked."

"I should call her," I said. "In fact, we should all call our taps. What are our plans for finishing the initiation?"

Odile put down her cup of coffee. "We've only got three more who need the final steps of the initiation. Blake had truly crappy timing."

"Well," said Nikolos, "he could hardly get hold of Michelle *after* she'd taken her oaths."

"How did he get hold of her at all?" Kevin asked. "How did he get into the tomb?"

"Who knows?" said Clarissa. "With all the people bustling in and out yesterday, maybe he just sneaked in."

"Sneaked in?" Jenny repeated. "But it's the Rose & Grave tomb. Who can just sneak in and out at will?"

Clarissa shrugged. "Lots of people have, over the years."

I remembered the meeting on the quad, remembered the scene in the hall last night. "Maybe," I began, my voice shaky as I considered the implications. "Maybe he had help?"

You wanted a Bugaboo? You got her.

"From whom?" Kevin asked.

I took a deep breath. "From his best friend. Topher."

THE TRAITOR INTERROGATION: 12 STEP METHOD

Step One: Invite Topher Cox, a.k.a. Achilles of D178, into the tomb of Rose & Grave. Verify that he comes *alone*.

Step Two: Array knights not currently suffering from severe bone fractures in a semi-circle in the Inner Temple, dressed in full society regalia: robes, hoods, candles obscuring our faces.

Step Three: Let Hale lead initiate inside. Direct him to sit in chair and begin trial. Ask him if he ever betrayed the Order, either before or after taking oaths not to.

Step Four: Ignore his denials. Ask again.

Step Five: Inform initiate that certain knights had seen him colluding with his longtime friend and current Barbarian Enemy #1 on previous day. Coincidence? We think not.

Step Six: Observe initiate's wormy little upper-crust expression melt into terror as he wonders which of the stories his grandfather told him about Rose & Grave are actually true.

Step Seven: Listen as initiate continues to prevaricate. Make threatening noises.

Step Eight: Watch initiate break down and admit to gathered audience that he had informed Barbarian Enemy #1 of his fellow tap's presence at a Rose & Grave tap party, and had wondered aloud to his friend if we were considering tapping her. (Initiate adds that he had considered it highly unlikely.)

Step Nine: Receive further intelligence that initiate identified one Miss Amy Haskel as a member of Rose & Grave to Barbarian Enemy #1.

Step Ten: Determine manner of Barbarian Enemy #1's entrance into tomb on Initiation Night. Confirm that initiate had no knowledge of this event. Let him promise up, down, and backwards that this is the case.

Step Eleven: Remind initiate that the word "secret" exists in the phrase "secret society" for a reason—even when it comes to close, personal barbarian friends. Remind him, also, that oath violations are punishable offenses. Remain vague on nature of punishments. Try not to exchange glances with fellow knight who may be dating your roommate and who shares with you an inability to keep your society a secret from her.

Step Twelve: While preparing to administer a punishment to initiate, receive cell phone call from college dean summoning you to the Office of the Dean of Student Affairs tout suite. Learn that you have become a party of particular interest to the case. Appeal to the aforementioned fellow knight dating your roommate for his legal guidance. Leave before the fun stuff starts.

"Do you think he was telling the truth?" Josh asked me along the way.

"Yes," I said. My nerves tightened with every step closer to the Eli Dean's office. "Michelle has already told us how Blake could get into her apartment, how he stole her stuff, how he managed to vandalize the car of one of her T.A.s. We broke into Micah's apartment last fall. We broke into the Dragon's Head tomb this spring. Is it such a stretch to imagine that Blake sneaked in, with all the hustle and bustle this Initiation Night?"

Josh had to concede the point as we headed up the stone steps and into the office of the Dean of Student Affairs.

In four years at Eli, I'd never done more than pass by this building on my way to and from classes. This is where troublemakers went. The freshman who'd burned down his dorm room. The group of rowdy sophomores who, drunk at Spring Fling, had dumped over a porta potty. The Bio major who'd stolen his classmate's lab notebook and turned it in as his own. The newspaper editor who'd published photos of all the disguised bodyguards who protected the Prince of Qatar. All those famous bits of gossip came back to me at that moment, as well as their denouements: suspension, expulsion, rustication. The Dean of Student Affairs—Becky Pasternak, or Becky P, as the students all called her—was known for being strict but fair. She loved the students, and she loved to nail their asses to the wall.

I don't know what I expected from her domain. In my mind, it had looked a bit like the bridge of the Death Star. Instead, Josh and I were greeted by wooden paneling, blue upholstered armchairs, and a large vase of daisies.

"I'm Amy Haskel," I said to the secretary. "I was called to—"

"Amy." I turned to see Dean De La Roche. "Have you seen George? I haven't been able to get in touch with him."

"He's asleep," I said. "The pain meds—"

"Who is this?" The petite yet powerful figure of Becky P appeared in the doorway to her office. She pointed at Josh. "He's not Prescott."

"I'm Joshua Silver, ma'am." He stuck out his hand.

"Hello. You can't be here. Only invited parties."

Josh took a deep breath. "I'm the secretary of this year's class of Diggers. No decision gets made in our society without my knowledge or permission." Okay, that was a stretch, but I wasn't about to disagree with him. "It is our understanding that Blake Varnham is claiming that he's been hazed as part of our initiation ritual, and I'm here to explain to you that this is categorically not the case."

"We didn't call you in. We called Miss Haskel and Mr. Prescott."

Why me? Only George was involved in the fight. "Anything you can possibly have to ask me about Rose & Grave," I said, "could be better answered by Josh."

Becky P raised an eyebrow at me. "Indeed? Well then, come in, illustrious Diggers. Grace us with your presence."

Josh shot me a look. We were so screwed.

In the room sat the dean of Strathmore College and Blake Varnham, looking remarkably well for a guy who'd just taken a knife to the back. (He was, it should be noted, *not* leaning against his chair.) Indeed, I think he got off better than George in the injury department. Maybe flesh wounds stung less than broken bones. Beside him sat a man who was either his father or a lawyer, and off in the corner, looking very much alone, sat Michelle Whitmore.

No wonder she hadn't answered any of my calls. She'd been stuck in here all morning. I went to her immediately.

"Are you okay?"

She shrugged without looking at me. I supposed I deserved that. After all, I'd promised that Rose & Grave would protect her from Blake, yet she'd hardly stepped foot in our tomb before he'd launched his most grievous attack on her yet. Was Becky P blind? Here was this young woman, obviously traumatized, sitting alone while her dean—the Eli faculty charged with protecting her—palled around with the likes of Blake Varnham and his support crew.

"Please take a seat, Miss Haskel," said Becky P. I looked around the room. Dean De La Roche had already resumed his seat near the other men, and there was an open chair next to him. I picked it up and moved it over to Michelle, then plopped down. Josh, failing to hide his amusement, took a seat on her other side. We were Diggers, even if Michelle hadn't been initiated yet. We stuck together.

Becky P didn't miss the nuance. She sat down behind her desk and folded her hands in front of her.

"It is well documented that I have zero tolerance for the abominable tradition of campus hazing," she said. "It makes no difference to me who the perpetrators of this crime are: sporting teams, fraternities, or even the oldest secret society on campus. It is naive of the secret societies to believe that because they operate outside the aegis of the Hellenic Society, Singing Group Council, or any other governing body, they are also exempt from the rules of this university and of the State of Connecticut. Do I make myself clear?"

Josh spoke up. "I understand the hazing statutes of the State of Connecticut, ma'am. I am curious to see how they apply in this case."

"This young man was stabbed in the back when he failed to comply with your bizarre initiation rites."

"We weren't initiating him!" I said. "We didn't tap him. He broke into the tomb on his own."

"We didn't stab him, either," Josh clarified. "He fell on

that knife—a knife, I might add, that he was using to threaten Michelle. It was an accident, brought on by his own outrageous behavior."

The man next to Blake turned and glared at us. "I see you three have your story all worked out. This is precisely what I'm talking about. These people don't operate within the law."

"That's rich," Michelle mumbled.

Becky P pursed her lips. "This is a conundrum. Miss Whitmore claims that Miss Haskel and her fellow society members were inducting *her* into their organization when the incident occurred. Mr. Varnham says that he was the inductee—"

"Of course he was the inductee," sputtered the man at his side. "Who is Rose & Grave more likely to tap? The straight-A student, the prep school graduate, the pillar of his residential college and his department of studies, the Eli legacy? Or some girl whose grades are so mediocre and whose mental state is so fragile that she had to drop out of school?"

Michelle's harsh little intake of breath was the only indication that the words stung.

"Excuse me," I said, cocking a thumb at the man next to Blake. "Who is this guy?"

"*This guy*," he hissed at me, "is Walter Varnham the Third."

"Blake's father," Michelle added, entirely unnecessarily.

"Apple doesn't fall far from the tree, does it?" I said. Josh stifled a groan.

"Miss Haskel, have you any idea the severity of this situation?" Becky P asked. "Your actions last night could have caused the death of an Eli student. Please do not be so flippant."

"I'm not being flippant, Dean Pasternak," I said. "But I

can guarantee you that we did not tap Blake Varnham. We find him hateful and unworthy of membership in Rose & Grave."

"They say that now," said Mr. Varnham, "because they're in trouble. These societies are a blight upon our Ivy League schools. Everyone knows how much research they do on their members. They dig up any dirt they can so they can keep them under their thumbs. No doubt they found out about Blake's unfortunate situation with *that girl* and now they're trying to use it in some bizarre, childish revenge scheme to sabotage my son's future!"

"I take it you weren't tapped, Walter," I said drily.

Josh jumped in to save me from myself. "As you may already be gathering, Amy is a bit of a renegade, and her choice of tap—Michelle—reflects those tastes. I'd be happy to provide you with documentation and witnesses proving that we invited Michelle to join our organization and not Blake."

"Of course he would!" said Mr. Varnham. "All the members of Rose & Grave are going to tell you precisely the same thing so they can keep their asses covered."

"Documentation can also be obtained from any number of other societies on campus," Josh added, "with whom we shared our tap lists."

"More collusion, no doubt," Mr. Varnham said. "An increased amount of scrutiny would be a disaster to any of these organizations. They protect their own. Why don't you look at real sources. Speak to Dean Ryan here. He can tell you about that girl's history of trying to spread lies about my son."

Michelle looked like she'd had enough. "Would you kindly," she said at last, "stop referring to me as *that girl*?"

"Dean Ryan?" Becky P asked.

The Strathmore College dean sitting next to Blake

shrugged. "Since the moment Miss Whitmore has returned to campus, she has repeatedly approached me about
some incident she claims happened last year. However,
there are no records in the files of the previous Strathmore
dean, she can provide no evidence or witnesses, and from
what I know of Blake after working together with him so
closely on the Strathmore College Council, I simply cannot give credence to any of these stories."

Michelle dropped her head against the back of the
chair. "Ugh, what's the point?"

"That's pretty appalling," I said. "A student comes to
you for help not once, but several times, and you rebuff
her? Is it just you, or are all deans so incompetent?" I
turned to Dean De La Roche. "What would you do if I
kept coming back to you, over and over, saying that my ex-
boyfriend was threatening me? Would I need to have actual bruises before you took action?"

Dean De La Roche was silent.

I gaped at both of them, then turned to the Dean of
Student Affairs. "Good system you've got here, Becky."

"There are countless cases of lovers' quarrels on this
campus," said Dean De La Roche. "Every semester, we get
complaints about someone's ex stalking them or threatening them or behaving erratically. You Eli students are intense and passionate, and sometimes this spills over from
your studies into your personal lives. But yes, we take real
threats very seriously."

"No you don't," said Michelle. "You cover your own
asses just the same as you claim Rose & Grave is doing.
You don't want the scandal, so you pretend it isn't happening."

"Shelly," Blake said, speaking for the first time. His
voice was hoarse, and thick with false innocence. "I don't
know why you don't just drop it. We broke up. It was over

a year ago. I got over it. I don't know why you can't do the same."

"Perhaps," Michelle said, "it would help if you stopped breaking and entering places like my apartment or society tomb and trying to force me to give you blow jobs."

Even my mouth dropped open. Becky P looked ready to explode.

Blake just shook his head at her, his eyes wide. "You really are a nutcase." He turned to Becky P. "I don't know what I'm supposed to do here. What if—" his expression turned to one of revelation "—what if they are telling the truth that they wanted to tap Michelle? What if I was some sort of initiation rite for her benefit? Destroy her enemy or something. Do societies do things like that?"

We destroyed enemies, sure. But not with knives. And Blake knew it.

"What if I only thought I was being initiated, and they were planning to hurt me all along?" He threw in a coughing fit for good measure. I wanted to deck him, stitches or no.

But Becky P's face remained thoughtful. "I think we've brought this situation as far as we can with this preliminary meeting," she said. "I'm going to need to see the documentation of the tap lists, and I'm going to need to speak privately to each of the society members, as well as Mr. Varnham and Miss Whitmore. I would also like to hear from Mr. Prescott, whenever he can be bothered to answer his phone."

"George Prescott broke an arm and a collarbone last night," I said to the dean. "He's on a lot of pain medication and it's possible—"

"*I was stabbed in the back last night,*" said Blake. "And I'm here, trying to make sure the truth is heard. All you people try to do is conceal it."

Also true. Hoisted by our own petards. How about that? Blake and Darren could laugh about this in hell.

"Enough," said Becky P. "This is more than we can resolve today. I am calling a meeting of the Executive Committee for a formal hearing."

"Dean Pasternak—" Josh began, beginning to look far more frightened than I'd ever seen him.

"This is an unusual case. Final exams are almost upon us, almost every student involved is on the cusp of graduation—"

Oh my God. She couldn't be considering expelling us. Suspending us? We had to take our finals. We had to graduate! I had to be able to turn in my thesis!

"But pass this along to your cronies, Mr. Silver and Miss Haskel. Until this matter is resolved, every person in Rose & Grave is on probation."

I hereby confess:

We created a monster.

14.
Diplomacy

The fun thing about being on probation is— No, wait. There's no fun thing. The week passed in agony and anticipation. I completed and turned in a thesis I wasn't sure would be graded, I attended classes I might not receive credit for, I studied for exams I didn't know if I'd be able to take, and I booked a flight to England for a colloquium whose invitation might be rescinded any moment.

Oh, and I talked to lawyers. Lots of them. Who knew that so many Diggers went on to pass the bar? All the law-and-order folks were incredibly optimistic. Blake's story stood not a ghost of a chance; there were too many witnesses that claimed the exact opposite—so what if they were all members of the same secret society? So what if the societies that may have had access to our shared tap lists were part of the same corrupt culture? So what if there wasn't any evidence at all that Michelle had been subject to a history of abuse at Blake's hands? The truth would rule the day.

I sure hoped so. My parents already had their flights

and their hotel room for Commencement Weekend. How could I call them up and tell them that I might get expelled, weeks before graduation, for hazing someone as part of an initiation ceremony for a secret society they didn't even know I was in?

The administration had temporarily closed the tomb on High Street, "pending investigation." Since we couldn't get inside, we were forced to suspend the rest of the initiation, as no one really wanted to induct new members into our order in Clarissa's apartment. Nikolos suggested we sneak in the back way, through the barrel-vaulted basement room that emptied out into the Eli Sculpture Garden, but we voted against the measure, since being discovered breaking into our tomb after the administration had forbidden it would hardly help our precarious positions.

Naturally, our closed tomb was cause of much speculation on campus, in the media, and most of all, on the Internet (where such things usually popped up). What had happened to the beleaguered society of Rose & Grave *now*? What unspeakable line had we crossed during this year's initiation? Was there something to all those rumors of sacrificing virgins? Had we killed someone?

There was even a story about the tomb's closure in the *Eli Daily News*—though we'd all been hoping that Topher could squash anything like that before it went to press.

"On the contrary," Topher had written in his brand-new phimalarico account, "keeping our name in the news at this juncture only further emphasizes the mystique surrounding our order. Besides, five inches on page 7 is nothing. It would have caused more attention if I'd killed it."

I had to admit it: My tap had a point. Maybe he wasn't a complete screwup. Also, he'd been trying so hard to make up for his part in the fiasco.

But the most interesting article in the paper that day was an op-ed on a most unexpected topic.

ACKNOWLEDGING THE PROBLEM IS ADMINISTRATION'S FIRST STEP

By Kalani Leto-Taube, Editor-in-Chief

When a student comes to Eli, she and her parents are putting their faith in the university to keep her safe. Is there a dedicated campus police force? Are there emergency phones dotted about the campus? What is the school's policy on drugs, weapons, violence, and hazing? What preventative measures have been taken by the university? Are there dedicated hate speech and tolerance workshops as well as rape, suicide, or general crisis hotlines? If the unthinkable happens, can a student turn to the university for help?

It is in this capacity that the administration is failing the students of Eli. While the university celebrates decreased crime and improved campus safety ini-tiatives, representatives at the Eli Women's Center as well as the GLBT co op are reporting increasing number of students who are falling through the cracks of these stopgaps. They may be getting advice on the crisis hotlines, but the university itself is turning a blind eye to situations that are occurring in their very buildings.

According to the recent, mandatory annual reports from school special interest groups, there is a growing trend among university administrators to encourage students to take non-official measures to remedy their problems. While occasionally such strategies work to reduce rancor and resolve issues amiably, in other cases, all they do is keep the problem under wraps. After all, if you never file a report about the man beating you up, then the university can retain its plausible deniability when it comes to statistics on campus domestic abuse.

Perhaps the university administrators believe that cooking the books will help avoid a scandal—no, we have no problems with racism, with violence against women, homosexuals, minorities. But what happens when an even bigger scandal comes along and it's revealed that the university could have stopped it, yet chose instead to bury its head in the sand?

Here's another question, readers of the *Daily*. What were the chances that Kalani spontaneously chose to write about this issue, today of all days?

In the absence of the usual tomb socializing, the new club had opted for a far more pedestrian format of getting-to-know-you: the group lunch. So it was in Commons that Demetria, Clarissa, and I found them, commandeering one of the large tables near the back, where they could chat freely without fear of being overheard.

But when we arrived, they seemed to be discussing only barbarian matters: internships, classes, coming exams. Michelle was calmly explaining to Clarissa's tap, Meredith Van Zandt, how the pork supply is actually comprised of psychopathic pigs driven crazy by awful farm conditions.

"You're eating the equivalent of a porcine Norman Bates," she said. Meredith eyed her BLT warily.

Beside her, Demetria's tap, Tamar, laughed and took another spoonful of lentil soup.

"Tamar," Demetria said, and slid in at the end of the row. "How's things down at the Women's Center?"

The junior shrugged and bowed her shaved head over her bowl. "The usual."

"Really?" Demetria asked. "Then what is this nonsense about mandatory annual reports?"

"It's the complete truth," she said. "Every year we have to reapply for our student organization fund grant, and as part of the process, we have to explain what we do. Ergo, mandatory annual report."

"It's not a grant study, Tamar," said Demetria. "It's a questionnaire."

"In which I specifically stated that we had been receiving reports of students urged by their deans not to press formal charges against other students harassing them or in cases of what I'll charitably term 'domestic disputes.' " She returned to her soup.

"And when did you receive these reports?" Demetria asked.

Tamar consulted her watch. "Um . . . Friday?"

"Initiation Night?" I said.

"Huh." Tamar pretended surprise. "How odd."

Michelle giggled. At the other end of the table, Topher watched the exchange and said nothing.

"Reports, the article said," I pointed out. "Plural."

Meredith raised her hand. "When I told my dean about the scary, desperate e-mails I was getting from Andrew, she said that he just regretted the way he treated me, sleeping with my best friend and all, and wanted a chance to reconcile. She said he'd give up eventually if I just ignored him."

"But that *is* what he wanted," Clarissa said. "And he *did* give up."

Meredith smiled. "Yes, but the outcome isn't important. The point is, the dean told me to ignore it."

"It counts," said Tamar.

Topher was still watching us from his end of the table.

"Hey," I called. "Managing editor. Get over here." As he dutifully trotted over, I considered the fact that he would have had to review Kalani's article. Perhaps he'd even suggested it. "What do you know about this?"

"I know it's an ongoing issue on the campus that deserves a little extra newsprint," he replied simply. "Anything else?"

Now every tap at the table was looking at us. The other two seniors and I exchanged glances.

"You know, guys," I began, "if you have any plans up your sleeve, it may behoove you to run it by us first."

"Why?" Michelle asked. "Aren't you busy with exams and theses and maybe being expelled? Don't you have enough on your plate?"

"Yeah, but—"

"That *was* the excuse you used for not turning in your problem set this week, isn't it?" she went on.

"Yeah, but—"

"We're changing the dialogue," Tamar said simply. "The administration is trying to use our society—*our* society—as a scapegoat to appease minority factions of alumni who have their panties in a twist."

"And ignoring actual problems on campus that they themselves have created," Michelle added.

"Exactly," said Tamar. "The administration has let us down in barbarian matters and pissed us off in society ones. Do you think we're just going to lie back and take it?"

"Or let you face it on your own?" asked Meredith.

"What did you tap us for," said Brianna, on the other side of the table, "if you didn't think we could handle stuff like this?"

"And not necessarily in the ham-handed manner we all witnessed at The Game last fall," piped up Paul, farther down the row. "Much as I may have been amused at the time."

"The media is power," said Topher. "You used it last year with Genevieve. We know that. We're using it, too."

"And because the article was written by Kalani," said Zoë Ponsonby, Greg's tap, "It's a bit hard to connect it to us." She looked over my shoulder. "Arielle, darling! Come here for a moment."

I turned to see Arielle with a tray in her hands and a Quill & Ink pin prominently displayed on her shirt collar. "Hey, Zoë," she said brightly. "Amy." A curt nod.

"Arielle, did you give any more thought to the suggestion I made at our *Faerie Queene* seminar yesterday?" Zoë asked.

"About the theme for the commencement issue of the Lit Mag?"

"Yes, wouldn't it be grand? Highlighting the ongoing struggle that women have had to undergo at the hands of the patriarchy at this university, whether through official or *unofficial* channels. A worthy theme, don't you think, seeing as how this year is the thirty-eighth anniversary of the first female class at Eli?"

"Thirty-eight," Arielle said drily. "How momentous. And curious, too, that you're giving so much thought to this, considering that the poem you submitted is about pollution."

Zoë waved it off. "The raping of our Mother Earth for masculine commercial gain and those in power's continued attempts to shut out her 'cries for help' by ignoring the obvious signs of global warming?"

"Right on," said Michelle.

"Seems apt to me," said Zoë.

Arielle did not appear convinced. "I just don't know how timely it is."

"Believe me," said Tamar. "It's about to become the most timely topic on campus."

My fellow Diggirls and I just sat in mute amazement.

———

True to the word of the knights of D178, over the next week, no one talked about anything but the administration's "policy" of sweeping domestic scandals under the rug in order to save face. There were no fewer than three more articles on the subject in the *Daily*. That weekend the *Eli Herald*, the campus alt-weekly, even published the anonymous account of a former student who had actually been encouraged to switch schools rather than deal with the prejudice she was facing as a transgendered Political Science major.*

As one might expect, the liberal student body, en masse, was quick to grab their pitchforks and fall in line. By the day of the Executive Committee meeting, there was even a small protest going on outside the Office of the Dean of Student Affairs, which was also, in a most provident coincidence, the location of the meeting.

I'd given up believing in coincidences.

It was a sunny spring morning, and the stones of the courtyard and the nearby rare book library gleamed a smooth, bureaucratic white.

"Hey there, Amy," said Kalani, meeting me on the steps. As usual, she looked like she'd just stepped out of a Wall Street high-rise to grab a bagel. Beige skirt and jacket, hair in a gloriously perfect bun. If only I didn't know she'd rather be wearing a corset and a hoop skirt. "Nice suit."

———

*The confessor cannot speak to the veracity of this account. One would assume that the ACLU would have been all over this by now, but then again, if the victim just went away quietly, as the confessor realizes victims are occasionally wont to do . . .

I smoothed my shell and skirt. "Thanks." This suit had seen me through last year's summer internship interviews, my society interview, and every important meeting in D.C. Now, I hoped it would survive this meeting and live to be worn under my robe come graduation day. "What are you doing here?"

"I'm press."

I gave her a skeptical glance. "You're not the kind of press that works the Dean's office beat for a protest."

"I am when it's an issue I brought to the attention of the student body," she said. "And you? What brings a model student like yourself down to the Dean's office so spiffed up?"

"I—"

Kalani grinned. "Just kidding, Amy, I'm no fool. Knock 'em dead, okay?" She reached over and folded up my lapel to reveal my Rose & Grave pin.

I gaped at her. "How long have you known?"

"Just a few days." Kalani's smile did not diminish. "Topher told me."

"Topher?" Dude, how many oaths did this kid plan to break in his first month as a Digger? Who did he think he was? Me?

"Of course. Topher and I have worked together for three years now, and he hasn't once tipped me off to a story. I knew there was something going on. I'm a reporter, too, you know. And though he has many good—or at least, *interesting*—qualities, holding up under interrogation isn't one of them."

"So I've found." I studied her. "Do you think less of me now?"

She laughed. "To be honest, I think more of Rose & Grave. I mean, if you can't have the Hall, I guess being a Digger is an adequate substitute."

Inside the dean's office, the other knights had already gathered. Odile and Jenny were trying to figure out a way to conceal the dirty sketch covering a large portion of George's cast.

"Don't worry about it," he said. "It's not as if we're actually appearing in front of the Dean of Student Affairs."

At the advice of our counsel, we'd opted to petition for a meeting of the ten-member Executive Committee's Coordinating Group, a small, three-person fact-finding subset whose job it was to determine whether or not the accusations against us held water. We theorized that the student members of the full committee were more likely to be swayed by campus rumor and give credence to Blake's wilder claims than the faculty-only coordinating group.

We were ushered into a small, classroom-like chamber. Three of the chairs in the triple row across from the table where the committee sat were already occupied: Blake, Michelle (as far from Blake as she could get), and Topher.

I tapped him on the shoulder as I took my seat in the second row. He merely tightened his grip on the manila envelope in his hand and said nothing.

"What is he doing here?" Jenny whispered to me.

"No clue." I was the worst big sib on the face of the planet. I tapped him again. "Hey—"

The chairwoman of the committee glared at me. "We'd like to get started." I sat back in my seat.

Blake's accusation was presented first. According to him, we had been engaging in a steady diet of hazing and psychological torture for weeks, culminating, he claimed, in threats and assault when, on Initiation Night, he finally refused to perform the "abominable rituals" we required to grant him entrance to Rose & Grave.

No, he did not specify the nature of said ritual. Natch. However, he did say that he was stepping forward to urge others who'd received similar treatment at our hands to speak out against our abusive ways.

Ooh, nicely put. Steal that line from Michelle?

While the committee chair read these bald-faced lies out loud, Blake glared at each of the Diggers in turn, reserving special amounts of venom for George and Michelle. Oddly, he didn't look at Topher at all.

"Topher," I whispered. "What you got there?"

He stared resolutely down at the envelope.

Uh-oh.

"George Prescott," the chairwoman said. George raised his good hand. "Would you please explain to us what happened on the night you initiated Mr. Varnham into Rose & Grave?"

"We didn't," George replied.

The chairwoman pursed her lips. "Fine. The night you attempted to—"

"We didn't do that, either," said George. "We didn't do a single one of the things he's got listed there, except for the part where I shoved him down a staircase. You *could*, reasonably, describe it like that, though really, we both fell." He waved with his cast and I saw one of the other committee members raise his eyebrows at the sketch gracing the plaster.

"Mr. Prescott," the chairwoman said wearily, "hazing is a very serious charge. Please describe for us what it is that your society does on Initiation Night."

George smiled his million-dollar grin. "I don't have any idea what that has to do with this investigation, ma'am. It's just location. If my fight with Blake had occurred at a Chinese restaurant, would you be asking me to describe the egg rolls?"

All the Diggers were wise enough to refrain from snickering.

George continued. "Focusing on what may or may not occur at our initiation is the wrong approach because if you don't believe me that Blake was in no way included in the ceremony, why would you trust any description I have of our rituals?"

"He's been coached to say that," Blake argued. "They're all in league to parrot the party line."

"I haven't been coached to say *this*," George directed at Blake. "Six generations of Diggers are going to be furious with me, but our initiation? It's nothing. More like a carnival's house of horrors than whatever this jackass is describing. It's laughable—and under any other circumstances, we *would* be laughing at this disgustingly transparent attempt to get us to reveal our secrets. The same way we laugh at all the urban legends surrounding Rose & Grave. The reason we aren't laughing in this instance is that after this guy *broke into* our tomb—uninvited, unannounced—he held a girl captive with a knife. Yeah, I jumped him. I admit it. I was trying to get both knife and girl away from him. Go ahead and withhold my degree for that. I dare you."

Oh, crap. George, please don't threaten the nice executive committee who holds our fates in their hands. We don't all have campus buildings named after us.

"Not because I'm a Digger, not because I'm a Prescott, and certainly not because of those people outside. But because it's obvious who is really to blame in this instance. I know what he did, and I've already overpaid trying to stop it."

No matter what George said, at that moment, he'd never looked more like a Digger, more like a Prescott, more like a son of Eli. Even the chairwoman had to gather her composure before speaking again.

"We seem to be at an impasse here. It's a case of he said/she said—"

"More like a dozen she saids to one he said," grumbled Mara.

"You and your cronies are all telling the same lie!" Blake said.

"Oh, yeah," said Michelle. "*We're* the ones who are all about the cover-up. That's right. I'm sure if we could get in touch with Dean Wiatt, you'd be singing a different tune."

But the old Strathmore College dean was doing research in Borneo. Without Internet access. We'd tried to get hold of her, to no avail. So much for the inexhaustible Digger influence.

Blake simply snorted. "She didn't believe your lies last time, either."

"So you're admitting that I didn't just start complaining about your behavior last week in an attempt to help my Digger buddies," Michelle pointed out. "Who's involved in a cover-up now?"

"Everyone quiet down," said the chairwoman, who, to her credit, had been watching the entire exchange with some interest. "As I was saying, in most instances where the version of events delivered by every witness differs so immensely from the version offered by the victim..."

Yeah, yeah, yeah. I'd heard this before. But of course you couldn't trust these witnesses. Diggers lie to protect their own. After all, we were all in training to be the secret leaders of the world.

"...without additional evidence—" the dean was saying.

"But we offered you statements from members of other campus societies, verifying that Blake was not a tap we discussed with them—"

"More secret society cronies?" Blake scoffed. "Right."

"I have additional evidence," said Topher Cox. "Right here." He stood up and crossed to the table, laying the manila envelope down on it. "This is a notarized statement from a girl named Jessica Townsend. Blake and I went to high school with her, and Jessica explains here what happened between them."

The chairwoman pulled out the sheet of paper and scanned it. "What does this have to do with the current situation?"

Topher shrugged. "You doubt the uniform accounts by the members of Rose & Grave, despite the fact that they are consistent with the incidents that Michelle describes—incidents that also, mysteriously, have no evidence to back them up. Well, the same thing happened to Jessica. She's at Kenyon now and has no connection to any secret society on the Eli campus. Call her if you want. Blake did what they say. All of it. He's done it for years and he's never, ever gotten into trouble for it." His expression turned thoughtful. "Given the current atmosphere on campus, I'd hate to hand this statement over to the press."

"You asshole!" Blake shouted. "You sold me out."

Topher turned and looked Blake in the eye. "You were my best friend, Blake. I'm really sorry it had to go down like this."

"Yeah. You picked Rose & Grave over me."

Topher nodded. "Yes. I did." But he didn't look happy about it.

———

Unsurprisingly, the Executive Committee decided that there was not enough evidence to back up Blake's hazing claims. D177 was safe. However, they did ask Michelle and Blake to stay behind to discuss the other incidents that this case (and Topher's Jessica papers) had brought to light. I asked Michelle if she wanted me to remain with her for moral support.

She shot Blake a look of triumph. "Nah," she said. "I think I've got him this time around."

I shook my head. "I should really take lessons from you sometime."

"Why?"

The committee returned to their tables and the secretary began closing the doors.

"Tell you later."

Michelle had tried to bring Blake to justice, and had been hampered by bureaucracy and stacked decks. If I allowed Darren to go unpunished for what he'd done to me over Spring Break, would this be him in a few years? Would I be like the girl at Kenyon, getting a phone call and being asked to testify as to what he'd done to me, oh so long ago? After he'd hurt someone else?

Speaking of . . . I hurried off to catch Topher, who had shocked us all, and found him on the front steps speaking to Kalani. And Felicity Bower.

"Hello, Amy," Felicity said to me. Topher and Kalani appeared to be in deep conversation.

"What are you doing here?" I asked.

"Waiting to see if you got expelled." Felicity gave me her most cloying smile. "Did you?"

"No."

"Pity." She stared off over the square and the protest. "Actually, I was waiting to see if Blake Varnham got what was coming to him. You may not have known who he was until recently, but he was on Dragon's Head's radar for a bit, before we saw what lay behind the façade."

"Wait. You knew? You had proof?"

Felicity shrugged. "You did, too. What you didn't have was the ability to influence your own knights." She nodded at Topher, then walked away.

Topher was already being mobbed by the Diggers in

my club. With all the backslapping and general congratu-
lations, his demeanor quickly shifted from resentful and
ambivalent to his usual smug triumph.

"Of course," he was saying, "I took an oath. I'm a
Digger, aren't I?"

Someone shushed him and called for discretion, but the
boy was clearly on a roll.

Felicity was right. I hadn't trusted Topher to do the
right thing, but with good reason. He hadn't brought evidence about Blake's past because it was true. He'd brought
it because he realized it behooved him more to keep our
secrets than Blake's. Still an ass, but one on our side.

I only hoped it stayed that way.

I felt my cell phone vibrating in my purse, but the number on the digital readout was not one I recognized. My
heart did a little flip. Could it be Jamie, calling from his
undisclosed location? Could he have finally gotten my
message? I answered it.

"Hello, this is Deputy Morgan from the Lee County
Sheriff's Office. May I speak to Amy Haskel?"

Lee County? "This is she."

"I'm calling to follow up on a report filed two months
ago regarding an incident on Cavador Key."

Oh. *That* Lee County.

"It says here that you were 'unavailable to provide
statement due to severe physical and emotional duress.' Is
that so?"

"It says that?" I asked. I didn't remember that. I'd been
out of it, sure. Between being drugged and almost drowning, I'd slept for about two days straight after getting off
the island. But I could have talked to the police. After all,
I'd talked plenty to the other Diggers. I'd been incredibly
firm that I didn't want Darren prosecuted, that I didn't
want to press charges when the police came—

Wait a minute. "So you're saying that you've been waiting for my statement all this time?"

"Well..." the sheriff began. "We sort of had a paperwork snafu in the office. The attending officers seemed to be a tad confused about whether or not there was an open case or even if the parties were pursuing prosecution. And when the powers that be alerted us to it the other day, we went back to computers and there you were."

"The powers that be alerted you," I repeated. In other words, the feds stuck their noses into a minor assault case? What were the chances of that? And which feds? He hadn't said the FBI. Perhaps he meant the State of Florida?

Perhaps he meant some other government agency. One with a brand-new employee who knew very well how to work the system.

"They, um, sometimes get interested when stuff happens out at Cavador," the sheriff explained. "You know it's owned by one of those northeast Ivy League secret societies, right?"

"Oh, yes," I said. "I know."

"So, ma'am, I was wondering if you would be in a position to give me a statement now. It would probably only take a few minutes. And, um, if you have any pictures..."

Was I in a position to give him a statement now? Good question. I cast a glance over my shoulder, back at the Dean's office, where even now, Michelle was probably providing her own statement to the Executive Committee.

"Yes," I said. "I think I am."

———

That night, in the Inner Temple of the Rose & Grave tomb, a hundred candles gleamed—some from skull-shaped sconces on the walls, and far more from the many-forked candelabra and vine-like rows of tea lights. The star-spangled dome could hardly compete, and the flickering light cast hundreds of eerie shadows all over the paneled walls. Even the painting of Connubial Bliss seemed sinister and mysterious, standing there in her proudly naked glory.

The knights of D177 and D178 gathered in a circle in the center of the room and chanted "Drink it!" as Michelle, in the center, quaffed the ceremonial pomegranate concoction from a skull-shaped bowl.

Initiation was long over, but we still had a few knights left to induct.

They hooted and hollered as she took her oaths, and then I stepped forward, my cloak flapping about my heels. There was no Don Quixote costume this time, no mask of wilting red roses. But we didn't need it. I held out the rusted sword as Michelle knelt before me.

"From this moment on, you are no longer Barbarian-So-Called Michelle Anastasia Whitmore. By the order of our Order, I dub thee Gaia, Knight of Persephone, Order of Rose & Grave."

Gaia stood up and smiled at the group. "So now we party?" she asked.

Indeed.

After removing our costumes and cleaning up a few splashes of stray pomegranate, we adjourned to the Firefly Room, where a nervous-looking Hale was presiding over a small bar and keeping careful eye on a knot of barbarians, lest any of them choose to bolt toward the private areas of the tomb.

"I can't believe I'm standing here," Lydia said to me as I joined her.

"What do you think?" I asked, as the dance music started up. Around me, the friends and lovers of the Diggers were meeting up with their pals. A few had already started dancing. Kalani was describing how the parties at St. Linus Hall were much better, but we'd eventually get the hang of letting barbarians into part of our tomb. We just had to give it a few decades.

Hale stood in the corner and wrung his hands. I was almost positive I heard him mumble about "the end of days."

"Honestly?" Lydia asked. "A little shabbier than I expected."

"Things always are." Josh came up and slipped his hands around Lydia's waist. "Want to dance?"

I watched them spin off and join Demetria and her mysterious Shannon and George and Devon on the dance floor. Michelle came over and handed me a glass of wine.

"You know, I don't really like pomegranate all that much." She wrinkled her nose. Her lips were stained a deep red.

"Couldn't be helped," I said.

"Apparently not." She smiled. "Now, what was that story you had to tell me? I paid attention to those oaths, you know. We're not supposed to have secrets from each other."

"Does that mean you're going to tell me what questions are on my Geology exam?"

"Not unless you have a burning desire to attend another meeting of the Executive Committee."

I shuddered. "Pass."

"Thought so." She took a sip. "So . . . was this all worth it?" She gestured around the Firefly Room.

I watched my friends laughing, talking, dancing. "Was what worth it? Letting the barbarians in?"

"No," she said with a laugh. "Being a Digger."

"I'm always a Digger," I said. "Got the tattoo to prove it."

"I mean being a knight," she said. "Was it worth it?"

The drama, the heartache, the stress? The friendships, the conspiracies, the pranks, the bonding... Was it worth it?

Oh, yeah. But then her words sunk in. *Was.* Past tense. For I was no longer an active knight of Rose & Grave. I was a patriarch.

I hereby confess:
If I never see a robe again,
it'll be too soon.

15.
Pomp and Circumstances

On the morning of my last day at Eli, I rose and looked around my bare room. My boxes and trunks had already been put into storage until I found a place to live, and just last night, Lydia and Josh had gathered up our couch, microwave, and coffee table for transport into Lydia's new off-campus apartment.

On Orange Street. In New Haven.

She'd decided to attend Eli Law. Only time would tell what this meant for Josh and her.

The last few weeks had been characterized by two things: nostalgia and major life decisions. Though Lydia was planning to spend at least three more years on campus, we'd spent a lot of time revisiting old haunts. Our last 3 A.M. call to the local Chinese food place. Our last shared "small Greek salad" that could feed a large family. Our last late night spent studying in the Stacks. Our last evening spent imbibing Gumdrop Drops.

After exams were over, most of my friends made the

usual senior trek down to Myrtle Beach (Michelle had offered to mouse-sit for Reepicheep until I came back from
England). Odile had rented a house for us right on the
shore, and twelve Digger and Digger-friends spent the
week fighting over bathroom time and rotating who got to
share private rooms with their sweethearts (or the random
"last chance" hookups they dragged home from clubs,
bars, and beachcombing). As someone who had more than
had it with Myrtle Beach hookups, I found myself relegated to sleeping bags in the living room a lot of the time.
I didn't begrudge my companions their prurient activities.
Heck, in a different frame of mind, I might have been up
for a few last-chance encounters myself.

One last encounter with Jamie would not have been
unwelcome.

I'd tried to contact him again. And again. No phone
numbers worked. And though his Eli alumni and Phimalarlico e-mail addresses remained active, I doubted highly
he was checking them. At least, I hoped he wasn't. The
idea that he could see four or five notes from me and still
not respond triggered blunt pains in my chest cavity.

I spent a lot of time with Jenny and Harun, who'd managed to turn restraint and courtly love into an art form, and
Clarissa, who'd recently placed a moratorium on her own
amorous existence in order to get the rest of her life in
peak shape. "I've got a company to run," she explained. "I
don't have time for heartbreak."

Was that what this was? Heartbreak? In the past, it had
floored me, too. But my separation from Jamie had felt so
different, and I still didn't fully understand why. Maybe it
was because it came without betrayal. We both cared for
each other. We just couldn't make it work. Or maybe it was
because every time I checked my e-mail, I held my breath

for a moment, hoping against hope I'd see his name in my in-box.

Given my choice of company, was it any wonder that I at last acquiesced to their persuasion? As soon as I returned from England, I'd be moving to New York City and working as the brand-new public relations chair of Jenny's company, Caritas. As it turned out, all my protests amounted to a lingering guilt that Jenny's offer was made out of pity. Eventually, they convinced me otherwise.

"I read the narratives you put together at your D.C. job last summer, Amy," Clarissa pointed out. "You were able to capture both the plight of these women and their hope for a better future."

"We want you to craft the same kind of narratives, just on a global scale," Jenny pointed out. "Caritas is going to be like the eBay for micro-loans. But some of these entrepreneurs—well, they aren't going to have the writing skills necessary to describe where they come from, what they face, and what's so good about their projects. You're going to be marketing for them as much as you are for the company."

I'd loved my job in D.C. I'd loved knowing that the writing I was doing was directly affecting people's lives.

All that, four weeks of paid vacation per year, and full health and dental. How could I resist?

So here I stood, on the morning of commencement, suit freshly pressed, graduation gown feeling very cheap and flimsy next to the society robe I'd been wearing two nights a week all year long. My mortarboard and tassel were waiting for me on my dresser, my parents were waiting in the café at their hotel, my diploma was waiting in a stack in the Prescott College dean's office. This was it. I was graduating from college.

Maybe I should wear a different blouse?

I was down to my bra and pantyhose, digging through my suitcase, when Lydia knocked on my door. "Are we going?"

"Just a minute," I called. I picked up the pink shell and held it against my jacket. Hmmmm...

"Are you decent?"

"You know the answer to that: hardly ever." What about the yellow top?

Lydia stuck her head in the doorway. "It's just that my little brother is out here and I don't want to spoil his virgin eyes with glimpses of college co-eds in bras."

"Aren't you and Josh supposed to be at that Phi Beta Kappa reception?"

"Been and back, honey," said Lydia. "It's almost ten."

"What?" I cried. "No!" But of course. With my alarm clock packed up, I had no way of keeping track of the time. "I was supposed to meet my parents—"

"They're here, too. But if you don't come out in thirty seconds, they are giving the English muffin and mocha they are saving for you to my brother. And you really don't want to see what he's like on caffeine."

"Okay." I looked at the three shirts in my hands. Ugh, why couldn't I make this choice? I was a college graduate—pretty soon anyway. Couldn't I dress myself?

"Overthinking again?"

"You know it."

Lydia tapped one. "The white. It's classic. Now come on."

"What am I going to do without you?" I slipped the shirt on and grabbed my graduation gown.

"Luckily, New Haven is just a short commuter train ride away."

I began to follow her to the door, then stopped,

snatched yesterday's jeans off the floor and pulled my Rose & Grave pin free of the belt loop.

One last time.

———

Ivy League commencement ceremonies are interminable. We'd already had one whole day of celebration, wearing gowns, but not our caps. We listened to our commencement speaker and met with the president for his commencement address followed by a reception at his house. Today consisted of a march through the New Haven Green, culminating in a giant ceremony at Old Campus, marked by honorary degrees, recognition of graduates in every graduate field of study as well as the undergraduate program, more addresses (some in Latin), and special awards to exceptional graduates. I was pleased to recognize a few faces on the podium that day. Omar received an award for outstanding scholarship in the face of significant personal tragedy, as most of his family were still political prisoners back in his home country—a story that his friends and fellow knights already knew far too well. Howard First, who had been a Digger for all of thirty seconds, received an award for his public service. I guess he did use his time well.

After the group event, all undergrads split off to attend smaller ceremonies in their respective colleges. As there was no way I'd be able to find my folks in the crush of families and students, we'd arranged to meet back at Prescott. I paused for photo ops with Jenny and Harun, Odile and Clarissa, Ben and Greg and Demetria and, hell, even Mara. I peeled Lydia away from Josh, promised her that we'd see him again at dinnertime, gathered up George (whose voluminous robe almost completely concealed his cast), and headed back to Prescott College, only to find another madhouse. The second we entered the gates, the under-grads working commencement gathered us up and herded everyone in a black robe into the dining hall to be orga-nized by last name and given instructions about how to ap-proach the stage to receive our diplomas.

Another commencement speaker, another host of awards. And then they handed out diplomas, preceded by the caveat that, in the interest of time, we should save our applause for the end. Amen to that. I was ready to get this robe off once and for all. I toyed with the Rose & Grave pin on my lapel as the dean and the master of Prescott worked their way through our graduating class.

"Amy Maureen Haskel, Literature, Honors in the Major."

I walked up the stairs and across the stage. Shook the dean's hand, shook the master's hand, took my diploma, and we all paused, smiling, for the photographer to take my picture. Out of the corner of my eye I finally caught sight of my parents, who'd somehow managed to snag cov-eted seats in the shade. In total defiance of the dean's or-ders, they were clapping and cheering. My mother lifted her camera to take a picture.

Later, my parents told me that I totally ruined my grad-uation photo and that my expression should have been more in the neighborhood of happy and triumphant than fish-mouthed and flabbergasted. But what could they expect?

Somehow I made it back into my seat, clutching my diploma folder and craning my neck back at the audience in vain. My parents' seats were nestled into an alcove—comfortable spot, to be sure, but I couldn't see them.

Or whoever they might or might not be sitting with. Because for an instant, up there on the stage, I swear I saw someone most unexpected standing at their backs.

Maybe it was a trick of the light? I spent the rest of the

ceremony trying to find out. When George cartwheeled across the stage, one-armed, my classmates hooted and hollered without me. When Lydia's summa cum laude, Phi Beta Kappa, Honors in both of her double majors was announced, it barely registered.

I couldn't have been hallucinating. I knew that face. In half light, in full light, in no light at all. In quiet or cruel moods, in happy, restful ones. Heck, I knew it in the throes of passion. Jamie had come to my graduation.

The second the ceremony was over, I bolted from my seat, vaulted over the laps of the graduates who actually chose to throw their caps in the air, and beelined for the alcove. My parents met me halfway.

"Sweetie!" my mom said, enveloping me in a momentum-ending hug. "We're so proud of you!"

"Smile, kiddo," my dad said, pointing his camera at me. "Get that tassel out of your face."

Students and families swirled around us, but there was no sign of Jamie.

"What a madhouse," said my mom. "We thought we'd never find seats here, but it turns out your friend had them saved for us."

"My friend," I repeated, still craning my neck over their shoulders. My mother has this habit of saying "your friend" in a tone of voice that manages to convey all of the following:

1) The individual to whom I refer is a person of the opposite sex,
2) Who clearly has carnal knowledge of my daughter,
3) But I'm not going to judge,
4) And I'm certainly not going to assume that their relationship is quantifiable by any pedestrian term such as "boyfriend" or "betrothed,"

5) Because who knows what passes for a romantic relationship in my daughter's mind,

6) A behavior of hers I wholly disapprove of, by the way (though as I stated, I'm not going to judge),

7) And while I'm on the subject, he'd better watch it. Just saying. Not judging.

"Do you think he'll want to come to dinner with us?" my father asked.

"Weird that he recognized us, don't you think?" my mom asked. "He said he'd seen a picture of us."

Well, yes, that's what happens when you spy on the families of your potential taps.

"I—" There he was, standing back from the crowd, as always, in a new black suit, with his arms filled with white lilies. He was watching us, his expression unsmiling but expectant. My heart almost burst out of my graduation gown.

"It's no big deal, at any rate," said my mother. "We're already eleven with Lydia's family and Josh's mom and siblings. A twelfth won't change the seating arrangements too much—"

"Oh, look, honey," said my father. "There are the Travineceks. Amy, sweetie, ask your friend if he wants to have dinner with us."

"You want him to, right, dear?" asked my mom, taking my diploma out of my hands.

Want him to what? I'm sure I mumbled an answer of some sort, but I was already floating past them and up to Jamie, who'd materialized out of the crowd. "Hi."

"Hi," he said, and held out the lilies. "For you. Thought you might be sick of roses."

I took the flowers, though my gaze did not leave his face. "What are you doing here?"

"I had a burning desire to see my little sib graduate."
He smiled. "The cartwheel was especially enjoyable."

I called shenanigans on that explanation. "I thought
you were gone for good."

He hesitated. "Right. So here's the thing. That job?
Turns out it's not really me. Or it was for a different me."

"You quit?" I whispered. "But what will you do now?"

"I'm going back to Eli Law. If they'll have me." He
studied me carefully. "I made a mistake."

If *they* will have him? "Jamie, I don't know if—"

"Please don't think I did this for you," he broke in. "I
did it for me. The guy who wanted those secrets, that life?
I'm not that guy anymore. I haven't been for a while."

I said nothing, just stood there, clutching the lilies.

"That part, I think, *can* be attributed to you," he admitted. "Or at least the time I've spent with you."

Somehow, I remained silent. I may have been pos-
sessed. Amy Haskel doesn't keep her mouth shut. Has
never kept her mouth shut. But I had no idea where he was
going with any of this.

"I know you've been through a lot since I left," he said.
"And I don't have the right—"

"I'll be in New York," I blurted out. "I'll just be in New
York. If you come back here—"

He gave me the biggest smile I've ever seen from Jamie.
"New York."

"I decided to take a job with Caritas. Jenny's company."

"God bless Metro North," he replied. For a second we
just stood there, neither of us wanting to make the first
move. Around us, families and friends embraced, but there
was more than an armful of lilies that separated me from
Poe. I wanted to ask him what trick he'd pulled with the
Lee County Sheriff's Office. I wanted to tell him that at

this very moment, Darren Gehry was preparing for his case in front of the juvenile court. I wanted to know what was the trigger that made him come back.

"I read your e-mails," he said at last. "I—wished I could have been there."

"We managed." Heck, D177 hardly needed to be there.

"Yes, you did. And in a way I never would have expected."

"It wasn't us, honestly," I said. "The new club is full of surprises. They have their own way of doing things."

Jamie chuckled. "You could say you deserve that."

"You could," I said. "*You* would probably relish it."

"Oh, believe me, Amy, I have been." He took a deep breath. "I—uh, got you a graduation present."

I brightened. "Where?"

He pointed at the lilies. "Check in there."

I peered into the bouquet. There, nestled among the blooms, was a red and blue énvelope. "These are tickets to England." I looked closer and gasped. "First-class tickets to England!"

"I decided you needed an upgrade. Notable international scholars such as yourself should always travel in style." He pointed at the ticket. "I hear you get to sleep in some sort of pod. It sounded very cool."

I flipped through the paperwork. "Jamie, you can't afford—" I froze. "There are two tickets here."

He stuck his hands in his pockets. "Yeah. I took a chance. I don't have a job this summer anymore, so I'm free. I mean, I may come back here and do research for a professor or two, providing they let me re-enroll, but..." He trailed off. "I've always wanted to see England."

"With me?"

"No, not always to see it with you, but now, yes, absolutely." He began speaking very quickly. "I know you're going to be staying at Oxford for the conference and that's fine. I've got some friends in London who probably wouldn't mind my crashing at their place for a few days."

"Friends?"

"Yes, Amy. Friends. I do have them. And afterward, well, I don't know what plans you've made in terms of sightseeing, but I thought it could be fun if we traveled together. I'll even do the Jane Austen thing if you want—"

"Yes!" I beamed at him. "Yes, yes."

"—but I'm more of a Tower of London type of guy."

"Figures." Torture, murder, mayhem, beheadings. Just his style.

Hey, Mom and Dad, this is my "friend" Jamie. My boyfriend Jamie. We're going to England together. Also, I met him in a secret society. We're Diggers, folks. And Eli graduates. And in love. What do you think?

But all that was for later, at the dinner I'd shoehorn him into attending with Josh and Lydia and our respective families. He'd get his double date and then some. Right now, I just wanted to drink him in, press into his arms. He was staring at me the same way.

I bit my lip. "How in the world can you afford first-class tickets anywhere?"

And now he did wrap his arms around me. "I'm a Digger, Amy. We've got connections."

I laughed and kissed him as my graduation cap slid from my head. Yes, we certainly did.

The Rose & Grave Club of D177

1) Clarissa Cuthbert *(Angel):* CFO of Caritas
2) Gregory Dorian *(Bond):* Fulbright Scholar, Oxford, England
3) Odile Dumas *(Lil' Demon):* Untitled Odile Dumas Project, Paramount Pictures
4) Benjamin Edwards *(Big Demon):* Price Waterhouse Cooper
5) Amy Haskel *(Bugaboo):* V.P. of Publicity, Caritas
6) Nikolos Dmitri Kandes IV *(Graverobber):* Deputy V.P., Kandes Industries
7) Kevin Lee *(Frodo):* Assistant, Creative Artists Agency
8) Omar Mathabane *(Kismet):* Harvard Kennedy School of Government
9) George Harrison Prescott *(Puck):* Teach for America
10) Demetria Robinson *(Thorndike):* Berkeley School of Graduate Studies
11) Jennifer Santos *(Lucky):* President, Caritas
12) Harun Sarmast *(Tristram Shandy):* V.P. of Development, Caritas
13) Joshua Silver *(Keyser Soze):* Stanford School of Law
14) Mara Taserati *(Juno):* The Wharton School of the University of Pennsylvania

Acknowledgments

My endless thanks to the usual suspects at the venerable Bantam Dell: Kerri Buckley, Nita Taublib, Lynn Andreozzi, Kelly Chian, Pam Feinstein, and Carol Russo. Thank you to the folks at the Knight Agency, especially Deidre Knight and Elaine Spencer. I owe a deep debt of gratitude to my colleagues and critique partners, Carrie Ryan, Erica Ridley, Julie Leto, and Justine Larbalestier, for keeping me sane when under deadline. More thanks are due to my fellow writers at the Washington Romance Writers, Chick Lit Writers of the World, TARA, Novelists, Inc., and the Greater Pacific Seahorse Polo Team.

I would also like to thank my friends and family for their love, support, and inspiration. My parents, my brothers, my in-laws, Elizabeth, Glenn, Chris, Megan, Mackenzie, Nicola, and Lauren—you're the best! Thank you to Dan for bringing takeout Thai, back rubs, and kisses after a long day of writing, and to Rio for consenting to nap under my chair while I worked.

As always, thank you to my secret sources, especially you new ones.

Finally, and most important, I am grateful to you, the readers of this book. Thank you for following Amy's story.

About the Author

DIANA PETERFREUND is a graduate of Yale University and lives with her husband and dog in Washington, D.C. She is the author of three other novels about the members of Rose & Grave: *Secret Society Girl*, *Under the Rose*, and *Rites of Spring (Break)*.

www.dianapeterfreund.com